PAUL TEMPLE AND THE FRONT PAGE MEN

Francis Henry Durbridge was born in Hull, Yorkshire, in 1912 and was educated at Bradford Grammar School. He was encouraged at an early age to write by his English teacher and went on to read English at Birmingham University. At the age of twenty one he sold a play to the BBC and continued to write following his graduation whilst working as a stockbroker's clerk.

In 1938, he created the character Paul Temple, a crime novelist and detective. Many others followed and they were hugely successful until the last of the series was completed in 1968. In 1969, the Paul Temple series was adapted for television and four of the adventures prior to this, had been adapted for cinema, albeit with less success than radio and TV. Francis Durbridge also wrote for the stage and continued doing so up until 1991, when *Sweet Revenge* was completed. Additionally, he wrote over twenty other well received novels, most of which were on the general subject of crime. The last, *Fatal Encounter*, was published after his death in 1998.

Also in this series

FRANCIS DURBRIDGE

Paul Temple and the Front Page Men

COLLINS
CRIME
CLUB

COLLINS CRIME CLUB

An imprint of HarperCollins*Publishers*
1 London Bridge Street
London SE1 9GF
www.harpercollins.co.uk

This paperback edition 2015

First published in Great Britain by
LONG 1939

Copyright © Francis Durbridge 1939

Francis Durbridge has asserted his right under the Copyright,
Designs and Patents Act, 1988 to be identified as the author of this work

A catalogue record for this book is
available from the British Library

ISBN 978-0-00-812558-5

Set in Sabon by FMG using Atomik ePublisher from Easypress

MIX
Paper from
responsible sources
FSC
www.fsc.org   FSC™ C007454

CHAPTER I

Chief Inspector Charles Cavendish Mackenzie Reed

Chief Inspector Charles Cavendish Mackenzie Reed would certainly have delighted the heart of that famous Hollywood producer who, in a moment of sheer inspiration, insisted that all Scotland Yard detectives should have genuine Scottish accents.

Though Mac tried hard to conceal his dialect, he was never entirely successful. Unlike many of his fellow countrymen, he wanted to forget that he was once P.C. Reed from a tiny Scottish border town, who had won his way further and further South by sheer pertinacity, climbing a rung in the promotion ladder with every move.

It was his relentless perseverance which had brought him into the public eye as the man who had run down The Blade Kid, perpetrator of a long series of razor-slashing crimes in the Derby area. Reed worked on his pet principle that every criminal makes a slip at some time or other, and that it was merely a matter of waiting for it. In this particular case, he took the very obvious procedure of making a methodical daily round of all the shops that stocked cut-throat razors.

1

His colleagues had thought it a great joke at the time, but Charles Cavendish Mackenzie Reed merely set his stubborn jaw and went on with his business.

And then suddenly, on a peaceful morning towards the end of May, The Blade Kid did buy a new set of razors and this dour, sandy-haired Scot came to town. He was not altogether happy at Scotland Yard, for there were far too many public school and university men at the Yard for his liking. Their assured manners and open vowels made him more conscious than ever of his homely Scottish accent, but he would never have dreamed of betraying this suggestion of an inferiority complex.

Nevertheless the Chief Commissioner had come to rely upon Mac, particularly in cases which called for unfailing patience and ceaseless attention to detail.

At this particular moment, however, Mac was none too pleased at the way the Chief was treating him. Sir Graham Forbes had carelessly informed him that another of these ex-public schoolboys was to join him on his latest case. Mac chose to construe this as a reflection on his capabilities, but he had not dared to say so.

Inspector Hunter stood before him now in his little private office, which was kept in scrupulous order. Hunter was a personable young man in the middle twenties, who had a wide and peculiar knowledge of the London underworld. He always gave the impression that he did not take life very seriously, and rarely wore uniform if he could avoid it.

'The Chief says ye're to come in with us on this Blakeley case,' began Mac in dubious tones. He had heard that Hunter was brilliant, but erratic.

'Why, I'll be glad to, Mac. I've always wanted to study your methods,' Hunter assured him fervently. Fortunately, Mac had very little sense of humour, and did not detect the merest twinkle that flitted over Hunter's smooth features.

'It's a most peculiar case,' continued Mac, disregarding the flattery, 'and ye'll have to be patient, I warn ye. I've got Marshall, Rigby and Nelson checking up every clue, but so far—'

'Perhaps you'd give me the history of the case, Mac,' put in Hunter. Reed's face hardened a trifle. He resented young Hunter addressing him with this familiarity. These college cubs were no sooner inside the Yard than they were running the show, he reflected. However, Mac selected a small batch of cards from a file on his desk and motioned Hunter to a chair.

'Early in January, Mitchell and Bell published a novel called *The Front Page Men*—'

'Jolly good yarn, too,' broke in Hunter. 'You've read it, of course?'

'I have no time for reading detective novels. Nelson and Rigby went through it and made a report.'

'Oh …' Hunter subsided. 'I see.'

'As you're a literary sort of feller, maybe you already know that the book sold very well indeed, both here and in America,' continued Reed, with a hint of sarcasm in his voice.

'Eighty thousand copies to date. It was in the paper this morning,' Hunter informed him, cheerfully.

'That's beside the point at the moment,' said Mac, who did not relish these constant interruptions. 'The thing that interests us is a raid at the Margate Central bank, and the murder of the head cashier – a young fellow called Sydney Debenham.'

'Yes, nasty business that,' agreed Hunter. 'Seems to have been hushed up lately. Weren't you looking after the case?'

3

'I am still looking after it,' retorted Mac in no uncertain manner. 'But I don't propose to broadcast it in the B.B.C. news bulletins!'

'Sorry,' murmured Hunter.

'By the side of Debenham's body,' continued Mac, 'we found this card.'

He handed over a piece of white cardboard, a little smaller than an ordinary playing-card, and Hunter regarded it with a puzzled frown.

'The Front Page Men. So this was the card, eh? I read about it, of course. You've investigated the writing?'

Reed nodded indifferently. What did this youngster take him for? But the youngster seemed to be ignoring him and thinking of other things.

'Of course this business would boost the sales of the novel,' concluded Hunter, at length.

'Are ye interested in the novel, or the case?' demanded Mac, acidly.

'Surely they have a bearing on each other?'

'If ye'll let me finish,' went on Mac impatiently. 'Well, about a fortnight after the Margate affair, there was a smash-and-grab in Bond Street. Lareines, the big jewellers. Inside the window of the jewellers, we found another card.'

He passed it over, and Hunter put the two cards together. 'Exactly the same,' was his verdict.

'Humph!' grunted Mac, who had examined the card under a microscope, and submitted it to the handwriting and finger-print experts with no better success.

'What about the author of this novel?' asked Hunter, passing the cards back. 'Wasn't it written by a woman?'

'It was published under the name of Andrea Fortune.'

'Can't say I've heard of her before. Was it a first novel?'

'Apparently.'

'Then who is this Andrea Fortune?'

'That,' replied Mac, 'is one of the many things the dear Chief Commissioner expects you to find out!'

'What about the publishers?'

Reed shook his head. 'They say the manuscript came from a back-alley agency in Fleet Street. We've been on to the agency, but they tell more or less the same story as the publishers. The novel was sent to them with instructions that all royalties should be handed over to the General Hospital in Gerard Street.'

'Any use my seeing the publishers again?'

'I don't want to discourage ye,' answered Mac, 'but I saw young Gerald Mitchell – he's the boss – only this morning. He swore he'd never set eyes on Andrea Fortune. I think he's telling the truth. In fact, he seems pretty scared about the whole business.'

Hunter took a cigarette from his case, caught Mac's quizzical glare, thought better of the matter, and replaced it. He shut the case with a snap. 'You seem to have covered the ground pretty thoroughly,' he commented.

'Ay, that's what I'm here for,' said Mac in even tones, taking up a new card from his desk. 'Now,' he announced solemnly, 'we come to the Blakeley affair.'

Hunter smiled. 'The papers have certainly been full of the Blakeley affair,' he said.

Mac frowned. 'I canna understand how it leaked,' he murmured irritably. 'The Chief has even had the Home Office on the phone five times.'

'Well, the Front Page Men have certainly "made" the front page this time. Is the Chief doing anything about it?'

'Now, hasn't he put you on the case?' demanded Reed, unable to conceal the sarcasm in his voice. 'Apart from that, he seems to be labouring under the impression that this business might have some connection with the Granville kidnapping.'

'But surely that was ages before we'd heard of the Front Page Men?'

'We may not have heard of them, but they could have been there just the same,' said Mac, who believed in covering all contingencies.

'It was a sad affair about Lester Granville. Apparently the child was the only thing he had left in the world after his wife died.'

'Granville completely went to pieces over that business,' said Mac. 'Gave up the stage and everything. The Chief was upset, too. But that's no reason for jumping to conclusions that it's anything to do with the Blakeley affair.'

'I wonder,' murmured Hunter, thoughtfully wrinkling his forehead.

'Now, look here ...' began Mac, peevishly.

Hunter laughed. 'All right, Mac, let's have the rest of the Blakeley story.'

'I expect you've read all there is to tell. Last Friday, Sir Norman Blakeley's only son disappeared under rather mysterious circumstances and—'

'By the way,' put in Hunter, 'who exactly is Sir Norman Blakeley?'

Before Reed could reply, there was a sharp knock at the door, and a burly sergeant entered.

'Sorry to trouble you, sir, but there's a man outside causing a lot of bother. Says he wants to see the Chief, but he refuses to fill up the form.'

Chief Inspector Reed's sandy eyebrows went up in disapproval. There were too many people walking in and out of

Scotland Yard these days, and it was time they put a stop to it. But before he could give instructions, the unruly visitor was standing behind the sergeant.

He was a man of about fifty, obviously in a highly nervous condition; correctly dressed in the customary City uniform of a morning coat, striped trousers and cream gloves. His tie was a shade crooked, his hair somewhat ruffled, and one button of his waistcoat was unfastened.

'When am I to be allowed to see the Chief Commissioner?' he began in high-pitched, petulant tones, and Chief Inspector Reed, who had risen to administer a stern reproof as only he knew how, straightened up smartly.

'At once, Sir Norman,' he answered politely.

CHAPTER II

Mr. Andrew Brightman

Once inside the unpretentious office that has been described as the nerve centre of Scotland Yard, Sir Norman's overbearing manner fell from him, and he began to tremble in patent distress.

Sir Graham Forbes looked up from his desk, and at once appreciated the situation. He took his visitor's arm and led him to a comfortable chair, then went across to a cupboard and poured out a glass of whisky.

'Drink this first,' he ordered, and made a pretence of carrying on with some work while Sir Norman gulped down the mellow liquid.

'Now,' said Sir Graham, carefully blotting his signature to a letter, 'any news?'

'Yes,' answered Blakeley, in a voice that had sunk almost to a whisper. 'I heard this morning.'

'Tell me exactly what happened.' The manner in which he fidgeted with his paper-knife betrayed that Sir Graham had caught some of his visitor's nervousness.

Blakeley set down his glass. His hand still shook appreciably, but he appeared to make an effort.

'At about a quarter past ten, the telephone rang. A girl's voice said: "We want nine thousand pounds. We want it in twenties. The notes must not be numbered consecutively. Put the money in a brown leather suitcase, and leave it in the telephone-booth at the corner of Eastwood Avenue, Mayfair. The money must be there by four o'clock tomorrow afternoon."'

'Is that all?' asked Forbes, who had been making rapid notes on a scribbling-pad.

'Not quite. After that, she said, "Don't worry. The child is safe." Then she rang off.' The visitor leaned forward in great agitation.

'Sir Graham, do you think he is safe? Because if anything's happened to him, I'll ...'

The Chief Commissioner leaned back in his chair.

'You can rest assured, Sir Norman, that we shall do everything in our power, but please remember that this is a far more serious business than a mere case of kidnapping. There's a lot more at stake than just getting back your boy for you.'

'He's my only son, Sir Graham, the only son I'm likely to have,' said Blakeley, quietly.

'Believe me, I sympathise,' replied Forbes. 'I am merely trying to impress upon you the fact that we are doing our utmost to track down the organisation that's responsible.'

'Then you really think it's a big organisation?'

Sir Graham shrugged non-committally. 'I suspect ... but I'm not certain.' He went across to the cupboard. 'Another whisky?'

'No, thanks.'

Sir Graham poured himself one.

'Your men were at the house yesterday,' pursued Sir Norman. 'Did they discover anything?'

The Chief Commissioner consulted a sheaf of papers.

'Inspector Nelson inclines to the opinion that the boy was snatched out of his bed at four in the morning. All the same, it's difficult to see how they got him out of the house.'

'It is, indeed. I have the room next door, and I'm a very light sleeper.'

'Who was the first to discover that the boy was missing?'

'I did. I went into his room about half past seven. The little chap is usually awake by then, and pretty frisky with himself.'

'And on this particular morning?'

'The room was very untidy – bed-clothes all over the place.'

'Was it shortly after that you received the message warning you not to communicate with the police?'

Sir Norman nodded. By this time he had recovered some of his old assurance, probably due to the influence of Sir Graham's old Scotch whisky. But he was still considerably agitated, and his face twitched with emotion as he answered Sir Graham's questions. The Chief Commissioner was lost in thought for a while; once he made a move to telephone, then changed his mind, and decided to continue with the questioning. He picked up a typewritten list, and looked across at Sir Norman.

'You gave Inspector Nelson full details of all the visitors to your home during the week. Now this list looks surprisingly short to me. Are you quite sure there's no one you've overlooked?'

'Absolutely certain,' said Blakeley, with a trace of his City aggressiveness.

'On Tuesday, for instance,' pursued Sir Graham, 'apart from the usual tradespeople, a Mr. Andrew Brightman called, and also a Mr. J. P. Goldie.'

For a moment Blakeley was nonplussed. 'Goldie? I don't remember saying anything about a Mr. Goldie?'

11

'I understand that he came to tune the piano.'

'Oh yes, of course! The piano-tuner! I never knew his name.'

Sir Graham was toying with his paper-knife again. 'Is Mr. Andrew Brightman a friend of yours?' he asked at length.

'Hardly a friend. I've known him about two years. We met at a City banquet, and I gave him a lift back to Hampstead. After that we became quite friendly – we're both interested in old china – but we don't see a great deal of each other.'

'Then why did he come round on that particular evening?'

'He'd brought a piece of china he'd had repaired for me by a relative of his. Suddenly, in a fit of desperation, I poured out the whole story to him. As you can imagine, I was very cut up, and to console me, I suppose, he started to tell me about his daughter.'

'His daughter? What about her?'

Sir Norman Blakeley hesitated.

She was kidnapped too – by the Front Page Men.'

The paper-knife fell with a clatter.

For a moment, the Chief Commissioner seemed too astounded to speak. Then he recovered abruptly. 'Are you sure of this? What happened to the girl?'

'He got her back.'

'The devil he did! How? He never informed us—'

'No. It cost him eight thousand pounds, Sir Graham.'

The Chief Commissioner was obviously staggered.

'Eight thousand! How soon can I get hold of Andrew Brightman?' he asked.

'He's outside in a taxi,' said Sir Norman. 'I thought you would probably want to interview him, so I persuaded him to come along.'

'I'm very grateful to you,' acknowledged Sir Graham, pressing a button at the side of his desk. As if by magic, the door opened, and Sergeant Leopold stood waiting for instructions.

'There's a gentleman in a taxi outside, a Mr. Brightman. Ask him to come up, Sergeant.'

When the door had closed, Sir Graham turned to Blakeley again. 'I suppose you've seen the papers today?'

Sir Norman started in alarm. 'You don't mean it's got into the papers?'

'I'm afraid so.'

The colour rushed to Sir Norman's face.

'They warned me not to get in touch with the police,' he almost shouted, 'and you promised to keep it out of the papers!'

Sir Graham clasped his shoulder. 'Don't alarm yourself, Sir Norman. They must have seen the papers before you had the message this morning. Now, tomorrow morning, take a taxi and go straight to your bank. Arrange for the nine thousand pounds exactly as the girl instructed you. Tomorrow afternoon, take the money yourself and deposit it in the telephone-box at the corner of Eastwood Avenue. As soon as you've deposited the money, leave the telephone-booth and return home. Is that clear?'

'Then you want me to give in to these swine?' stammered Sir Norman.

'I want you to do as I tell you and leave the rest to us,' answered the Chief Commissioner. 'Now I'd like to see Mr. Brightman alone, if you don't mind waiting.'

'Yes, yes, I'll wait,' agreed Sir Norman, collecting his hat and umbrella.

Sir Graham ushered out his guest, and returned to telephone for a map of the Mayfair district. He had just replaced the receiver when Mr. Andrew Brightman was shown in.

The Chief Commissioner surveyed him shrewdly. 'Please sit down, Mr. Brightman,' he murmured politely, and his visitor complied. He was a fairly stout individual in the middle fifties. A man who was obviously the life and soul of the party. He reeked with self-assurance, and was never at a loss for a reply of some sort, whatever the situation might be.

His hail-fellow, well-met attitude was calculated to disarm most people, and doubtless accounted, in no small measure, for his prosperous appearance. He did not seem in the least overawed by his surroundings, and faced Sir Graham with a pleasant smile, as if they were about to discuss a business proposition.

'I have just been having a chat with Sir Norman Blakeley,' began the Commissioner. 'He tells me that your daughter disappeared under rather mysterious circumstances, and that you paid a certain sum of money for her return.'

'That is so,' asserted Brightman. For a second or two, Sir Graham appeared to be puzzled.

'When did this happen?'

'March of this year. The eighth to be precise, a date I shan't easily forget,' Brightman assured him.

'Why didn't you consult us about this matter, Mr. Brightman?' suddenly demanded the Commissioner, with a hint of anger in his tone. But his visitor was not in the least perturbed.

'To perfectly honest, Sir Graham, because I didn't wish to take any risk.'

Forbes' anger was obviously rising. 'It seems to me that you took a very grave risk.'

That,' murmured Andrew Brightman politely, 'like so many things, Sir Graham, is a matter of opinion.'

Once again the Chief Commissioner was at a loss, finally he asked, 'Is your daughter in town at the moment?'

'She's at school in France. A small place near St. Raphael. She's been there six months. I thought was advisable to send her away after that business.'

Sir Graham gave a nod of understanding. 'Now, Mr. Brightman, when you handed over this money, did you retain the numbers of the notes?'

Brightman shook his head. 'I was told to deliver it in twenties – I remember that rather surprised me. However, I cashed a cheque at Floyds, in Manchester Street, my private bankers. I daresay they could tell you the numbers. I understand it's usual to keep a record.'

Sir Graham waved aside the suggestion. 'How did you receive your instructions about delivering the money?' he asked.

'By telephone. It was the Monday after Margaret had disappeared. I didn't feel like going to the office in case something should turn up, and I was wandering round the library when the phone rang.'

Sir Graham seemed incredulous. 'Do you mean to tell me you waited two days without making any move?'

Mr. Andrew Brightman was still very sure of himself, however. 'I had a reason for waiting,' he answered quietly.

'Then I should very much like to hear that reason.'

'When Margaret vanished,' continued Brightman, 'naturally my first thought was to get in touch with the police. I was actually on the point of doing so when my butler brought me a small card. There was nothing unusual about it, except that it had no address and had obviously been delivered by hand. Morgan, my butler, thinks it must have been left in the letterbox while we were all rushing over the house looking for Margaret. This must be true, because he had already cleared the first delivery of letters out of the box and put them on my desk.'

'H'm, very interesting. Now tell me, who was the first person to discover your daughter was missing?'

'The maid. She used to take Margaret a glass of milk at about eight o'clock every morning. On this particular day she was surprised to find Margaret was not in her room, and that apparently the bed had not been slept in. Naturally, the poor girl was quite bewildered, so she called Morgan.'

'And you were about to phone the police when Morgan brought you this card?'

Brightman nodded. 'Yes. We'd searched the house from cellar to attic, and I was getting more and more alarmed. By the way, I thought perhaps you'd be interested to see the card.'

He handed over a slip of pasteboard, which Sir Graham examined carefully through a small but powerful magnifying glass. It bore the simple message:

Don't call the police. Wait 48 hours. The child is safe.
The Front Page Men.

'Thank you,' said Sir Graham at length. 'I should like to keep this for the time being, if I may.'

'Of course, sir,' agreed Brightman, who now appeared to be more at ease than ever, and spoke in the slightly pompous manner of the chairman of a company who is about to disclose the payment of an extraordinary dividend. 'You can imagine,' he went on, 'what a state I was in when I received that note. I didn't know what to do. Suddenly I made up my mind to wait.' Brightman paused. 'I needn't tell you what that week-end was like, Sir Graham. Every minute seemed an eternity. I wouldn't go through it again – not for a million!'

Suddenly the recollection of this experience seemed to upset his urbanity for the first time. He swallowed hard, shifted uncomfortably in his chair, and ran a finger round the edge of his collar before continuing. 'Both Morgan and the maid wanted me to send for the police. In fact, Morgan threatened to go over my head and get in touch with Scotland Yard himself. The poor devil is devoted to Margaret, and he was completely unnerved. Then, at about half past nine, another note was delivered.'

He handed over the second card, which read:

Be near the telephone tomorrow morning. The child is safe.
  The Front Page Men.

Forbes examined it carefully, but it appeared to offer no clue.

'How long have Morgan and the maid been in your employment?'

'Oh, quite a while – long before my wife and I parted. Morgan was with my father for some years. They both worship Margaret, if that's what you're thinking, Sir Graham.'

'What time did you receive the phone call?'

'At about 10.15. Naturally I answered the phone myself. A woman was at the other end. She sounded young and quite pleasant. "We want eight thousand pounds,' she said, 'we want it in twenties. The notes must not be numbered consecutively. Put the money in a brown leather suitcase, and deposit it in the cloakroom of the Regal Palace Hotel. The case must be there by 12.30 tomorrow morning." '

Sir Graham snatched up his pencil and made several notes. Then he nodded to his visitor to continue.

'The next morning, I turned up at the Regal Palace Hotel complete with suitcase and money. At the cloak-room they gave me a ticket for the suitcase, which rather worried me.

I couldn't quite see how anybody could get the suitcase out without the ticket – and so far, at any rate, I'd received no instructions about sending the ticket on anywhere. I was still thinking about this when I arrived home.'

He paused, took out a handkerchief, and rather nervously wiped his lips.

'I opened the front door, and the first thing I heard, was Margaret's voice. She had arrived just after I left the house with the money.'

If this mystified Sir Graham, he did not betray the fact. He inquired if the child was in good health.

'Perfectly normal, except for one thing,' replied Brightman. 'She couldn't remember anything that had happened. I talked to her for hours, trying to bring back her memory, but it was no use at all. That weekend had just been erased from her consciousness.'

'You made no attempt to retrieve the money?'

'I did consider that point, I admit. I even got as far as starting out for the hotel, but at the last moment I turned back. It struck me that even if I did get the money, something terrible might happen to Margaret again.'

Sir Graham re-read his notes with a worried frown before asking Brightman if there had been any callers at the house on the day his daughter disappeared, Brightman thought for a while, appeared to be about to reply in the negative, then recalled that the only visitor was a piano-tuner.

Sir Graham looked up quickly.

'A piano-tuner?'

'Yes.'

'Do you know his name?'

'I'm afraid I don't,' confessed Brightman. 'Morgan did mention it, but—'

'Was it Goldie, J.P. Goldie?' broke in the Chief Commissioner, unable to repress a hint of eagerness in his voice.

'Why, yes. I believe it was,' replied Brightman in surprise. 'But he's quite a harmless old customer, he couldn't have had anything to do with this awful business.'

Sir Graham smiled. 'That, like so many other things, Mr. Brightman, is a matter of opinion.'

A rather awkward pause was suddenly interrupted by Sergeant Leopold, who entered with a large map, which he placed on the Chief Commissioner's desk.

'I think you've told me pretty well everything,' said the Commissioner, 'and if you'll excuse me ...'

'Why, certainly, Sir Graham. And if I can be of further service, don't hesitate to telephone.'

'Thank you. Sergeant Leopold will show you the way out.'

As soon as Brightman had gone, Sir Graham rang for Inspector Nelson, a dark, alert young man, and ordered him to telephone Floyds Bank in Manchester Street and find out whether their customer, Andrew Brightman, had cashed a cheque for eight thousand pounds on March the eighth.

'And tell Reed and Hunter I want them,' he added as an afterthought.

'Well, Mac, did you check up on Brightman?' Forbes demanded, as the stocky figure appeared in the doorway, closely followed by Hunter.

'I did that. He's a stockbroker – lives in Hampstead. Divorced his wife in 1928, and has the custody of the child.'

'H'm, that seems to tally,' agreed Sir Graham. 'What else?'

'Brightman and the piano-tuner were the only people who visited Sir Norman Blakeley on the day the boy disappeared.'

19

'What about the piano-tuner?'

'I checked up on him, sir. He used to be with Clapshaw and Thompson's in Regent Street. Started on his own about six years ago. Lives at Northstream Cottages, Streatham.'

'That sounds fair enough. Now I've some news for you, Mac. Sir Norman's had a message. They want nine thousand pounds by four o'clock tomorrow afternoon.'

Even Mac's inscrutable poker face reacted to this information, and Hunter made no secret of his astonishment.

There was a moment's silence.

'Nine thousand?' repeated Reed. 'Did he get any instructions?'

'Yes, it must be left in twenties – inside the telephone-box at the corner of Eastwood Avenue, Mayfair.'

'Eastwood Avenue! They've certainly got a nerve!' exclaimed Hunter.

Sir Graham pulled the map towards him, and they all bent over it. They traced the position of the telephone-booth without much difficulty, and the Commissioner began to formulate a plan.

'Mac, I shall want six of your men here on the corner of Lenton Park Road,' he said, 'that will give you a clear view in both directions.'

'We'll be there, sir.'

'And, Hunter, you'll be on the other corner, opposite the booth. I want everybody there by three o'clock at the latest.'

The two assistants acknowledged their instructions and made certain of their positions on the plan. Then another idea occurred to the Chief.

'This block of flats here has a perfect view of the telephone-booth if this map's accurate.'

'That's so, sir,' agreed Hunter, who knew the district quite well.

'See if you can arrange for me to be in the first floor flat. Ring the janitor, Hunter, and find out whom it belongs to. The address is Eastwood Mansions.'

Hunter went out to make the call, passing Nelson in the doorway. He had returned to inform Sir Graham that Floyds Bank had turned up Brightman's cheque, which corresponded in every detail with the Commissioner's description.

'Well, Mac, it looks as if things are moving,' mused Sir Graham.

'They always are moving, sir, in this business,' was the non-committal reply.

'By the way, here are two more cards for your collection. They were sent to Brightman.'

Before Mac could ask any further questions, Hunter returned.

'That flat, sir,' he began.

The Chief looked up.

'Whose is it?'

'The address is 49, Eastwood Mansions, sir.'

There was a rather peculiar smile on Hunter's mobile features.

'The flat belongs to Mr. and Mrs. Paul Temple, sir,' he said.

CHAPTER III

Sir Norman Blakeley

The morning after Sir Norman Blakeley visited Scotland Yard, a taxi drew up at the main entrance of Northern Bank in the Haymarket, and Sir Norman emerged, carrying a small leather suitcase. He was nervous and apprehensive, yet to the casual observer here seemed to be almost an attitude of resigned indifference in his manner. His eyes were weary, and the skin on his face was flabby and greyish-yellow. A doctor would have taken one look at him and immediately reached for his hypodermic needle.

'Wait for me; I shan't be long,' Sir Norman ordered, as he stepped out rather heavily, and the driver touched his cap respectfully in acknowledgment. It was a fine morning, the sort of morning on which people preferred to walk rather than take a taxi, and he was lucky to have picked up this fare so early in the day; with a bit of luck, this distinguished-looking passenger would demand to be taken to one of the outer suburbs like Richmond – it would be a nice run through the Park this morning. 'All the same, I'd sooner it was Croydon,' mumbled the driver to himself. 'It'd be nice

23

to get 'ome for a bit o' dinner.' It was surprising how very few people wanted to go to Croydon these days – at night he invariably had to make the journey home without a fare.

He was cogitating upon this point when another well-dressed man came on the scene, opened the taxi- door without warning, and declared briskly: 'Take me to Euston—quick as you can—I've a train in twenty minutes. ...'

'Sorry, guv'nor. The cab's taken—I've got a fare in the bank 'ere. There's a rank just up the road—'

The stranger immediately took a pound note from his pocket and unceremoniously pushed it under the driver's nose. 'I must get the 11.15 from Euston,' he snapped. 'And if you do it, there's a pound for you.'

With a puzzled frown, the driver looked inquiringly into the bank entrance. There was no sign of his former passenger. Then he looked at his meter, which registered three-and-sixpence. He made a rapid calculation on the question of the maximum fare to Euston and decided he would clear at least ten shillings on the deal.

'Get in, sir,' he invited, slammed the door after his new fare, clicked the flag down as he sprang into his seat, and briskly started the engine.

The Haymarket branch of the Northern Bank is one of the oldest of its London offices, and its fittings savour of the traditional baronial hall. All the clerks are similarly attired in dark coats and striped trousers, and one or two of them can still remember the days when they were all expected to wear top hats. In spite of the absence of toppers, however, dignity is still the prevailing note.

Sir Norman never particularly liked this bank. He kept his account there because his father had done so before him, and it would have been rather an effort to change. As he stood there now, he resented the slightly supercilious air with which the clerk examined the cheque he had passed over. The young man, who was new to counter-work, had never been asked to such a large cheque before. He turned it over several times in patent hesitation. Suddenly Sir Norman's temper got the better of him.

'If you wish to refer that cheque, please do so at once. I want nine thousand pounds in twenty-pound notes, and they must not be numbered consecutively.'

The young cashier blushed, then managed to stammer an apology. 'I won't keep you a minute, sir ... I just wondered if ...' Rather incoherently, he beat a hasty retreat to the other side of the counter. Sir Norman could see him talking to a small group of three other clerks in hushed whispers. One of them peered over the top of the counter, obviously to make certain of the customer's identity.

Meanwhile Sir Norman drummed his fingers impatiently upon the expensive walnut surface. After what seemed almost ten minutes, but which was in reality exactly ninety seconds, the door of the manager's at the far end of the counter was opened by the young cashier.

'Would you mind stepping this way, please?' he demanded politely, and Sir Norman had no choice but to obey. He had not the slightest wish to interview Mr. Percy Briggs, an obsequious little man who'd been appointed temporary manager two years ago, and had contrived by judicious methods, which his staff described in unprintable language, to make himself a permanency. None of his staff liked Briggs, but elderly ladies among the bank's clientele thought him the most charming man they had ever encountered, seriously considered recognizing the fact in their wills. Which was exactly what Mr. Briggs was aiming at.

*

However, his fawning tactics never deceived Sir Norman, and he always felt slightly nauseated when Briggs thrust out a flabby hand to welcome him.

'Good morning, Sir Norman – a very fine morning,' smiled Briggs, exposing two teeth heavily stopped in gold.

'I think it will turn to rain,' replied Sir Norman, as disagreeably as possible, 'and I want nine thousand pounds as quickly as you can let me have them.'

'Certainly, Sir Norman. There are just one or two formalities, if you wouldn't mind taking a seat.' He indicated the comfortable chair reserved for customers. Briggs delighted in entertaining what he invariably termed 'the upper classes'. At lunch he would mention Sir Norman's name at least three times – as casually as possible – and there was no doubt that his table companions would be suitably impressed, particularly as Sir Norman was so much in the news just now. The manager adopted an attitude of polite sympathy. He had followed the Blakeley case very closely in the papers, and he loved to know what was going on behind the scenes. He told himself that it was part of his job. ('Never be afraid to ask questions,' he always impressed upon his new juniors.)

'I was very distressed to read about your son, Sir Norman,' he began in smooth accents.

'Ah yes, nasty business,' growled Blakeley. This was the last subject he wished to discuss with Briggs.

'I was reading in the *Evening Post* that Scotland Yard consider that the Front Page Men are really an organisation of—'

'The newspapers print too much damn rubbish,' said Sir Norman abruptly.

'Yes, but all the same, Sir Norman, don't you think—'

'I think I'd like that money as soon as possible, if it isn't troubling you too much,' retorted Sir Norman sarcastically.

So he was going to be unpleasant, was he, ruminated Briggs. All right, he would have to be shown that two could play the same game.

'You realise, of course, Sir Norman,' he cleared his throat rather ponderously, 'this cheque will make you about four thousand overdrawn? Of course, there will be no difficulty about that, but I thought you may have lost track of your affairs lately in view of this—er ...' He cleared his throat again.

'That will be all right. I shall be paying in some big dividends during the next week or two,' Sir Norman informed him.

'Quite, Sir Norman; I hope you did not mind my mentioning the matter.'

'Not in the least; I presume you will charge the usual rate,' replied Blakeley, hoping that the note of sarcasm in his tones did not escape Briggs.

'It may take a little while to get the notes,' continued Briggs, moving a pile of red-sealed documents from one side of his desk to the other in a manner which seemed to suggest that Sir Norman was trying to get a glimpse of them. This was one of Briggs' favourite little tricks. 'You see our main stock of banknotes are numbered consecutively. We may have to send out to the other banks.' He shrugged his shoulders, as if to impress upon his visitor the many intricacies of the banking system.

Sir Norman fumed inwardly.

Meanwhile Briggs meandered on. He touched upon the refugee problem, National Service, unemployment and Sir Montagu Norman.

After what seemed an eternity, the young cashier returned, carrying a bulky package, and Briggs dismissed him with a curt nod.

'Would you care to run through the notes, Sir Norman?' he asked.

Sir Norman half-heartedly fingered the notes, then put them into his suitcase. He hardly imagined that the receiver would quibble if there were twenty pounds short. He took his leave of Briggs as rapidly as he could, but the manager insisted on following him to the outer door of the bank.

Curiously enough, Sir Norman's prediction concerning the weather had been fulfilled, and rain was falling sharply. He was both irritated and annoyed to find that the taxi was nowhere to be seen. He distinctly remembered telling the man to wait for him. 'Confound the impudence of the fellow!'

Sir Norman glanced down the practically deserted thoroughfare, and instinctively turned up the collar of his coat.

There was no sign of a taxi. Just as he was turning away from the bank, however, a powerful American limousine swung out of a side-street and came sleekly to a standstill level with the kerb. Sir Norman was delighted to find that he at once recognised the man sitting in the back of the car.

'Jump in, Sir Norman,' called Andrew Brightman smilingly as he swung open the door of the car. Sir Norman sank into the heavily sprung seat with a sigh of relief. He was feeling tired, and rather apprehensive about forthcoming events. Placing the suitcase on the floor beside him, he tried to relax.

'I had a taxi waiting for me, but the fool disappeared,' he explained, for Brightman's benefit. Brightman smiled again, and produced his cigarette-case.

'Lucky I was passing,' he commented. 'Where can I drop you?'

'Well, I'm really on my way home,' Sir Norman informed him, 'if that isn't taking you too far out of your way.'

Brightman shook his head. 'As a matter of fact, I was going home myself to pick up some documents, so it's only a question of a couple of minutes.' He produced a gold petrol-lighter and lit Sir Norman's cigarette.

Sir Norman puffed contentedly, and felt more at ease than he had done all day. 'By the way, Brightman, how did you get on at the Yard yesterday?' he asked at length, exhaling a cloud of smoke.

Brightman made a faint *moue* which might have meant anything.

'They were very polite, but rather vague. I suppose one expects that of a Government department,' he laughed. 'Though Sir Graham did seem rather interested in my information. He's a good man, Forbes, though inclined to be a little too independent. In a case like this, Sir Norman, I maintain that Scotland Yard cannot afford to ignore the most trivial clue.'

Sir Norman nodded. 'It was very decent of you to go along there and tell them all you knew,' he murmured, drowsily, flicking the ash off his cigarette. 'Very decent indeed ...' This was a very comfortable car, he reflected, though a trifle overheated. Like most of these latest American models, it was designed to nullify the rigours of their climate. Sir Norman leaned forward in an attempt to open the window. To his surprise, he found that his head swam alarmingly the moment he moved his body. He remembered that he had had no food that morning ... yes, that would be the trouble ...

He raised his hand to his forehead, and the cigarette fell through his fingers on to the expensive upholstery. Brightman picked it up and held it out to Sir Norman. For the first time, Blakeley noticed that the smoke was a peculiar bluish-green colour. There was a strange taste in his mouth, too. Brightman was looking at him intently.

'You must finish your cigarette, Sir Norman,' Brightman was saying. There was something strange about that smile of his. In spite of the fact that his head was swimming, and his vision was more than a little blurred, Sir Norman made a mental note that Andrew Brightman was not to be trusted. For some unknown reason, he reminded him of Briggs, the bank manager ... and he had never liked Briggs ... had ... never ... liked ... Briggs ... had never liked ...

Andrew Brightman opened the window of the car about two inches and tossed the cigarette into the road. At precisely that moment, Sir Norman fell from the seat across the brown leather suitcase.

CHAPTER IV

Mr. and Mrs. Paul Temple

'Why Mayfair?' several of Paul Temple's acquaintances had demanded when they heard he had taken a flat in that exclusive and somewhat 'Michael Arlenish' neighbourhood.

'Why not?' urbanely replied the novelist. 'We've got to live somewhere, and one might as well start married life in the best possible surroundings. Besides, I adore seeing Steve in a riding habit, and living so near the Row encourages her.'

Paul Temple was confounding the sceptics who declare that a bachelor is too settled in his habits to make a success of married life. Nowadays he took more exercise, had lost a certain amount of weight, and looked all the better for it. His wife had even persuaded him to cut down his smoking, thereby disconcerting various other cynics who hold the opinion that a man never changes after he is married.

So far, Paul Temple had only one complaint against married life – he was so immersed in the novelty of its routine after his bachelor existence that he found little time, and not a great deal of inclination, to concentrate upon his latest novel.

When Gerald Mitchell, his publisher, brought his wife, Ann, to see the new flat one day, Temple was only too well aware that the visit had a dual purpose. Gerald Mitchell was anxious to discover if the new book was likely to be completed to schedule.

Mitchell was an exceptionally tall, dark man, a distinct Varsity product, and apt to worry himself unduly over matters which he could not control, and which had a habit of straightening themselves out without his assistance.

His wife, Ann, was in some ways a useful sort of antidote. Self-centred and sophisticated, she waved aside all his fears and petty worries until he eventually began to see them in their correct proportion. Almost ash-blonde, and extremely good-looking, Ann Mitchell obviously spent as much on her appearance as would maintain a fair-sized, working-class family.

It was not long before the conversation veered round to the subject of *The Front Page Men*, and Mitchell was obviously more than a little troubled about the mystery surrounding this, his most successful publishing venture. Temple did his utmost to reassure him, but Mitchell was feeling the strain of the police inquiries and constant cross questioning.

Temple was sorry that Steve was not present to divert the conversation to more cheerful channels in that delightful way she had. She was out shopping, and Temple's mind wandered away from the conversation occasionally to picture her roaming around Selfridges', her small mouth set in determined fashion, as from time to time she consulted her shopping list.

'So you honestly don't think there's any need for me to worry about this business?' Mitchell was saying.

'Of course not, Gerald. If you hadn't published *The Front Page Men*, somebody else would have done so.'

'That's exactly what I've been telling him all along,' put in Ann. 'Isn't it, darling?'

'Yes, I know. But these detectives get me rattled. After all, my story does sound a bit thin, doesn't it? When a woman writes a best-seller like *The Front Page Men*, she doesn't usually go out of her way to keep her identity a secret. Not from her publisher, at any rate.'

'My dear, darling husband, don't be silly,' scoffed Ann Mitchell, screwing her head a little, to get a better view of herself in the full-length mirror that stood at one end of the drawing-room. 'It's as obvious as daylight. The woman who wrote the book is scared to death because some gang is putting her ideas into practice. I know I'd keep in the background if it were me – and I've never objected to publicity. Why, goodness, if she revealed herself, the police would be down on her right away. They'd immediately jump to the conclusion that she was the master mind behind these robberies.'

This idea seemed to intrigue Temple.

'I don't think the police are as stupid as all that,' he smiled. 'I have a feeling that Miss Andrea Fortune has a better reason than that for keeping her identity a secret. Still, there's nothing for you to worry about, Gerald.'

'Of course not. Come along, darling, we really must be going,' decided Ann, moving over to the mirror and adjusting a Suzy hat, which appeared to be in perpetual danger of dislodgment.

Temple saw his visitors to the door, and had just closed it when the phone rang. It was Sir Graham Forbes. Rather to the novelist's surprise, Sir Graham declared himself greatly interested in the new flat, and wondered if he could come round. Temple was inclined to feel a trifle dubious of this sudden enthusiasm, but his invitation was convincing enough.

As he replaced the receiver, there was a sound of someone lightly kicking the outer door He opened it, and there stood Steve, almost obscured by a huge pile of parcels, which seemed to hang from every part of her person.

'I couldn't ring or knock,' she informed him, her dark-blue eyes twinkling with glee. 'Quick, Paul, help me with these before I drop them.'

'What on earth have you been doing?' he asked, taking several parcels and carrying them into the lounge.

'Only a little shopping, darling,' she answered placidly. 'Just a few odds and ends.'

'But you've been away all afternoon,' he pointed out.

'Have I? Then you've had a good opportunity of getting on with the book ... oh, do be careful with that box—'

'What is it?' demanded Temple. 'An infernal machine?'

'It's a new contraption for peeling oranges. You've never seen anything like it. It's absolutely marvellous! You put the orange in at one end, turn the handle, and—'

'But, Steve, we don't like oranges!'

'I know, darling, but it was so frightfully cheap.'

'By Timothy, you are the limit!' laughed her husband, appraising her trim figure in its neat, dark-brown costume, and unconsciously making comparisons to the detriment of Ann Mitchell.

'And besides peeling oranges,' continued Steve, 'Carol Forbes says it will—'

'Have you been with Carol this afternoon?' he interrupted, quickly.

'Yes, why?'

34

'Her father was on the phone a moment ago. Invited himself to tea, in fact. He should be here at any minute.'

Steve looked surprised.

'Sir Graham? What does he want?'

'Presumably, a cup of tea,' grinned Temple.

'I do hope you were polite to him,' she murmured rather apprehensively. 'You've been in a fearful mood since you started the novel.'

'Nonsense! I was politeness personified. Why, his own pet detectives couldn't possibly have ...' His voice trailed away as he glanced through the window.

'Phew! Talking of detectives—'

'What is it?' asked Steve, following his gaze.

'Look! See those two men at the corner of the avenue?'

'Yes,' said Steve, peeping over his shoulder at the stalwart individuals who stood on the pavement. 'They were there when I came in. I've seen them before somewhere, haven't I?'

'They're from the Yard,' Temple told her. He went right up to the window and looked out in all directions.

'Good Lord, there's Hunter – and Reed over the other side! Now what the devil are they up to?'

'They seem to be watching that telephone-booth,' decided Steve, after they had observed the Yard men for some time. Temple nodded rather reluctantly. The cream of Scotland Yard playing sentry to a telephone-box didn't seem to make sense.

'Isn't that Richards in the car?' queried Steve.

'Yes, I believe it is.'

'I wonder if that's why Sir Graham invited himself to tea, so that he could keep an eye on his flock,' she mused.

'That's it!' Temple had almost simultaneously reached the same conclusion. He suddenly became very cheerful.

'Steve, my girl,' he laughed, 'things are looking up round the old homestead.'

His wife found it difficult to respond to his mood. The series of adventures in which she had been involved following the death of her brother had quite satisfied Steve's thirst for adventure.

Since the adventure which had culminated in the capture of Max Lorraine, *alias* the Knave of Diamonds, Paul Temple had completed one book and started another. Now he had apparently arrived at a degree of satiety which demanded a certain amount of extrusion before his inspiration could be renewed.

Pryce, the Temples' elderly manservant, suddenly announced Sir Graham Forbes, and the Chief Commissioner entered briskly.

'I do hope I'm not butting in, Temple,' he began, as Paul Temple went forward to greet him.

'Of course not,' his host assured him. 'You know my wife, I believe?'

'Rather,' said Sir Graham. 'How are you, Mrs. Temple? Married life seems to suit you. You're looking much better than on the last occasion we met at that dilapidated inn near Evesham. Remember the place?'

'The First Penguin? Brrr – shall I ever forget it?' shuddered Steve.

Paul Temple laughed, and a reminiscent smile lit the Chief Commissioner's rugged features.

Steve regarded them curiously. Here they were, making light of that terrible experience. Had they forgotten? Or was her imagination running away with her?

'I read your last novel, Temple,' Sir Graham was saying. 'The detective was a bigger fool than ever.'

'He had to be, Sir Graham,' answered Temple seriously. 'He was practically the Chief Commissioner!'

Steve joined in the laughter, then rang for Pryce and ordered tea. Sir Graham left his chair and strolled across to the window in casual fashion.

'Nice place you've got here, Temple,' he commented. 'Pretty handy for most things.'

'Very handy indeed,' suavely agreed the novelist. 'And such a delightful view. On a clear day we can see practically the whole of Scotland Yard.'

Sir Graham was momentarily disconcerted. 'So you've noticed them?' he grunted.

Temple nodded lightly. 'Is that why you came here, Sir Graham?'

'Yes. I wanted to be able to keep an eye on everything, and picked on this flat as the most likely spot. I got something of a shock when I discovered it was yours.'

'We haven't used it a great deal,' explained Steve. 'We've spent most of our time at Bramley Lodge.'

'I see, just a sort of *pied-a-terre*, eh?' said the Chief Commissioner. 'Well, I've lived in worse places.'

'Why are they watching that telephone-booth?' asked Temple, unable to restrain his curiosity any longer.

Once again Sir Graham was rather taken aback.

'Is it so obvious?' he asked.

'No, I don't think so. Not to the casual observer, at any rate. But I recognised Reed.'

Sir Graham looked at his watch. It was just turned twenty minutes to four. Time enough to give his host a brief outline of the case. He might be able to make some suggestion. Temple was certainly never lacking in ideas, reflected the Chief Commissioner.

'You've heard of Sir Norman Blakeley?' he began.

'You mean the motor magnate? Why, yes, of course.'

'The man whose child was kidnapped – it's in all the papers,' put in Steve.

'Yes, it's in the papers all right,' said Sir Graham ominously. 'But I'm going to tell you something that the reporters haven't got hold of yet.'

He went on to give details of the instructions Sir Norman had received.

'And he's going to deposit the notes?' softly queried Temple when Sir Graham had finished.

'Yes,' answered Forbes, slowly nodding his head, 'he's going to deposit them.'

'Did Blakeley receive any visitors the day the child disappeared?'

'Two. A friend of his named Andrew Brightman and an old chap called Goldie, a piano-tuner.' The Chief Commissioner then gave Temple a resume of the Brightman case and the strange coincidence of Goldie's presence on the day of the abduction.

Temple seemed particularly interested in the piano-tuner, and was about to fire a series of questions at Sir Graham when Pryce entered. For once, the imperturbable Pryce actually appeared to be in a hurry.

'Chief Inspector Reed has called to see Sir Graham,' he announced, and Reed himself was right on the servant's heels, somewhat out of breath and more than a little excited.

'Sorry to burst in like this, Sir Graham, but ...' he paused to shoot a dubious glance at Temple before imparting his news, 'it's Blakeley.'

Sir Graham was on his feet at once.

'What about Blakeley?'

'He's—dead.'

'Dead!' gasped Forbes, incredulously.

'Where is he?' demanded Paul Temple, briskly.

'He's in the telephone-booth downstairs. We've been watching it for two hours, and the poor devil was on the floor all the time.'

'But supposing someone had wanted to telephone?' queried Steve, in amazement.

'Yes, you can't tell me that nobody used the box for two hours in a district like this,' insisted the Chief Commissioner.

Reed shook his head, dismally.

'There was a large board against the booth which said "Out of Order". It was there when we arrived. If it hadn't been for that, we should have seen the body.'

'Then what made you go to the box?'

'The bell started ringing, sir. Hunter answered it.'

'Anyone there?'

'No, sir.'

'Was the suitcase there?'

'No. But there was this card on the ledge, sir ... near the telephone.'

Forbes took the card and read:

Unlike Mr. Andrew Brightman – he talked.
  The Front Page Men.

He passed the card to Temple, who examined it, and returned it to Reed. 'You'll be getting quite a collection, Mr. Reed,' he smiled, but Mac did not deign to reply.

'Come along, Mac, I want to see the body,' ordered Sir Graham presently. 'I'll be in touch with you again, Temple.'

'Always at your service, Sir Graham,' murmured Temple politely as they walked to the lift.

*

When he returned, he found Steve deep in thought. She looked up quickly as he entered. There was rather a strained expression in the dark-blue eyes.

'Paul,' she demanded earnestly, 'you're not going to have anything to do with this, are you?'

The idea seemed to amuse him.

'Me? Good Lord, no! What makes you think I have time to play around with the Scotland Yard boys? My dear Steve, I'm a hard-working novelist with an expensive wife to keep, and a novel as good as promised for—for—'

He stopped, and seemed to be listening intently. Steve, too, was suddenly alert.

'What is it, Paul?' she asked.

'Listen!'

As from a distance, came the sound of a piano being played; rather slowly, and with a soothing, delicate touch. Heard like this, there was almost a weird charm about the performance.

'There's … there's someone in the drawing-room,' whispered Steve, rather jerkily.

'Yes,' murmured Temple. 'Ring for Pryce.' She crossed the room, and almost before she had returned to her seat the door opened, and the sound of the piano became clearer and more purposeful.

'Is that someone in the drawing-room, Pryce?' asked Steve.

'Yes, madam. It's the piano-tuner. He called while you were with Sir Graham. I—I didn't wish to disturb you.'

Pryce appeared to be unconscious that his announcement had any dramatic possibilities.

'The piano-tuner … ?' said Paul Temple softly.

'Yes, sir. A Mr. Goldie … Mr. J. P. Goldie.'

CHAPTER V

Mr. J.P. Goldie

Temple looked at Steve and hesitated. Then he said, 'All right, Pryce, thank you.'

'Shall I bring the tea now, madam?'

'As soon as it's ready,' Steve replied. Pryce departed, noiselessly closing the door behind him.

'Wait here – I'll go and see if I can find out anything.'

Steve was obviously uneasy, but made no effort to restrain him. Temple went to the drawing-room, pausing for a moment outside, while the playing continued. Softly, he turned the door handle and entered. Though his back was to the door, and Temple imagined he had made no sound, the piano-tuner turned swiftly.

'Good afternoon, sir. I trust I did not disturb you.'

He spoke in a mellow, quiet voice, with every evidence of culture. Temple regarded the piano-tuner curiously. He was apparently a little below average height, for he looked tiny, seated at the piano. His clothes were inclined to be shabby, his hair rather too long, and he wore a bow tie. His greyish eyes were obscured to some extent by slightly tinted rimless glasses.

'You didn't disturb us at all,' said Temple in reply to his question. 'You play very well.'

'Thank you, sir. I could not resist the temptation – it's such a beautiful instrument.'

'Is this the first time you've been here?'

'Oh no, sir,' murmured Goldie, taking a large and some-what soiled handkerchief from his pocket and carefully wiping his hands. 'I came in March and November of last year. I attend at most of the flats in this building, and I must say I rather look forward to it. They have some lovely instruments ... there's a Bechstein in Number Twenty-two ... '

'I don't think we can have met before,' put in Temple.

'No, sir,' said the little man, whose memory appeared to be quite methodical. 'On the last two occasions you have been away, if I remember correctly, and the janitor had the key.'

'Oh, I see,' smiled Temple rather lamely. Mr. Goldie's manner was so completely disarming that he felt very like an intruder. 'Well—er—I mustn't interrupt you any longer,' he stammered at length.

'Not at all, sir. My work is finished. There is never much required on this instrument. It's always nicely up to pitch. I was just amusing myself.'

'By the way, your name's Goldie, isn't it?'

'That's right, sir,' answered the little man, turning a fraction in Temple's direction, and blinking mildly at him.

'Weren't you with Clapshaw and Thompson's for a number of years?'

'Yes, sir, almost fifteen.'

'By Timothy, that's a long time!' commented Temple.

'Yes, sir, but it passed quickly. I liked the work.'

'By the way, do you ever see Mr. Paramore now?' Temple went on, adopting a conversational tone, and doing his best to avoid any suspicion of cross-questioning in his manner. But something in Mr. Goldie's expression changed immediately, and he was obviously on his guard.

'Mr. Paramore?' he repeated, rather coldly.

'Yes, surely you remember Mr. Paramore. He used to be their general manager.'

There was a pause. Temple could almost feel the tension.

'No, sir,' said Mr. Goldie, finally, and there was almost a hint of reproof in his voice. 'I'm afraid I do not remember a Mr. Paramore.'

'Oh,' subsided Temple, flatly. 'Perhaps I am mistaking the firm. Er, if there's anything you want, just ring. My man will attend to it for you.'

'Thank you, sir,' replied Mr. Goldie with frigid politeness 'Good afternoon, sir.'

He turned to the piano and began to play a melancholy study by Chopin about which there almost seemed to be an air of grievance. Paul Temple returned thoughtfully to the lounge, where Pryce was laying tea.

'Well, what's he like?' was Steve's greeting.

'He seems rather a nice little fellow,' Temple told her. 'Apparently he's been here before, when we were down at Bramley Lodge.'

'Mr. Goldie is more or less the official piano-tuner for all the flats, sir,' explained Pryce.

'I see,' smiled Temple. 'Thank you, Pryce.'

'Not at all, sir. Will there be anything else, madam?'

'No, thank you, Pryce.'

'Muffins!' cried Temple. 'That was a good afternoon's shopping, after all. And what a treat Sir Graham's missed.' Steve passed him a large cup of tea.

'You seem very curious about this business,' she declared.

Temple stirred his tea reflectively. 'Yes, it's no use pretending that I'm not interested,' he admitted.

'I understand, darling.' But she did not sound very enthusiastic.

'There are one or two points which rather fascinate me,' continued Temple. 'For instance, this man Goldie ... and Andrew Brightman ... and Andrea Fortune ...'

'Andrea Fortune?'

'Yes, the woman who wrote *The Front Page Men*. I'm not absolutely certain that she doesn't fit into all this, somehow or other.'

Steve began to show some interest. Her reportorial instincts were slightly aroused.

'Has it occurred to you that Andrea Fortune may be just a pseudonym?' she suggested. 'In fact, Andrea Fortune might even be a man.'

'Yes, I had thought of that,' said Temple, taking a large bite out of his muffin. 'Pryce does these muffins to a turn,' he murmured, inconsequently.

'Yes, he is versatile for a man his age. He seems capable of anything from toasting muffins to throwing out inquisitive female reporters. Maybe he wrote *The Front Page Men*,' laughed Steve, rather delighted at the idea.

'I wonder if he could get the heroine of this cursed novel of mine out of her present distressing situation,' said Temple, thoughtfully.

They continued this light-hearted banter until tea was over. Then, rather casually, Temple said, 'We haven't anything special on tonight, have we?'

Steve wrinkled her brow for a moment. 'No,' she answered, 'nothing important.'

'Good. Then if you don't mind my leaving you alone, darling—'

'Not at all. I saw Morgan of the *Daily Gossip* this afternoon, and he asked me for an article.'

'On what?'

'He hadn't the least idea. Editors never have.'

'All right. Then I'll take the opportunity of looking up an old friend of mine. A Mr. Chubby Wilson.'

'Chubby Wilson,' murmured Steve.

'He's a disreputable sort of devil, and I wouldn't trust him with a brass farthing, but I'm really rather fond of him, and besides ...'

Steve smiled. 'I understand, darling. He talks!'

CHAPTER VI

Rev. Charles Hargreaves

Any self-respecting stranger to Rotherhithe would have thought twice before entering the Glass Bowl for a drink, unless, of course, he was particularly hardened to the drab appearance of riverside taverns. It stood on the corner of an uninviting street leading up from the river; its creaking sign portraying a bowl of dejected goldfish was so faded that only the fish were now faintly visible.

There were usually half a dozen loungers, very much down-at-heel, reclining listlessly against its crumbling walls, waiting for an acquaintance to come along and invite them inside for a drink.

A good proportion of the Glass Bowl's customers were seafaring folk; sailors from tramp steamers of every nationality, many of them looking every bit as desperate as their prototypes in the more bloodthirsty class of film.

On this particular evening, however, the bar-parlour was rather quieter than usual, and Mrs. Taylor, the hostess, had taken the opportunity to embark upon a long account of some grievance for the benefit of one of her customers.

She was a large, flamboyant woman of about forty-five, obviously a little too much inclined to sampling her own wares. Although it was still comparatively early in the evening, Mrs. Taylor's tongue had received sufficient lubrication to set it going merrily.

'"My Gawd!" I said to 'er,' she ended her story, '"to 'ear you talk anybody would think your ole man were a blasted admiral, instead of a yellow-bellied first mate on a perishin' tramp steamer."'

This seemed to tickle Jimmy Mills, a shifty young man of about thirty, who was rather too well dressed for his surroundings. He had a cruel mouth, which rarely relaxed from its thin, set line, except when he laughed rather too loudly, and he wore an expensive soft felt hat, pulled a little too far to one side.

'I bet she was nonplussed, Mrs. Taylor,' he remarked, stressing the long word, as if proud of his vocabulary.

'It took the wind out of 'er sails, I don't mind telling you,' nodded Mrs. Taylor. 'Can I get you anything else, love?' she suggested pleasantly, noticing that Mills' glass needed refilling.

'Yes,' ruminated Mills, 'I'd like another dry ginger; but this time you can put in a drop of—'

Suddenly his jaw dropped, as he caught sight of Paul Temple standing in the passage outside.

'Who is it?' asked Mrs. Taylor nervously. She had always been a little jumpy since the place had been raided last year. 'Who is it?' she repeated urgently.

'A fellow called Temple,' Mills told her. 'The last time I saw him was—'

'Phew! You 'ad me all of a jitter for a minute. I thought it was that dirty swine Brook, or one of his river cops.'

'Sh, he's coming in here,' cut in Mills. 'Now, the name's Smith – remember that!' he ordered curtly.

48

*

Temple came up to them and leaned against the bar, slightly nauseated by the odour of stale beer, foul tobacco-smoke, and the general uncleanliness of the bar-parlour.

'Good evening, sir. What can I get you?' primly demanded Mrs. Taylor, in her politest manner.

Temple ran a speculative eye over the bottles at the back of the counter.

'Well now, I think I'll have a ginger ale,' he decided.

'Yes, sir, very good, sir,' answered the obsequious Mrs. Taylor, and busied herself with bottle and opener. Meanwhile, Temple moved over to her late companion.

'Well, well! Look who's here! If it isn't Jimmy Mills!' he ejaculated.

'The name's Smith,' retorted Mills, shortly.

'Smith?' Temple seemed amazed. 'Not one of the Devonshire Smiths?'

'Don't try to be funny!' snapped Mills, savagely, and Paul Temple laughed.

'Still the same old Jimmy. Tell me, what happened to that Canadian gold mine of yours? Don't say there wasn't any gold. Dear me, what *did* the shareholders have to say at the general meeting? Or perhaps there wasn't any general meeting, Jimmy?'

Apparently the shot went home.

'Look 'ere, Temple,' snorted Mills, 'there's no need for any of this funny business. If a fellow can't keep to the straight and narrow without some busybody shovin' 'is nose where it's not wanted, then it's come to something!'

'Jimmy, I'm disappointed in you,' pronounced Temple, appearing to be hurt. 'You're dropping your aitches again. It's a bad sign, Jimmy, it's a bad sign!'

'Ah, you are a one, Mr. Temple!' laughed Jimmy, but his laugh was somewhat reluctant and rather hollow, and he was by no means at ease. He had decided that his policy was to play up to Temple without giving anything away.

'I'm glad to see you again, Mr. Temple,' he went on. 'Looking pretty fit, too. I heard you was married. Is that right?'

'That's right, Jimmy,' nodded Temple.

'Seems to agree with you. I suppose you've gone out of the business now.'

'Business?' queried Temple.

'Yes … you know …'

Paul Temple smiled enigmatically. 'That depends …'

'I thought of settling down meself,' pursued the other. 'But, well, things ain't too good in my line just now, and—'

'What exactly is your line nowadays, Jimmy? You're so versatile, I never know quite—'

'I'm a commercial man now, Mr. Temple.'

'What sort of commerce?'

'Oh, buyin' and sellin' things you know,' said Jimmy vaguely. 'All above board and legitimate,' he hastened to add. 'I've got a cosy little office in the West End.'

'Really?' smiled Temple.

Mrs. Taylor placed a badly chipped glass of ginger ale in front of the novelist, and noticing Mills' empty glass, he invited him to have another drink.

'I don't mind if I do, Mr. Temple. Ginger ale, please, Mrs. Taylor.'

As she moved away, he turned to Temple. 'I'm on the wagon these days – going straight, you see, Mr. Temple.'

'I should have thought that there would have been rather more congenial pubs near your West End office,' said Temple pensively.

'Oh, I dunno. You get a hankering to see the old places,' replied Mills, with a shrug.

Mrs. Taylor brought the drink, and would obviously have had no objections to joining in the conversation, but neither of the men encouraged her, and she eventually returned to the tap-room.

Temple lifted his glass and sniffed it suspiciously. It smelt strongly of beer. He took a quick gulp by way of acknowledging Mills' salutation, and set the glass aside.

'It's always hard for a bloke like me to convince people what knew 'im in the old days that he's running straight,' persisted Mills, but Paul Temple was paying little attention. A newcomer had entered the bar parlour.

Dressed in sober black, the stranger had a thin face and ascetic appearance. He wore a clerical collar, but no hat. His dark hair was plastered smoothly, but free from any unguent, and Temple thought he detected a roguish glint in his eyes. He might have been any age between thirty and forty-five. For a second he stood in the doorway; then Jimmy Mills hailed him heartily.

'Mr. Hargreaves! Come over here and vouch for me to this gentleman.'

'Certainly I will!' agreed the newcomer, joining them.

'This is the Reverend Hargreaves – Mr. Temple,' Mills introduced them, and the parson shook hands warmly. 'He's in charge of the Seamen's Hostel just round the corner,' explained Mills for Temple's benefit. 'Knew me before I took to the straight and narrow.'

Hargreaves managed to get in a word at last.

'Not—Paul Temple, by any chance?' and there was a note of astonishment in his voice.

'Yes, that's right, Reverend,' corroborated Jimmy Mills.

51

'Well, indeed, this is a pleasure,' enthused Hargreaves. 'I've read so many of your books, Mr. Temple, that I feel as if, well, as if I've known you for years.'

'That's very kind of you,' replied Temple, who did not know quite what to make of this unusual cleric.

He was just a shade too effusive, and Temple did not like the way he constantly looked out of the corner of his eyes at the other occupants of the room.

'You never told me that you were a friend of Mr. Temple's, Jimmy,' reproached Hargreaves.

'Well, I don't know whether you'd call us friends or not, Reverend.'

Hargreaves seemed to understand, and was obviously amused. 'There's no reason why you shouldn't be friends now, Jimmy.' He turned to Temple. 'He's going straight, Mr. Temple, and making a very fine job of it.'

'I'm glad,' said Temple. 'Jimmy always made a very fine job of everything,' he added cryptically.

Mrs. Taylor intruded once more.

'Anything I can get you, Parson?'

'No,' smiled Hargreaves, as though deliberating the point. 'No, thank you very much, my dear. But I wonder if you would be so kind as to place these bills in a prominent position for me. I'm holding a special concert on Sunday afternoon, and I do hope the attendance will be a record.'

'Well, I'll do my best, Reverend,' offered Mills. 'I'll bring some of my City pals along.'

'Thank you, Jimmy, that's very good of you,' said Hargreaves, laying a friendly hand on Mills' shoulder.

'I'll see what I can do, Mr. Hargreaves,' said Mrs Taylor, taking the bills. 'I can't promise nothin', mind you.'

'Thank you, my dear. I know I can rely on you.'

'Well, I must be toddlin',' said Jimmy Mills at length, draining his glass. 'Good night, Mr. Temple.'

'Good night, Jimmy.'

'Good night, my son,' said Hargreaves, shaking Jimmy's hand.

'Cheerio, Lucy,' called Mills, with a significant wink and backward nod as he passed the tap-room.

Paul Temple tried to persuade his companion to change his mind about a drink, but the latter shook his head resolutely.

'I have great faith in Jimmy Mills, Mr. Temple,' said Hargreaves earnestly. 'He's changed a great deal in the last two years.'

'I hope you're right, sir. He used to be one of the cleverest confidence men in the country.'

'Yes, yes, I know, Mr. Temple. How dreadful, how very dreadful!' deplored Hargreaves, a shade too piously.

'I don't want to disillusion you, sir, but I think I ought to warn you that Mills has a knack of convincing anybody about anything he sets his mind on. Of course, it's no business of mine, but—'

'That's all right, Mr. Temple. I quite understand, and I appreciate your trying to warn me. But I want to give Jimmy a chance.'

'Do you spend much time here, sir – I mean in this part of the world?' demanded Temple, abruptly changing the subject.

'Oh, a great deal, Mr. Temple. I'm more or less in charge of the Seamen's Hostel, you know. It's uphill work, but I'm always doing my best to persuade those unfortunate fellows to regard our hostel as a sort of home from home.' He added with a sigh, 'My task isn't an easy one, Mr. Temple, by any means.'

'I'm sure it isn't,' said Temple sympathetically.

'However, one mustn't grumble. There's never a dull moment; I'll say that for my daily round.'

'I can quite appreciate that,' smiled the novelist. He looked round the smoky parlour, which was now filling up with men from all the seven seas. Temple noticed their looks of suspicion and lowered his voice.

'Mr. Hargreaves, do you know a man called Wilson, Chubby Wilson?'

'Why, yes, I know him quite well,' admitted Hargreaves with some slight hesitation. 'A delightful fellow, but – well, I hate to say this – thoroughly untrustworthy.'

He seemed reluctant to pursue the subject, and continued hastily: 'Let's talk about yourself, Mr. Temple. I'm really quite thrilled at meeting you like this. I've often wondered how you get those charming little eccentricities into your characterisation – but of course I see now. You come to places like this and study your types at first hand.' He paused. 'You know, it may sound rather funny, but I've always thought that, given the opportunity, I should be able to write.'

Paul Temple began to feel rather bored. He had not come to the Glass Bowl to swop enthusiasms with a literary amateur.

'Oh, I know it sounds frightfully conceited,' persisted Hargreaves deprecatingly, 'and I suppose rather priggish in a way, but when one studies human nature in the raw, as it were—'

'Talking of life in the raw, have you read *The Front Page Men*?' asked Temple, quietly.

Whether Hargreaves resented this diversion from the subject of his ambitions, or whether he was taken aback by the question, Temple was not certain. But he paused for a moment before replying.

'*The Front Page Men*? No, no, I haven't read the book. I'm told it's very good.'

'Yes,' said Temple, 'extremely realistic.'

'I really feel quite—er—reluctant to read it,' confessed Hargreaves, ingenuously. 'I mean, with all these terrible robberies, and that shocking case of Sir Norman Blakeley's. Although I suppose one can hardly hold the dear lady who wrote the book responsible. After all, according to the newspapers, she is devoting the royalties to a worthy charity.'

Temple absent-mindedly picked up his glass, set it down again, and lit a cigarette.

'Well, this is a coincidence,' said Hargreaves suddenly, in a surprised voice. 'Here's the gentleman you were asking about.'

'Chubby Wilson? Where?' demanded Temple.

'In that far corner, Mr. Temple. I only just caught a glimpse of him.'

'Then would you excuse me?' said Temple rather abruptly.

'Why yes, yes, of course. But I hope we may meet again on some future occasion.'

'Yes, I hope so too,' hastily agreed Temple, as he quickly shook hands, and moved over to the corner of the bar which Hargreaves had indicated.

As he approached, he could hear Chubby Wilson's voice rising above the hubbub of general conversation. Apparently Chubby was trying to impress his political opinions upon one of the loungers from outside, whom he had brought in for a drink.

Chubby was not exactly worthy of his cognomen. Rather was he inclined to be pudgy and flabby. His complexion was a dirty yellowish brown, and a shabby scarf concealed a none-too-clean neck. He paused occasionally in his harangue to draw a deep breath.

'Hallo, Chubby, still on the soap box?' Temple greeted him. Chubby Wilson seemed surprised, but quickly recovered.

'Why, hello, Mr. Temple!' Then he turned to his former listener. ''Op it, Larry!' he ordered. The lounger leered questioningly at Temple, then slunk away.

'Sit down, Mr. Temple,' invited Chubby. 'Quite like old times seeing you again.'

Temple did not obey. Instead, he leaned over and spoke authoritatively. 'Chubby, I'm a very busy man, and I want to talk to you. Where can we go?'

'Well now, let me think,' mused Wilson. Then a solution suggested itself. 'Follow me, guv'nor.'

He led the way outside and along the passage to a tiny sitting-room, meanly furnished and shabby to a degree. Chubby closed the door after them very carefully.

'How's this?' he asked.

'It's not the Ritz, Chubby, but it will do,' decreed Temple, choosing a particularly uninviting bent wood chair, and sitting down. 'Well, how's life treating you?'

'Very nicely, Mr. Temple. I never was one to grumble.'

'Still in the dope racket?'

'Mr. Temple!' Chubby gave a very good imitation of shocked innocence, and Temple laughed.

'All right, Chubby – let's skip the part about going straight. I've just had one dose of that from Jimmy Mills.'

'Jimmy Mills, oh, 'im!' Chubby spat expressively.

'Now tell me,' continued Temple, bluntly, 'what do you know about the Front Page Men?'

At last Wilson appeared to be genuinely frightened, and made no pretence of concealing the fact.

'Nothin—nothin' at all,' he gasped. 'My God, if Basher's talked, I'll break every—'

'Oho,' chortled Temple. 'Still friendly with poor old Basher, eh? When did he get out?'

'About a month ago, Mr. Temple. He's a sick man, is Basher. His heart's in the wrong place.'

'You're telling me!' said Temple with a short laugh. 'It was certainly in the wrong place when he beat up that poor old Chelsea pensioner.'

Chubby was still very uneasy. His yellow streak was never very far from the surface.

'Have you seen Basher lately, Mr. Temple?' he blurted out at last.

'No, Chubby, I haven't. So he hasn't done any talking. Not to me at any rate.'

Chubby brightened up at once.

'I'm going to America at the end of the week, Mr. Temple,' he announced. 'Wonderful country, America.'

Temple leaned forward somewhat aggressively.

'Chubby, you haven't answered my question.'

'What question?' The little man tried vainly to avoid the issue.

'What do you know about the Front Page Men?' repeated Temple deliberately.

'I've told you, nothin'. Why the 'ell should I know anythin' about 'em?' cried Chubby, hysterically. He spread out his hands pleadingly. 'I've bin a lot of things in me time, Mr. Temple, but if there's one thing about me to the good—'

'There isn't!' snapped Temple, 'so you can cut the cackle. You're a dirty-minded little crook, with about as much backbone as a filleted plaice – but I like you.'

After this outburst Temple took a wallet from his inside pocket.

'I want information, Chubby, and I'm willing to pay for it.'

'How much?' demanded Chubby, licking his lips.

Temple pocketed the wallet again.

'That's better,' he approved. 'Now we're getting somewhere.'

'Mind you,' whispered Chubby guardedly, 'I don't say I've got anything to tell.'

'Chubby, you know you can trust me,' said Temple persuasively.

'Oh, sure, Mr. Temple, but—'

'Who are the Front Page Men?' asked Temple, in his quiet determined tones.

Wilson hesitated. 'I don't know, Mr. Temple. Nobody knows,' he declared.

'But you've had dealings with them,' pursued Temple, not to be outdone.

Chubby seemed to be struggling to make up his mind before replying. He went across to the door, opened it, looked around and closed it again. Then he came back to where Temple was sitting.

'Mr. Temple, have you heard of "Amashyer"?' he said softly.

'Amashyer?' repeated Temple, rather puzzled. 'Can't say I have. What is it?'

'It's a drug – a very strange and very rare drug,' explained Chubby, mysteriously.

'What effect does it have?'

'It makes people forget. Forget every blessed thing that's 'appened to them in the last forty-eight hours.'

Temple was obviously interested. His mind flew at once to the return of Brightman's child who had no recollection of what had happened to her. 'Go on, Chubby,' he ordered.

'In Holland it's called the Time drug. Nobody seems to know where it comes from in the first place – all I ever found out was that it's difficult to get 'old of, and worth its weight in gold.'

'All this is news to me,' confessed Temple. 'Tell me how you came to handle this drug.'

'I was in the Seamen's Hostel one night – it'd be about two or three months ago now – 'avin' a game o' cards with a feller, when up comes the parson chap and gives me a note which says: "Be at Redhouse Wharf tonight at nine."'

'Just a minute, Chubby. Which parson are you referring to?'

'Why 'im as calls 'imself the Reverend Hargreaves – bloke what runs the place.'

Temple whistled expressively, and nodded to Chubby to continue.

'Well, I never did like to miss a good thing, Mr. Temple, so to cut a long story short, I turned up at the wharf. There was a bloke waiting for me – a little feller with a high, falsetto voice. He said he could do with as much of this Amashyer as I could get 'old of. I told 'im peddlin' dope was a risky game, but all 'e did was to put 'is 'and in 'is pocket and take out a wad of notes. I counted 'em when I got back – they were hundreds, and the total was four thousand quid!'

'Phew!'

'So I didn't lose any time, I can tell yer,' continued Chubby with a wink. 'I got in touch with a feller called Cokey Williams, and he got me all the Amashyer stuff 'e could lay his 'ands on.' Chubby paused, and after a little while Temple nodded for him to continue.

'This chap with the falsetto voice arranged to meet me at a warehouse up the river. They had a boat waiting for me at the wharf, and off we went. The little feller seemed very pleased when I gave 'im the stuff, and once I'd 'anded it over I was politely dismissed, and taken back to Redhouse Wharf.'

'Did you recognise anyone at the warehouse?'

'Not a soul, at least ...' Chubby seemed to hesitate.

'Well?' demanded Temple.

'I couldn't swear to it, but just before I stepped into the boat I had an idea I saw Hargreaves – the Reverend Hargreaves, I mean. But I must have been mistaken, because I came straight back 'ere, and who should be the first person I bump into but the Reverend 'imself.'

'H'm,' mused Temple. 'Of course, we really have no proof that all this has anything to do with the Front Page Men.'

'Oh yes it has!' insisted Chubby.

'What makes you so sure?'

'Because when I left the warehouse the little feller gives me a funny sort of look. Then he says, "If you feel like talking, Chubby, remember Sydney Debenham."'

'Sydney Debenham?'

'Yes, it was the week after that murder – you remember – he was the head cashier at the Margate Bank—'

'I remember,' said Temple quietly. Apparently the Front Page Men left nothing to chance.

'Where is this warehouse, Chubby?' questioned Temple, presently.

'Don't ask me, guv'nor. I've got no bump of locality, as they calls it. As far as I could make out, it seemed to be about a mile up river from Redhouse Wharf.'

Temple weighed up this information carefully. 'Thanks, Chubby. Drop in and see me before you sail. You know my flat.' He handed over a small bundle of notes.

'Yes – thank yer, guvnor. And mum's the word!'

'Of course. How can I get out of here without going through the bar?'

'That's easy,' Chubby assured him. 'Follow me, Mr. Temple.'

He opened the door, and they stood for a moment just inside. Temple suddenly became conscious of a piano being played in one of the rooms upstairs. He recognised the melody even above the hubbub of conversation and roars of laughter from the bar and tap-room.

'What's that?' he demanded swiftly.

Chubby looked alarmed. 'What's up, guvnor?' he whispered, hoarsely.

'That music!'

Chubby laughed reassuringly. 'Oh, that's just a piano in one of the rooms upstairs. They often 'ave smokers and lodge meetin's up there.'

'I see,' said Temple gruffly, and followed Chubby along the passage and out into the murky backyard, where his companion indicated a passage which led back to the waterside.

As he was about to go, the novelist turned and looked up quickly at an illuminated window. Faintly, in the background, he could still hear the sound of the piano.

It was the melody that Mr. J. P. Goldie had played in the drawing-room of Paul Temple's flat.

CHAPTER VII

A Message for Paul Temple

Paul Temple caught a bus going to Charing Cross, climbed the stairs, and thoughtfully lit a cigarette, preparatory to reviewing the situation.

It had been a stroke of luck finding Chubby, though, once found, Temple knew the odds were in favour of Chubby having had some transaction with the Front Page Men. There was scarcely a gang in the London underworld that had not employed Chubby at some stage in its existence.

But his reputation as a squealer had been getting around a little too actively for Chubby's liking during the past few months. His income had dropped accordingly, and he had even been reduced to attempting petty thefts from time to time.

If he really did intend to cross to America, then both police and crooks were in for some lively times, reflected Temple with amusement. Chubby's double-crossing propensities were bound to make trouble for somebody – trouble that Chubby himself had an eel-like trick of wriggling out of.

All the same, the Front Page Men must have been very sure of themselves to have taken a chance with Chubby Wilson.

Temple was inclined to reproach himself for not making certain whether it really was Goldie in that upstairs room. Anyhow, it certainly looked suspicious. How often did one hear Liszt played in a low riverside tavern? All the same, there was a chance that if he had gone upstairs he would have bumped into the Reverend Hargreaves, and he wished to avoid any such meeting at that juncture.

Temple was frankly puzzled about Hargreaves. According to Chubby Wilson, the cleric was implicated to some extent with the Front Page Men. How else could one construe his delivery of the note? Was the Seamen's Hostel a cloak for these nefarious pursuits? Temple decided to lie low and watch the Reverend Charles Hargreaves' activities very carefully.

He got off the bus at Charing Cross and turned up to the left through the streets of Soho, animated with the arrival of late diners and the departure of others on their way to the theatres. He eventually reached Mayfair, arriving in a mild glow as a result of his exercise. Pryce heard him come in, and met him while he was delving in the letter-box for any letters by the late delivery.

'Hello, Pryce,' Temple greeted him cheerfully. 'Is Mrs. Temple upstairs?'

'No, sir, she's out. She left about twenty minutes ago to meet Miss Forbes.'

'To meet Miss Forbes?' queried Temple, in some surprise.

'Yes, sir. Madam received a telephone message from Miss Forbes, shortly after you left.'

'Oh, about something they bought this afternoon, perhaps,' speculated Temple.

'Mr. and Mrs. Mitchell arrived about five minutes ago, sir.'

'Back so soon?' murmured Temple with a slight lift of the eyebrows. 'Oh—er—all right, Pryce.' The manservant returned to his kitchen, and Temple made for the drawing-room.

'So here you are at last, you old reprobate,' Gerald greeted him, excitedly.

'Hello, Gerald! Hello, Ann! What's all the fuss about?'

'You've been holding out on me, you old sinner,' said Gerald, reproachfully.

'Don't tell me you've discovered that I am Andrea Fortune,' replied Temple, solemnly.

They all laughed.

'It isn't you at all,' explained Ann, who looked her best in an expensive black evening frock that revealed her lovely figure to every advantage. 'Gerald's just heard that Steve is writing a novel, and he wants to get her signature on the dotted line, before any of the other publishers.'

'Well, you haven't lost much time,' laughed Temple. 'I wish Steve made such rapid progress. Why, she's been working on it for at least six months, and she hasn't even finished the prologue yet.'

'Not finished the prologue?'

'I told you there was no hurry,' laughed Ann, amused at her husband's bewilderment.

'How on earth did you hear about it, anyhow?' asked Temple.

'The editor of the *Daily Courier* told me about it two days ago, and I happened to mention it at dinner tonight,' said Ann. 'Gerald nearly passed out with excitement.'

'If Steve is half the novelist that she was a reporter, that's good enough for my money,' declared Gerald emphatically.

'Then what about fifty pounds in advance on royalties?' laughed Temple. 'Remember Steve has a husband to maintain ...'

'Now I see why you married, Paul,' riposted Ann.

'Seriously, though, Gerald, the subject of Steve's novel is absolutely taboo in the Temple household. We had our first and only row over that blessed novel – or should I say prologue?'

'So you'll just have to be content with an optional agreement,' Ann told her husband.

At that moment Pryce entered carrying a silver salver on which lay a card. It was rather smaller than a playing-card.

'This was in the letter-box, sir. I thought perhaps it might be important.'

'It certainly wasn't there when I came in,' murmured Temple, turning to take it.

'No, sir.'

The Mitchells watched him examine it carefully, saw his jaw drop as its significance dawned upon him.

'Paul, it isn't bad news, is it?' asked Mitchell quietly.

Temple did not seem to hear. His brain was working so frantically that it excluded everything outside itself. Then, with a distinct catch in his voice, he asked, 'Have you got your car here?'

'Why, yes—'

'I want to get to Scotland Yard as quickly as possible,' Temple heard himself say, as if from a great distance.

'Paul, what is it?' exclaimed Mitchell in alarm.

'It's—it's the Front Page Men,' said Paul Temple, in that peculiar tense voice.

Ann jumped to her feet in dismay.

'The Front Page Men!' she cried.

'Yes,' nodded Temple deliberately. 'They've got Steve.'

CHAPTER VIII

The Front Page Men

Mr. Andrew Brightman was inclined to be irritable. He had
been summoned peremptorily to Scotland Yard, where Sir
Graham Forbes was putting him through what might have
been described as a refined version of the third degree.

And Mr. Brightman was showing some signs of feeling
the strain, though outwardly his manner had lost little of its
pristine pompousness. Sir Graham liked him less and less,
and was doing his utmost to find a flaw in his story. But
Brightman had been equal to him so far.

'My dear Sir Graham, why on earth you brought me
here to ask me the questions I have already answered half
a dozen times is completely beyond my comprehension,' he
was protesting in his oily, assured tones.

Forbes ignored this outburst.

'Mr. Brightman, I am anxious to get to the bottom of this
business,' he persisted quietly. 'And there is just one more
point. You say you deposited the suitcase in the cloakroom
of the Regal Palace Hotel?'

'Yes, yes!' snapped Brightman, his patience almost exhausted.

'And the cloak-room attendant gave you a ticket for the case?'

'Yes.'

'You're quite sure of that?'

'Of course I'm sure,' said Brightman wearily, as if he were dealing with an inquisitive child.

'Thank you,' said Sir Graham, pressing a button on his desk, which brought in Chief Inspector Reed.

'Mac, Mr. Brightman is leaving,' said Sir Graham shortly.

His visitor seemed surprised that the ordeal was over, and a little uncertain as to what he should say.

'This way, sir,' prompted Mac.

'Oh—er—thank you,' said Brightman, recovering. 'Goodbye, Sir Graham.'

'Good night,' grunted Forbes. The more he saw of Andrew Brightman, the less he liked that obsequious smirk of his.

Forbes seized the telephone, intending to give orders to have Brightman followed, then thought better of it. He was still pondering on the problem when Reed looked in again and announced, 'Mr. Temple, sir!'

'Hallo, Temple, what brings you here at this time of night?' demanded Sir Graham, who did not seem any too pleased at this intrusion. Then he noticed Temple was not his usual urbane self, and that there was a strained expression in his eyes.

'Sir Graham, I'm sorry to burst in like this—'

'Why, what's the matter?'

'It's—it's Steve,' said Temple, chokingly.

'Steve? What do you mean?'

'They've got her ... the Front Page Men!'

Sir Graham leapt to his feet, pushing his chair back with a bang. 'Impossible! It can't be true!' he gasped incredulously. 'Here – sit down – let me get you a drink.'

He went to the cupboard and splashed a generous quantity of Scotch whisky into a tumbler. Temple gulped it down before speaking again.

'Earlier this evening I went to a pub on the river called the Glass Bowl—'

'I know it verra well,' put in Reed, but Sir Graham silenced him with a look.

'While I was there, Steve apparently received a telephone message which she believed came from your daughter.'

'Maybe it was. You know how friendly they are.'

Temple shook his head. 'No, it couldn't have been Carol. Half an hour ago I had this card.'

'Good God!' breathed Sir Graham, recognising the familiar warning.

'Wouldn't it be as well if ye 'phoned Miss Carol?' suggested Reed.

'Yes, yes, of course,' said Forbes, snatching the receiver from his desk.

There was a short pause, during which Reed gloomily inspected the card, and Temple paced nervously up and down the office.

'Is that you, Davis?' said Sir Graham suddenly. 'Yes, Sir Graham here ... is Miss Carol in? Oh ... I see ...'

He replaced the receiver.

'She left the house about an hour ago,' he informed them.

'Then it's all right after all,' hazarded Reed. 'She's gone out to meet Mrs. Temple. Mebbe that card is only—'

'It isn't all right! I don't like it!' snapped Sir Graham, who had begun to look very worried.

Temple paused in his restless pacing.

'I went to the Glass Bowl to see a man named Chubby Wilson,' he said slowly, obviously deep in thought.

'Ay, ye'd find him there, no doubt,' agreed Mac.

'I found him all right. And he talked. He told me about an empty warehouse a mile from Redhouse Wharf.'

'What about it?' queried Forbes.

'It's used by the Front Page Men,' Temple informed him.

Even the dour Reed was aroused by this.

'You think mebbe they've taken ye wife and perhaps Miss Carol—' he was beginning, when Sir Graham cut him short again.

'Mac, get the Thames Police,' he thundered. 'I want a launch at the North Pier; tell Brooks and Donovan.'

Again he snatched up the telephone.

'Hunter? Meet me at the North Pier in twenty minutes.' He paused to give some brief instructions to Reed, then snatched up his hat and followed Temple, who was already half-way downstairs.

Outside, Gerald Mitchell was waiting for them. 'Ann took the car home,' he explained. 'I thought perhaps I might be able to help in some way ...'

'Sir Graham, this is Gerald Mitchell, a friend of mine. Would you mind if he came along?' asked Temple.

Sir Graham sized up Mitchell with a rapid glance. 'All right,' he consented gruffly, 'as long as he understands he isn't coming to a picnic.'

They all entered a fast police-car, and were whirled through a succession of back streets which the driver used to avoid the heavy traffic.

Temple's face was white and set beneath the glare of the street lamps that shone in on them in monotonous succession. Nobody talked much, and Mitchell was patently nervous, though nonetheless, determined.

Hunter was already seated in the launch with the two sergeants, Brooks and Donovan, lean, weather-beaten river police, whose eyes appeared to be perpetually focused on some distant object. Sir Graham's party settled themselves in the launch, and Donovan started the engine.

This was not the usual type of police-boat maintained for patrolling purposes, but a rakish, speedy craft reserved for emergencies, and fitted with a powerful miniature searchlight.

They slipped out into the river, and Temple noticed for the first time, that there was a considerable amount of fog over the water. Sir Graham murmured some instructions to Sergeant Donovan at the wheel, and soon they were travelling at a fair pace in the direction of Redhouse Wharf.

The fog was so patchy that at times they had to slow down to a mere crawl. Then it would drift away, and the lights on the Embankment would be visible once more. Donovan opened the throttle, and the black waters slid swirling behind in their wake.

Save for the distant siren of a departing tramp steamer and the dim roar of the city traffic, the river was very quiet. They might have been in another world, reflected Mitchell, buttoning up his coat, for it was very cold on the water. A tug came into view, towing a line of four barges, and chugged its way into the distance, and the mysterious silence, broken only by the roar of their own engine, descended upon them again.

Brooks and Donovan exchanged a clipped comment occasionally on the subject of their bearings, but none of the others spoke, until Temple murmured, 'The fog seems pretty bad, Sergeant.'

'Nothing to what it is sometimes, sir,' Brooks told him. 'I've been in it that thick that you couldn't see the water under you, and there hasn't been a soul on the river except the police-boat.'

They had progressed the better part of two miles when Hunter asked, 'What's that place over there?' He indicated a large building that had loomed up at a bend in the river.

'Fisher and Watkins, sir. They're the coal people,' Brooks informed him.

'Then that couldn't be it.'

'No, sir. That place is pretty well known. There isn't a tug on the river that doesn't call there at some time or other.'

'You seem to know the river pretty well, Sergeant,' commented Mitchell.

'Well, I've been up and down a few times, sir,' was Brooks' laconic reply. 'I could write a book on the things I've seen ...'

'If ever you do, you must give me the first chance of publishing it.'

'Are we anywhere near the place they call "People's Wharf"?' asked Forbes, recalling the name in connection with a notorious case.

'That's the other direction, sir. You mean the place where we found the Wapping Kid the night he was all shot to pieces. I shall never forget that night as long as I—'

'Listen!' interrupted Mitchell, gripping Temple's arm.

'What is it?'

'I thought I heard something,' said Mitchell, nervously. 'It sounded rather like a revolver shot.'

'A revolver shot?' queried Sir Graham sharply.

Brooks seemed sceptical. 'This old river's full of strange noises, sir – until you get used to 'em. You might imagine almost anything.'

'I don't think that light is imagination, Sergeant,' interposed Paul Temple.

'Light, sir? Where?'

'To the left, George. Look!' called out Sergeant Donovan, before Temple could reply.

'H'm, that's a light, true enough,' admitted Brooks. 'A pretty powerful one, too. Why, it must be—'

'Listen!' hissed Donovan.

From the distance, somewhat muffled by the fog, came the familiar 'chug-chug' of a motor-launch, like a quickened heart-beat. Its light swept the river inquiringly, but so far had not picked up the police launch.

'That must have been the boat I heard before,' observed Mitchell.

'Not one of your men, by any chance, Sergeant?' queried Temple.

Brooks shook his head. 'Not our type of engine, sir,' he declared, positively.

'Perhaps it's Ginger Ricketts. He often comes down to his tinworks about this time,' suggested Donovan.

'I'd know the sound of his old tub anywhere,' said Brooks.

'It's a pretty powerful light they've got,' said Temple, peering across the water.

'They're getting closer,' announced Donovan from the wheel.

'Give 'em a hail,' ordered Sir Graham.

Brooks stood up, cupped his hands and shouted:

'Ahoy there! Ahoy!'

There was no reply, but the oncoming launch appeared to change her course slightly.

'Turn the light on, Harry,' ordered Brooks.

There was a click, and a thin, powerful beam pencilled its way across the river towards the light in the other boat, which was immediately switched off.

73

'They've gone right over to the other side,' declared Temple, who was watching closely. 'They're trying to dodge us. Bring the light over to the right, Sergeant. A bit more ... now back to your left a shade ...'

The sound of a shot echoed clearly over the water, and everybody ducked instinctively as there was a sudden crash of splintered glass. The lamp on the police-launch was out, leaving them in a darkness that seemed more intense than ever.

'What the 'ell *is* this?' gasped Donovan, completely bewildered. To him, an attack on a police-launch was akin to high treason.

'Get the reserve lamp, Harry, and look sharp,' snapped Brooks.

Donovan began to fumble in a locker with his free hand, and Brooks went to help him.

'Where the blazes did Thompson put that flex?' Temple heard one of them mutter, then another shot was heard and a bullet whined away to their left. This was followed by a rapid fusillade.

'Keep down! For God's sake keep down, Sir Graham!' shrieked Brooks, and they all crouched as low as they could in the well of the launch. Again the staccato racket that obviously emanated from a machine-gun.

'Keep down, Donovan,' called out Forbes. But the man at the wheel had straightened to a sitting position.

'We must turn her round and get after them,' he answered, and was about to add something further when there was another spurt of machine-gun fire, this time much nearer and more prolonged.

Temple saw Donovan clutch his shoulder and sink slowly into his cockpit. Brooks went over to him at once.

'Are you all right, Harry?' he asked.

'Yes—yes—' gasped Donovan weakly, and with a queer strangled sigh relapsed into unconsciousness. He had switched off the engine, and the boat was drifting aimlessly with the tide.

'Get him in the corner if you can,' suggested Mitchell.

Suddenly the light from the other launch blazed on them, and Brooks ducked quickly. To all outward appearance there was no sign of life on the police launch. For the better part of a minute, the relentless glare swept the boat, then snapped out. Apparently the strangers were not tempted to investigate further.

Temple made for Donovan and hastily examined his injury. 'He's in a pretty bad way,' he announced.

As he spoke they heard the steady beat of the engine of the other boat amplified to a roar which gradually faded into the night.

'The swine have gone!' said Mitchell.

'Donovan is getting worse. We'll have to turn back,' declared Brooks.

'Yes, better wait a couple of minutes till they are clear,' advised Sir Graham.

'Paul – you don't think that Carol and your wife are in that boat?' blurted out Mitchell.

Temple shook his head helplessly.

Brooks was struggling to restart the engine.

'All right, Sergeant, I'll take the wheel,' offered Mitchell. 'You look after Donovan.'

'Think you can manage it all right, sir?'

'Perfectly. I've got a boat of my own up at Maidenhead.'

He lowered himself into the cockpit and gingerly felt for the starter.

'Perhaps it would be as well if we made for the bank and telephoned the nearest hospital,' Brooks was suggesting, when there was a sudden exclamation from Forbes.

75

'Temple! There's something in the water!'

Temple leaned over the side and peered in the direction Sir Graham indicated. 'It's a man!'

'My God, he's right!' confirmed Brooks.

'Over to the left, Gerald – cut out the engine – that's it …' instructed Temple.

The wavelets washed listlessly against the launch as the engine spluttered to a standstill. Brooks produced a long boathook and dragged in the black object that bobbed gently up and down on the dark waters.

'Have you got him, Temple?'

'Yes,' gasped Temple, as he clutched at the body and lifted it slightly. But it was so sodden that getting it aboard was quite another problem. Forbes and Hunter went to his assistance, and eventually they succeeded in heaving this strange, inert mass over the side, though at one time there appeared to be some danger of the boat capsizing.

They laid the pitiful object full length in the well of the launch.

It was a man, quite heavily built, and his face was swathed in yards of bandages.

'He looks a goner,' announced Mitchell, kneeling on the driving-seat to get a better view.

'Yes, I'm afraid he is,' agreed Temple, bending over the body.

'Better get that cloth off his face,' suggested Brooks.

'Afraid it's too late,' grunted Sir Graham.

Temple had carefully pulled a sodden card away from the man's sleeve. He passed it on to Sir Graham without comment. The Chief Commissioner ignited his cigarette lighter and looked at the card, though he knew what to expect before he did so. Hunter leaned over.

'The Front Page Men,' he murmured.

'Hadn't we better untie this bandage stuff round his face, sir, and then we'll be able to see who—'

'I'll do it,' said Forbes. He produced a penknife and cut away some of the soaked outer wrappings.

'They've certainly tied this tight enough – the poor devil must have died from suffocation,' he pronounced, struggling with various knots.

'Let me hold the lighter, sir,' offered Hunter. With both hands freed, Sir Graham worked faster. 'Ah, that's done it,' he announced at last.

'My God!' breathed Paul Temple, as the bandage fell away. He was looking at the face of Chubby Wilson.

CHAPTER IX

News of Steve

'Chubby Wilson?' echoed Forbes, letting fall the dripping pile of bandages.

'Yes, the man who told me about the warehouse,' nodded Temple.

'So that's why they put him out,' said Brooks.

'I'm afraid so, Sergeant.'

'Poor devil!' growled Forbes, placing a handkerchief over the face of the corpse.

Temple pondered upon the tragedy as the launch steadily chugged its way homewards. As far as he knew, only the Reverend Charles Hargreaves had any idea that he and Chubby had talked together. Of course, someone else in the Glass Bowl might have caught a glimpse of them. But Hargreaves was certainly a primary suspect.

'Donovan looks in a bad way,' muttered Forbes in a troubled voice, and Brooks also seemed anxious about his colleague.

At last, amidst the swirling mist, the lights of the pier were faintly visible, and Mitchell, who had by now mastered the little idiosyncrasies of the launch, steered her towards the lights.

'There's someone waiting for us,' said Forbes.

'Yes, it looks to me like Reed,' confirmed Temple. 'That might mean news of some sort.'

'It's Reed all right,' laughed Hunter. 'I can recognise that dirty old raincoat of his. Give me the painter, Sergeant.'

He sorted out the rope, then turned to help Brooks with Donovan, who had temporarily recovered consciousness. But he was in such pain that when they tried to lift him he fainted again.

'Hello, is that you, Mac?' called Sir Graham.

'Ay, I've got a message for ye,' answered Reed, running down the steps of the landing stage.

'Catch hold of the rope, Mac,' called Hunter, and the Scotsman deftly obeyed.

'Well, how's that?' sighed Mitchell, as he shut off the engine and leaned back in some relief.

'Thank you, Mr. Mitchell. We're very grateful for your assistance,' acknowledged Sir Graham.

'Yes, it was very lucky you came along, Gerald,' said Temple, noticing that Mitchell's hand shook slightly as he mopped his brow.

'Holy Moses!' ejaculated Reed in astonishment, when he came close up to the rather dejected party. 'Where the devil have ye been? An' what's the matter with yon laddie?'

'Bullet through his shoulder. He's pretty badly hurt, and I'm afraid of chill,' snapped Sir Graham, a little impatient at this questioning. 'Better phone the station, Brooks, and get them to send a hand-ambulance right away.' Brooks leapt ashore.

'Don't put the wind up the missis, George,' gasped Donovan weakly, in a fleeting spell of consciousness.

'That's all right, old man. Don't you worry,' Brooks reassured him, as he ran to the nearest telephone.

Reed was peering intently at the body in the well of the launch.

'I say, what's wrong with the other chappie?' he asked.

'Dead,' replied Temple laconically.

'Dead! Phew!' whistled Reed. 'It's been a pleasant little picnic you've been on, by the look of things.'

Temple nodded grimly.

'His face is familiar, but I canna just place him,' ruminated Reed.

'Then you can't have seen much of him lately. It's Chubby Wilson.'

'Chubby Wilson! The dope laddie! My, my! Ye've certainly been hobnobbing in high society. However, it'll save the police a lot of—'

Reed broke off abruptly.

'Good heavens, Sir Graham, I was forgetting all about the message!' he exclaimed.

'Message?' repeated Temple quickly. 'You haven't had any news?'

'Ay, it's from Mrs. Temple and Miss Forbes, sir. They're waitin' for ye at the flat.'

'At my flat?' queried Temple in amazement.

'Ay, that's right, sir.'

'Are you sure of this?' gasped Sir Graham, incredulously.

'Well, that was the message Nelson gave me, sir. He said Mrs. Temple telephoned the Yard about half an hour after ye left for the river.'

Temple and Forbes looked at each other blankly.

'At that rate, we'd better run along to your place, Temple, and see what it's all about,' decided Sir Graham at last.

'I'll get a taxi,' suggested Mitchell at once. 'Then I can drop you on my way home.' He moved over towards the roadway.

'Shall I stay with Donovan, sir, till the Sergeant gets here?' offered Hunter.

'Yes, I wish you would, Hunter. And you come along with us, Mac.'

'I will, sir,' agreed Mac with alacrity. 'And I hope ye've got a wee drop of Scotch handy, Mr. Temple. I'm nearly frozen stiff waitin' here for ye.'

Forbes took another look at Donovan, and shook his head dubiously. The wounded man was now in the early stages of delirium, and was talking wildly.

'Keep that coat over him, Hunter,' advised Sir Graham. 'If he gets pneumonia now ...'

Looking very worried, he rejoined the others, who were just about to enter the taxi.

Despite his native hardness, Chief Inspector Reed complained of the cold all the way to Mayfair. This, at any rate, relieved the others of making conversation. Outside Temple's flat they said good night to Mitchell, who promised to telephone Paul Temple first thing in the morning.

CHAPTER X

Story of a Rendezvous

With a hand that trembled slightly, Temple sorted out his latchkey, and let his companions into the flat. Then, with a muttered excuse, he went on into the lounge, which he had noticed was occupied.

As soon as he opened the door, Steve jumped up and came to meet him. Her eyes were shining and just a little moist.

'Darling!' she cried softly, clasping him tightly for a moment, and finding a response as he clutched her shoulders and held her to him.

Then they simultaneously realised that Carol was sitting in an armchair, and that Sir Graham and Reed were standing rather awkwardly in the doorway.

'Come in, Sir Graham, and you too, Reed,' said Temple hastily. 'Whisky for both of you?' He went to get the decanter, and everybody started talking at once.

'We've had a devil of a game, Carol,' Sir Graham was saying when his host brought the drinks. 'Temple and I have been practically at our wits' end.'

'You explain, Steve,' drawled Carol, a dark, slim young

woman in the early twenties, and rather too inclined to adopt a blasé pose, though perhaps this was incited by her father's continual activity. Carol did not seem to be taking the events of the evening particularly seriously, and her dark eyes smouldered with a twinkle of amusement from time to time. Crime and criminals were so much a part of her daily mealtime conversation at home that they no longer awed her.

'Well, it's all rather strange really,' began Steve, obviously rather puzzled. 'I must admit I can't quite make it all out.'

Temple replenished Reed's glass, which had rapidly emptied. 'My, but that's a grand drop o' Scotch,' whispered the Chief Inspector. 'Only a wee splash of soda, if ye don't mind.'

'Tell me about this mysterious telephone call, Steve,' urged Temple.

'It came through just after you had left. There was a girl at the other end, and I hadn't the slightest doubt that it was Carol. The voice was exactly the same, and besides, she said it *was* Carol speaking.'

'Naturally, you wouldn't question it,' agreed Sir Graham. 'Please go on, Mrs. Temple.'

'Well, she asked me to meet her at the corner of Half Moon Street shortly before nine. That struck me as rather queer, because Carol usually calls for me, but I thought she might have been seeing someone in that district and hadn't time to come on here. So I changed into a costume and left about twenty to nine.' She paused. 'Now this is the strange part. Before I got to the end of Park Lane, a taxi sailed past, and who should be sitting inside, gazing blissfully out of the window, but Carol.'

'I was on my way to the Fosters',' that young lady lazily explained.

'Naturally, seeing Carol like this rather surprised me,' continued Steve. 'Apart from the taxi going in the opposite direction to Half Moon Street, I noticed that Carol was wearing evening dress. This certainly didn't look as if she was on her way to keep our appointment. So I waved my arms frantically, and Carol stopped the taxi.'

'Lucky I saw you,' commented Carol, lighting the cigarette she had inserted in a holder. 'Even so, I thought poor Steve had gone potty!'

'What then?' asked Temple.

'There's really nothing more to tell,' said Steve. 'Carol swears she never went near the phone all evening, and most certainly didn't ring me up.'

'And yet you were sure it was Carol who spoke on the telephone?'

'I was certain at the time,' declared Steve, emphatically.

'And when did you arrange to go to the Fosters', Carol?' asked Sir Graham.

'Why, ages ago. I told you they were giving a dinner party to celebrate their fifth wedding anniversary. They were both so amazed the marriage had lasted so long they felt they had to do something about it,' explained Carol, cynically.

'Of course – they were the people you were telling me about this afternoon when we were shopping,' recalled Steve, and Carol nodded.

'Excuse me,' interrupted Chief Inspector Reed, who had been silent up till now, except for an occasional smacking of lips in appreciation of Temple's whisky. 'About what time would it be when ye received the telephone call, Mrs. Temple?'

'Oh, I should say ... shortly after eight,' replied Steve.

'We might trace the call, Sir Graham,' suggested Reed.

'That's an idea, Mac,' conceded his superior. 'May I use the phone, Temple?'

'Certainly, Sir Graham.'

The Chief Commissioner went out into the hall, where they could hear him dialling vigorously.

'Paul, who do you think would do a thing like that?' murmured Steve, wrinkling her forehead.

Her husband took out his wallet and handed her a card.

'This arrived later in the evening,' he told her.

'The Front Page Men!' cried Steve in dismay.

'Don't be alarmed, darling,' Temple comforted her. 'Whatever they were after, they didn't succeed – and in future we shall be on our guard. All the same, I'd like to have been on the corner of Half Moon Street at nine o'clock ...'

By this time Sir Graham had concluded his telephone investigations. 'Apparently the call came from the Medusa Club in Piccadilly,' he announced. 'They've got four or five call-boxes there.'

'The Medusa Club?' echoed Temple, dubiously.

'Ay, that'll be Tony Rivoli's new place,' supplied Reed. 'It's that swanky, we daren't even raid it.'

This seemed to amuse Carol, who had visited the club in question on several occasions.

'I think I've heard of it,' said her father.

'Who is this Tony Rivoli?' asked Temple, who had been rather out of touch with London night-life since his marriage.

'You've heard of him, Mr. Temple. He was the fellow mixed up with the big Holborn forgery case about four years ago. Nothing very much against him.'

'Oh yes, I remember,' recalled Temple, thoughtfully.

'Tony's doing well for himself,' declared Forbes. 'He owns the Rivoli Restaurant in Bruton Street, the Highspot on the bypass at Waring. And now this new place in Piccadilly.'

'Ay, his head's screwed on right,' sagely agreed Mac.

'Is he going straight?'

'As far as I know,' conceded Mac. 'He gambles rather heavily, but I don't think there's any real harm in him.'

Sir Graham dismissed this point for the time being, and returned to their first topic.

'I wonder why the Front Page Men wanted to get hold of your wife, Temple,' he mused.

'Ransom, of course,' Carol informed him in the tolerating tone of an indulgent parent. 'They intended to hold Steve until ...'

But Sir Graham would have none of this theory.

'No, I don't think that was the reason. In fact, I'm sure it wasn't,' he asserted, confidently.

'They've got a hunch that Temple is working on this case, and they want a means of keeping his mouth shut,' was Chief Inspector Reed's opinion.

'Yes,' said Forbes after a pause, 'I think you're right there, Mac.'

'I can't see any other reason,' admitted Temple.

Steve seemed about to speak, but changed her mind.

'Well,' concluded Sir Graham, draining his glass, 'I don't think there's anything else we can do at the moment. Are you ready, Carol?'

She nodded. 'I telephoned the Fosters and told them to expect me later.'

'Coming, Mac?' asked Sir Graham.

'Ay,' murmured Mac reluctantly, with a wistful eye on the decanter. 'I'm ready, sir.'

They took their leave, and after hearing the last echo of their voices and the clash of the lift-gates, Temple returned to find Steve gazing pensively into the fire.

He dropped on the rug at her feet and leaned his head against the arm of her chair. For a while neither spoke – they were just glad to be alone together after the nerve-racking events of the evening. Then Steve stirred uneasily.

'Paul, did you see that man at the Glass Bowl?'

He offered her a cigarette and lighted one himself before replying.

'Chubby Wilson? Yes, I saw him.' He paused, then tried to continue in a level voice. 'We dragged him out of the river about two hours ago.' Steve recoiled.

'You mean he was murdered? Oh, how horrible!' She threw the cigarette into the fire with a nervous gesture.

'Who did it?' she whispered. 'The Front Page Men.'

Steve shuddered. 'If I'd gone to Half Moon Street ...'

'Well, you didn't,' said her husband firmly. 'And thank goodness you're safe.' But they were both silent for some minutes, speculating on what might have happened.

'By the way, I've got some news for you,' said Temple at last in a more cheerful voice.

'You have?'

'Yes, Gerald Mitchell wants an option on your novel.' With a twinkle in his eyes, he added graciously, 'So all you've got to do is finish it!'

Steve could not repress a smile. 'You can be amused, Mr. Temple, but one of these days I'll write another *Anthony Adverse*.'

'That's what I'm afraid of,' sighed Temple, as the telephone started ringing. Steve went out to answer it.

After a little while she put her head round the door. 'It's Ann Mitchell – she says have you seen Gerald?'

'He's on his way home,' Temple replied, and she went out to resume her conversation.

'Gerald should have been home by now,' said Temple when she returned. 'Where did you leave him?'

'Outside. He dropped us, and then went on.'

'Maybe the theatre traffic held him up,' suggested Steve, making herself comfortable again.

'Paul, what did that man tell you?' she resumed.

'Which man?'

'The one you went to see … Chubby Wilson.'

'He told me about a warehouse on the river,' quietly answered Temple.

'Oh? What about it?'

But her husband made no reply. He was gazing reflectively into the fire, where the dramatic events of the evening flickered at the call of his imagination. Steve could see there was something perplexing him by the two tiny furrows which deepened above his eyes.

'Darling, you're not listening,' she murmured, reproachfully.

'Eh? What was that?' asked Temple, coming out of his reverie.

'What were you thinking about?'

'About a man I met at the Glass Bowl … I know his face frightfully well, and yet, somehow I can't place him,' confessed Temple. It always irritated him beyond measure if he could recall a man's face and nothing else.

'What was his name?' asked Steve, trying to be helpful.

'He said his name was Hargreaves,' murmured Temple sceptically. 'The Reverend Charles Hargreaves.'

CHAPTER XI

Paul Temple in Regent Street

The lavishly furnished showrooms of Clapshaw and Thompson's rarely failed to attract the footsteps of the lingering Regent Street shopper. Discreetly yet attractively lighted, they gave an impression of airiness calculated to appeal simultaneously to the artiste in search of a new piano or the blase denizen of Mayfair who was merely interested in the latest American swing classics.

Walking down Regent Street, carrying his hat in one hand, Paul Temple was enjoying the early spring sunshine to the full when the latest Remstein model caught his eye, just as Clapshaw and Thompson's had intended it should.

The piano stood in the centre of the larger window; it was, in fact, the only instrument displayed, surmounted by a neatly printed card in brown and gold which announced that it was the very latest in Remsteins. No mention of price, of course. That might deter a prospective customer from inquiring further. Even an old-established firm such as Clapshaw and Thompson's was not averse to arranging terms; they had to keep up with the times, and overheads in Regent Street were heavy.

Temple stood silently surveying the new Remstein for some minutes, lost in thought, and oblivious to the traffic that roared behind him. Then he appeared to make up his mind quite suddenly and pushed his way through the swing-doors.

A middle-aged man of rather prim appearance came forward to meet him, looking faintly surprised. Customers in a morning were comparatively rare; people usually waited for the afternoon or evening before indulging their musical whims.

'Good morning, sir. A very fine morning,' began the salesman, with the merest touch of deference in his tone. 'Can I help you at all?'

'I'm rather interested in the new Remsteins,' Temple informed him a little diffidently, for he had all the average man's reluctance of buying things.

'Ah, yes, the Remstein. They are becoming quite the rage, sir. We are continually replenishing our stock.'

'Indeed? Yet you have quite a large place here. Must need a fair-sized staff.'

'Oh yes, sir. Over thirty of us.'

'Really? I hope they treat you well ...'

'About the Remstein, sir,' gently interposed the salesman, nervously fingering his immaculate winged collar. 'I should like you to take particular notice of the wood, sir.'

'Oh yes, the Remstein,' repeated Temple, with something of an effort.

'This wood, sir, is what we call continental walnut.'

'How very interesting,' murmured Temple politely. 'It does seem rather—er—unusual ...'

'I think I may say, sir, that it is highly distinctive,' continued the salesman, 'and it also has several advantages over the more usual type of wood, such as mahogany ...'

The salesman sat down and ran his fingers lightly over the keys. 'You will notice, sir, that it has a very light touch – the keys are very responsive. It is very suitable to the sensitive performer.' He began to play a Chopin waltz with a mechanical precision and utter lack of inspiration.

'Very nice,' said Temple, when he had finished.

'Perhaps you would like to try the instrument, sir,' suggested the salesman, relinquishing his seat.

'I play very little, really,' confessed Temple, sitting down nevertheless and striking a series of chords. 'How much is this model?'

'Six hundred and fifty guineas, sir. And a remarkable bargain.'

'It's a lot of money,' murmured Temple reflectively. 'The price of quite an attractive car.'

'If it's a question of suitable terms, sir, then I am sure Mr. Thompson ...' The salesman waved an expressive hand.

'Then there is a Mr. Thompson,' said Temple with reawakened interest. 'And a Mr. Clapshaw?'

The salesman shook his head. 'Mr. Clapshaw retired from the business some years ago, during the last depression, in fact.'

'I see. You mean Mr. Thompson bought him out.' The salesman shrugged his shoulders. He was a little puzzled by this charming customer, whose face was vaguely familiar, and whose curiosity was so disconcerting to high-pressure salesmanship.

'Perhaps you would like to see Mr. Thompson, sir. I'll see if I can get him—'

'Please don't trouble,' smiled Temple disarmingly. 'I would like to see some of the smaller models. There is hardly room for a really large piano in the modern flat.'

The salesman nodded understandingly, and led the way along an aisle between dozens of new pianos of all descriptions. They came to a neat baby grand piano in a far corner.

'This is the Remstein Junior, sir. It has all the salient features of the larger model, and makes a most attractive proposition. I forgot to mention, sir, that a rather remarkable feature of the Remstein is that it requires very little tuning. You see, it incorporates a new device which keeps it well up to pitch and—'

This was the point in the conversation for which Temple had been waiting.

'But surely,' he said, 'that's rather hard on the piano-tuner, who has to earn a living the same as the rest of us.'

'Nevertheless, sir, it is a most attractive feature. Last month we sold over seventy Remsteins, which I think you will admit is pretty good going.'

Temple nodded. 'All the same, I can't help feeling sorry for the poor piano-tuner. I suppose you employ several?'

The assistant shook his head. 'Only one now, sir.'

'It wouldn't by any chance,' murmured Temple, slowly, 'be a Mr. Goldie?'

The salesman looked up quickly.

'Why no, sir. We did have a Mr. Goldie, but he retired some years ago. Do you know him?'

Temple smiled. 'He tuned a piano for some friends of mine. The old boy seemed quite a character.'

'You're right there, sir. And lately I'm beginning to wonder just what sort of a character.'

Temple swung round on the piano stool, obviously very much intrigued.

'But surely the old man is quite harmless,' he expostulated.

The salesman shook his head mysteriously.

'I wouldn't be so sure about that, sir. Of course, while he was here, I understand that his work gave every satisfaction. So much so that several of his favourite clients persuaded him to continue tuning their pianos after he left us. I believe he still has quite a connection.'

'Surely there's no harm in that,' said Temple.

'Of course not, sir. But ...' The salesman looked round, cautiously. 'There's been some queer folks making inquiries about Mr. Goldie this last week or two. An inspector from Scotland Yard only last Wednesday.'

'You surprise me. You don't think Mr. Goldie's done anything desperate, do you? He seemed such a harmless little man. I shouldn't have thought he would have hurt a fly.'

'You never can tell, sir. Look at Crippen.'

Temple obligingly looked at Crippen for a few moments, and nodded sympathetically.

'I said to Mr. Thompson, sir, I said, "If Mr. Goldie hasn't been up to anything, then what do Scotland Yard want with him?"'

'Exactly,' nodded Temple solemnly. 'Could you tell the Scotland Yard men anything?'

'Well, I didn't know Mr. Goldie very well, sir, and his work used to take him outside most of the time. I must say I always found the old chap very inoffensive, but I always say you can never tell what a man will get up to in his spare time. And with all these people asking about him, he must have been up to something.'

'You mean other people have been inquiring?'

'Well ... there's yourself, sir. You might be a private detective for all I know.' He smoothed his grey hair a trifle nervously. 'In fact your face is very familiar, if you will permit me to say so. I must have seen your photo somewhere.'

Temple took out his wallet and slowly extracted a card, which he handed to the assistant.

'Why, Mr. Temple! How stupid of me not to recognise you before, sir.'

'Now,' said Temple, 'as far as I know, there's nothing against Mr. Goldie, but I'm interested to find out one or two little things about him. First of all, have you had any other inquirers besides the Scotland Yard man and myself?'

'There was one less than an hour ago, Mr. Temple.'

He noted the novelist's start of surprise with obvious satisfaction.

'Could you describe him to me?'

The assistant looked rather shamefaced.

'As a matter of fact, sir,' he had to confess, 'the gentleman was a parson.'

'A clergyman?'

'Yes. He said that Mr. Goldie had once been a parishioner of his, and he was rather anxious to get in touch with him again. He seemed quite genuine, sir, but you never can tell, can you?'

'No,' smiled Temple, 'you never can tell.' His informant was obviously a lover of detective fiction, and Temple saw no reason to disillusion him on the subject of the sordid realities of criminal investigation. In his idle moments, Temple often speculated as to whether the public would ever buy detective fiction if they knew the real story of the painstaking, monotonous elimination that lay behind almost every case.

'This clergyman,' he continued, 'could you describe him at all?'

The assistant obliged to the best of his ability. There was little doubt in Temple's mind that the gentleman in question had been the Reverend Charles Hargreaves.

Temple idly played a scale or two, then asked, 'I suppose we are both talking about the same Mr. Goldie?'

'Of course, sir. A little man with rimless glasses and a bow tie. I never knew him very well myself, sir, but I've heard tell he was a brilliant pianist. Seemed quite kind-hearted too. Often used to bring us a bunch of lilies from his garden.'

'Lilies?' repeated Temple, with a lift of the eyebrows.

'Yes, sir. The old boy was an expert on lilies. And I must say he grew some beauties. They gave the showroom quite an air. I've missed 'em more than once since he left.'

'Rather an unusual hobby,' commented Temple.

'Yes, he wasn't what you'd call an ordinary sort of man, although he was only a piano-tuner. He was a character, sir, no doubt about that.'

Temple nodded thoughtfully. Somehow he couldn't forget the lilies. The assistant brought him back to realities with a start.

'About this Remstein, sir … were you really thinking of buying one?'

Temple frowned in deep deliberation. 'I think perhaps I'd better consult Mr. Goldie about that,' he announced at last, as he picked up his hat and made his way to the door. 'If he advises in favour of it, I promise to get in touch with you again.'

The assistant accompanied him to the door and politely held it open for him. But before Temple could leave, a well-built man in morning coat, striped trousers and spats, swung brusquely through the door and into the shop, where Temple heard him loudly demand the presence of the manager.

It was none other than Mr. Andrew Brightman.

CHAPTER XII

The Medusa Club

The time-honoured Services Clubs in Piccadilly were inclined to look down their nose when the latest newcomer opened its chromium-plated doors and illuminated a violent green and purple neon sign to tell the world that the Medusa Club had sprung into existence.

'Another of those damned dives!' commented retired colonels from the depths of their saddle-bagged armchairs. 'These bally places spring up in the night like mushrooms. Give it six months. Now I remember when I was in Delhi ...'

But, under the judicious management of Mr. Tony Rivoli, the Medusa's growth threatened to outpace even that of the despised mushroom. By now, it occupied the larger part of a complete building, and in addition to its public activities did a flourishing business in catering for private parties in superbly furnished rooms of all sizes.

True, you paid at least nine times the actual value for any food or drink at the Medusa, but, as Tony would point out to the very occasional protesting customer, one cannot run a place in Piccadilly without encountering the white man's burden, termed by manufacturers with delightful vagueness, 'overheads'.

Tony was always quite nice about these explanations. In his poorer days, he had been accustomed to his patrons arguing about charges. But if you dared hint that the Medusa Club's reputation was not quite all it should be, you were quite likely to be submerged in a flood of Sicilian argot, spiced with lively phrases from half a dozen other languages.

Tony was determined to preserve the prestige of the Medusa Club if it cost him his life. It was his favourite enterprise, dear to him as his overspoilt son. The Medusa represented the fulfilment of Tony's ambition of a lifetime. Already he had politely discouraged several dubious customers, either of whose combined bank rolls would have bought the club five times over.

And now Tony was just a little uneasy about a party that had been meeting a good deal during the past few months in Room Number Seven. Two of them, Lucky Gibson and Jimmy Mills, he knew had been mixed up with racecourse gangs some years ago, when he himself had gambled a fair amount on the turf. And he didn't like the looks of that Mr. Brightman, who arranged about the room. Of course, the money was always paid promptly, and as far as he knew the party might have been merely an occasional forgathering of old friends.

Standing in the foyer one cool spring evening, Tony saw Lucky Gibson airily pushing his way through the swing doors.

'Hello, Tony!' called the little Cockney quite perkily, pushing back a shabby opera hat which completely negatived any sartorial achievement of his expensive suit.

Tony nodded rather coldly in response to the greeting. As a rule, he was just a shade too effusive with his clients – but Lucky was different. Tony did not intend to encourage him. He would have refused to let the party take the room, but for the fact that he knew Brightman was an influential man in the City, and might do him considerable harm where other clients were concerned.

Lucky dropped his cigarette end and ground it under his heel, an action which irritated Tony profoundly. Apart from the fact that his carpet had cost three guineas a yard, he blenched when he thought of certain distinguished members of his clientele who might have witnessed the occurrence.

'Number Seven, Mr. Gibson,' he murmured hastily, moving away to the dining hall to welcome a group of guests who had just arrived.

Having progressed leisurely up a heavily carpeted staircase, Lucky poked his head cautiously round the door of Number Seven. The only other person he could see was Jimmy Mills, who was reclining in a luxurious armchair and toasting his feet at the electric fire.

'Hello, Lucky,' said Jimmy casually, lighting a fresh cigarette from the end of its predecessor.

'Isn't Brightman here?' demanded Lucky, in some surprise.

'No,' answered Mills calmly, leaning over to pour himself another drink from a decanter which stood on a tray beside him.

'Mix me a drink,' said Lucky, nervously licking his lips. He seemed far less self-assured now.

'You sound sweet, I must say,' commented Mills. 'Anything wrong?'

'I've had the jitters since last night,' confessed Lucky.

'Coo! What was the matter with last night?' demanded Jimmy, in some surprise. 'We 'ad 'em on the run proper.'

'That police-launch was too damn near for my liking,' admitted his confederate.

'You're losing your nerve,' sneered Mills. 'Here, drink this.' He passed over a large tumbler, which Lucky grasped eagerly.

'What's the lay-out for tonight?' he asked presently, when the drink had begun to take effect.

'The Chief's got something up his sleeve,' scowled Mills.

Lucky paused with the glass half-way to his lips. 'The Chief?'

'I mean Brightman.'

'Brightman isn't the big noise behind this outfit. Don't run away with that idea,' advised Lucky.

Well, he is as far as I'm concerned,' retorted Mills, nonchalantly flicking the ash off his cigarette.

Lucky eyed him shrewdly. 'You know, Jimmy, I've been thinking—' he began.

'Yes, I know,' nodded Mills. 'And it isn't always a wise policy. What you want to do, Lucky, is to make hay while the sun shines.'

'That's all very well,' growled Lucky, aggressively, 'but until I joined this outfit, I had a pretty clean record.'

This tickled Jimmy enormously.

'A pretty clean record!' he cackled. 'Lucky Gibson! Oh! Oh! That's rich!'

'You know what I mean,' said Lucky with an injured air. 'I've never done nothing like last night. That feller we dumped overboard – I knew 'im. 'E was a decent sort was Chubby, and—'

'My Gawd!' Mills spat contemptuously. 'You are in a mood!'

'What do we get out of this?' cried Lucky. 'That's what I want to know.'

'What do we get out of it?' echoed Mills, in a surprised voice. 'What the 'ell are you talkin' about? Didn't you make nearly two thousand quid last month? You've never seen that much money in your life before.'

'Money ain't everything,' protested Lucky.

'Then what the 'ell is? That's what I'd like to know.'

'Security,' blurted out Gibson.

'What d'yer mean by that?' queried Mills in a puzzled tone.

'Listen,' pursued Lucky hoarsely. 'There ain't a 'tec in London that wouldn't give four years of 'is life, and 'is blinkin' pension thrown in, to know who the Front Page Men are.'

'So what?' snapped Mills.

'Well,' Lucky paused meaningly, 'suppose they found out. Supposin' they got to know that the Front Page men are Brightman, Swan Williams, Jed Ware, Lina Fresnay and their old friends Jimmy Mills and Lucky Gibson. What do you think would happen?'

'Why, it'd be the end of the Front Page Men,' pronounced Mills. 'That's common sense, ain't it?'

'Would it be the end of the Front Page Men?' reflected Lucky. 'I wonder …'

'What d'yer mean?'

'There's another man behind this racket,' declared Lucky emphatically. 'A man with brains and initiative. Front Page Man Number One!'

Mills shrugged his shoulders.

'Who is he?' cried Lucky in desperation.

'Would you sleep any better if you knew?' demanded Mills, sarcastically.

'Yes, I would, and I don't mind admittin' it,' retorted Lucky, not to be denied. 'Why should we take all the risk? Don't you see, this bloke – whoever 'e is – 'as only got to tip off the Yard about one of us and—'

'Don't be a damn' fool!' barked Mills. 'Why should the Front Page Man go out of his way to do us down? We're making 'im a pot of money, and feathering our own nests into the bargain.'

'All the same, I'd feel a lot safer if I knew who he was.'

'Well, if you want my honest opinion,' said Mills, shifting his feet from one chair to another, 'the feller behind the gang is Brightman – and nobody else.'

'Then why should Brightman go out of his way to prove that there *is* someone else? At every meeting 'e tells us that 'e 'as received fresh orders from the Chief or—'

'It suits 'is purpose,' argued Mills. 'Brightman's a pretty wise guy. 'E knows that 'e can get better results by keeping us in the dark.'

'Well, I think you're wrong,' persisted Lucky. 'I think that Front Page Man Number One is a woman.'

'My Gawd!' gasped Mills, with a comical gesture. 'You are bright this evening!'

'Yes,' went on Gibson, unheeding, 'a woman by the name of Andrea Fortune.'

'Andrea Fortune? Didn't she write the novel called *The Front Page Men*?'

'She did. And in my opinion that's why—'

'Sh!' hissed Mills suddenly, as a step sounded outside. 'Here's Brightman.'

It was very much the Brightman of old; brisk, self-assured, and a little too suave. He might have been attending a meeting of shareholders, for he was dressed in a severe black coat, striped trousers and a neat-fitting collar. He shut the door carefully.

'Hello! Where's Jed and Lina?' was his first inquiry.

'They haven't arrived yet,' said Mills, who was now on his feet.

'We 'aven't seen Swan either,' supplied Lucky.

'Swan is downstairs. He'll be up in a minute,' said Brightman, crossing to the fire.

'Any news about Donovan?' queried Mills tentatively.

'Donovan? Oh, the police-sergeant. Yes, he died this morning,' announced Brightman, in the same tone one would imagine he adopted in reading a balance-sheet.

'D—dead?' stuttered Lucky.

'Yes. You pumped a fair amount of lead into him, Lucky, with that machine-gun of yours.'

Lucky was about to make some retort, but the door opened to admit Swan Williams, a dapper little man with a mincing gait, who was strikingly dressed in a suit of electric-blue material.

'Sorry I'm late, boys,' he apologised, in a peculiar falsetto voice. 'Where's Lina?'

'She isn't here yet,' Brightman told him.

Williams went and helped himself to a drink, and settled down in one of the more luxurious chairs.

'Jimmy, I want you to contact Mullins. Tonight if possible,' ordered Brightman, who was obviously anxious to proceed with the evening's business.

'Mullins? You mean the fence?'

'Yes.'

'He's a difficult man to get hold of ...' Mills was beginning to protest, but Brightman promptly cut him short.

'I don't care if he's Colonel Lindbergh. Get him!'

'O.K.,' said Mills, shortly.

'What do we want Mullins for? We 'aven't got any stuff on our 'ands,' put in Lucky, curiously.

'No, but we soon shall have,' significantly retorted Brightman.

Jimmy Mills was interested at once.

'What is it?' asked Lucky Gibson, suspiciously.

'The Falkirk Diamond,' smiled Brightman, rubbing his hands gently.

'I thought it was out of town,' said Mills, who was usually well up in these matters.

'It is,' Brightman told him. 'It's at a small jewellers in Nottingham.'

'Nottingham?' echoed Mills, rather taken aback.

In spite of Brightman's nod, Jimmy Mills seemed unconvinced.

'Jimmy, have you heard of Lord Cresset?' smoothly proceeded Brightman.

'You mean Cresset the brewer? Yes, I've 'eard of him.'

'Well, in spite of a somewhat alcoholic environment, his lordship's weakness does not happen to lie in that direction. He has rather more noble aspirations.'

'You mean 'e's got a lady friend,' interposed Mills.

'He has a lady friend,' murmured Brightman.

Swan Williams set down his glass. 'The Falkirk Diamond has rather an interesting story,' he informed them. 'It was brought from America in nineteen thirty-four, and then ...'

Brightman waved an impatient hand. 'The Falkirk Diamond is worth a quarter of a million. That's all the history that interests us,' he declared.

The door was suddenly flung open to admit a striking young woman of twenty-five. Slightly above average height, the pallor of her regular features contrasted effectively with the sleek black hair, parted exactly in the centre. Most men looked twice at Lina Fresnay.

Behind her was the burly figure of Jed Ware, agile as a cat for all his fourteen stone. Indeed, Jed included cat burglary among his many dubious accomplishments.

'Evening everyone! Sorry we're late,' smiled Lina, taking off her hat and flinging it carelessly on to a side table.

'My God! What a journey!' grumbled Jed, making for the decanter. 'Anybody'd think Nottingham was in the north of Scotland.'

He appeared far more irritable than Lina, due, no doubt, to the fact that he had been driving continuously for eight hours in heavy traffic. She settled herself comfortably, took a case from her bag, selected a small cigarette, accepted a light from Swan Williams, and puffed contentedly.

'Well, Lina – what do you think?' demanded Brightman impatiently. Lina placidly contemplated her cigarette, her lacquered nails contrasting sharply with its virginal whiteness.

'He's right. It can be done,' she announced at length.

'Good,' said Brightman, obviously relieved at the information.

'They're keeping the stone down there till Monday,' continued Lina, in her almost expressionless tone. 'If Cresset doesn't buy, Simpson is bringing the stone back to Town on the eight-ten.'

'Simpson? Who's Simpson?' asked Brightman.

'He's the insurance representative. Believe me, that stone is pretty well looked after. Our only chance is—'

'They mustn't get the diamond back to London,' declared Brightman. 'In that case we're done for.'

'They won't do that,' came the thick, coarse voice of Jed Ware. 'It's a perfect set-up.'

'Good!' applauded Brightman. 'Now Jimmy, listen ...'

But once again Lucky Gibson would not be denied.

'I say, I don't follow all this. What's the Falkirk Diamond doing in Nottingham in the first place?'

Brightman shrugged impatiently. 'I thought I'd explained that Lord Cresset has a lady friend. The lady friend has a weakness for diamonds. One and one make two; two and two make four. Good God, Lucky, pull yourself together!' he concluded in angry tones.

'How do we know that the Falkirk Diamond is in Nottingham?' persisted Lucky, quite undismayed.

'Because I have received information to that effect,' snapped Brightman.

'From whom?' asked Lucky, who quite obviously liked to get to the bottom of everything.

'You know perfectly well from whom I have received the information,' retorted Brightman. 'It came from the Chief—'

'Yes, I daresay, but who is he?' pursued Jimmy, his voice rising almost to a shout. 'Who is he? That's what I want to know!'

A sudden gesture from Ware reduced him to silence. Jed walked carefully to the door, placed a hand on the knob, and was about to open it, when there was a knock from outside. Jed flung the door open.

Tony Rivoli stood there.

'Dinner is ready, gentlemen,' he announced urbanely.

Brightman eyed him suspiciously, but Tony met his gaze blandly, and stood deferentially awaiting further orders.

'Thank you,' said Brightman, softly, and Jed Ware closed the door on Tony's retreating figure.

There was a moment's silence.

'One of these days, Lucky, that tongue of yours is going to get you into trouble,' declared Brightman, and there was a sinister glint in his eye. 'Over dinner, I shall outline the Nottingham details,' he proceeded. 'Afterwards, Jimmy, I want you to contact Mullins.'

'Yes, yes, all right,' agreed Jimmy, who obviously did not relish the job.

'Are you ready, Lina?' asked Brightman. She had been watching the proceedings with a flicker of amusement, and now rose to accompany Brightman, a queer little smile slightly distorting her highly sensual mouth.

CHAPTER XIII

The Falkirk Diamond

It was a pity that Swan Williams had not been allowed to enlarge upon the history of the Falkirk Diamond, for the Front Page Men, and Lina in particular, would have found it quite interesting.

In the first instance, the Falkirk Diamond had been bought from a negro by an Austrian Jew for three bottles of very indifferent whisky. The negro had smuggled the diamond out of the mines by the simple process of carrying the diamond in the palm of his hand. The officials, as usual, had made a detailed examination of the negro's person, but had quite naturally overlooked the ridiculous possibility of him carrying the diamond out under their very noses.

The negro was more than pleased with his bargain – he had never received more than two bottles of whisky on any previous occasion. But he was no more delighted than the purchaser, though the latter concealed his ecstasy more skilfully. In fact, he was so overwhelmed, that he felt justified in taking a trip to America to dispose of the stone and to enjoy the proceeds.

There was no difficulty about this, for the diamond realised forty thousand dollars in Chicago without much effort on the part of the seller. After that it changed hands with amazing rapidity, and usually under very similar circumstances. In fact, the Falkirk Diamond began to get a reputation as a token of marital infidelity, a sort of antithesis of the Dunmow Flitch.

It circulated around New York's exclusive Four Hundred for some years, figuring during that time in eight divorces and four *affaires* which were never the subject of litigation, but which were freely hinted at in the Yellow Press.

The diamond received its cognomen following a sensational case in which the principal was the Honourable John Falkirk, a ne'er-do-well member of the English nobility who had been sent to America in the vague hope that it would be the making of him. His main asset in life was a poker face which he used to such good purpose that he relieved an American millionaire of the diamond at the end of an all-night session. Before the month was out, it was adorning the person of Miss Betty Lemuir, of the Vanities chorus, who lost no opportunity of flaunting it, particularly in the presence of Miss Lesley Dane, its previous owner. But Miss Dane was soon to have her revenge.

Suffering from the effects of a rather too liberal dose of alcohol, the Honourable John Falkirk returned to his flat one night to find his lady love sleeping peacefully with one hand flung carelessly across the coverlet. On the second finger, the diamond sparkled.

Whether he was overcome by remorse at his extravagant generosity, greed for lucre, or whether he was too befuddled to know quite what he was about has never been ascertained, but the Honourable John started to make a clumsy effort to remove the ring.

'Darling!' murmured Miss Lemuir drowsily, mistaking this for a touch of amorous playfulness to which she had become accustomed.

Then she suddenly sat up in bed.

'Johnnie, what are you doing?'

'The ring,' muttered the Honourable John, thickly. 'Must have the ring ...'

Betty was now frightened. There was something peculiar about her lover's expression.

'Get away ... let me alone!' she screamed.

Falkirk's fingers left her hand and clutched at her throat.

Twenty-four hours later, Walter Winchell was telling anxious New Yorkers what really had happened to Miss Betty Lemuir.

The American police spread a wide net in search of the Honourable John, but he was never seen again. However, the Falkirk Diamond reappeared at Detroit in the hands of a receiver, who told the police that it had come to him *via* a certain Rod Nester, who generally managed to keep friendly with the police by methods best known to himself. So the Falkirk Diamond was allowed to return to legitimate circulation, and no further questions were asked.

It came to England in the possession of a certain film star whose Hollywood contract had expired, and who had told a score or two pressmen that she had decided to return to her first love, the legitimate theatre. Unfortunately for Miss Cranston, she considered it imperative that the play should be written by her cousin, presented by her nephew, and produced by a gentleman who Miss Cranston fondly described as 'a very dear friend of the family'. Unfortunately the very dear friend had very little knowledge of the theatre, and after a run of barely three weeks the play was withdrawn.

Still, Miss Cranston was a determined young lady if nothing else, and since the very dear friend was sure that this time he had found the right play, she sold the Falkirk Diamond to finance the second production. This time it was to be a large-scale musical with Miss Cranston playing the part of a celebrated opera star. The fact that Miss Cranston had a southern accent and no singing voice was overlooked by everyone except the audience, who, rather to the surprise of everyone concerned, took exception to the fact. So, in a fit of desperation, the film star picked herself a City stockbroker and relapsed into comparative obscurity.

Meanwhile the Falkirk Diamond was in active circulation. In fact, it was a staple topic of conversation at Mayfair cocktail parties. ('My dear, the way she's going on she'll qualify for the Falkirk Diamond!') It did not change hands quite so swiftly as it had done in New York, for the Englishman is rather less inclined to make extravagant gestures to his lady love. Also, there happened to be a depression on at the time, and money was flowing less freely.

There was a minor sensation when young Tony Macguire presented the much photographed and publicised Miss Sybil Lamont with an engagement ring in which the Falkirk Diamond was mounted. All his friends declared that he was tempting the gods, but he was very sure of Sybil, and considered nothing too good for her.

But their engagement did not come to a normal conclusion in church, or even registry office. It ended with Sybil eloping with a very wealthy Italian Count, who had a passionate liking for England and a private income of forty thousand a year.

Of course, being a lady – and since the Count insisted – Sybil returned the ring. Tony was forcibly restrained by his best friend from flinging it into the Thames, and when he had cooled down it was whispered around Mayfair that the Falkirk Diamond was up for sale again at a certain Bond Street jewellers.

The news reached Lord Cresset at a hunt breakfast near his Nottingham estate. With his cup of coffee half-way to his mouth, his eyes glistened. It was a confounded nuisance he couldn't get up to town just now. He'd ring up Mains and Shearing after lunch and see if they could get it down to Nottingham on approval, as it were. Besides, old Spears had always been quite decent – he might as well get a commission on the deal, if it came off.

Lorrimer Street provides a not unpleasing contrast to the wide, sweeping thoroughfares in the centre of the dignified city of Nottingham, which invariably make a pleasant impression upon the casual visitor.

A survival of the lace-making quarter, Lorrimer Street is a perpetual source of worry to the authorities, as it leads from a corner of one of the large squares in which the traffic flows freely. However, large limousines have a habit of sweeping into the narrow Lorrimer Street and parking themselves outside the two or three exclusive establishments which have remained faithful to their ancient premises and refused to move elsewhere. This frequently results in a minor traffic block. Until the authorities, driven to desperation, have decreed that Lorrimer Street shall be one way. This, despite the protests of the aforesaid establishments, who naturally welcomed any amount of car traffic and did not wish their clients to be inconvenienced.

Mains and Shearing's establishment – it was never vulgarly referred to as a shop – stands about half-way down Lorrimer Street, where the road has a slight tendency to form a bottleneck. This has the effect of bringing cars and other vehicles a shade nearer to the windows. The windows in question are arc-shaped and painted in rather a drab shade of brown, which certainly provides no distraction from the display of a quantity of shining silver-plate inside, and also a small but expensive display of jewellery in one corner of the window.

Mains and Shearing scorned the protective network which is effected by so many jewellers' establishments nowadays. Never in the hundred years' history of the firm had any marauder dared to lay a plundering hand upon any property of Mains and Shearing. Still, one had to admit that both Mains and Shearing had been old-fashioned (they were dead now) and neither had ever heard of such things as gangsters and G-men.

On a bright April evening, just before closing-time, a lorry clattered up Lorrimer Street, belching forth spasmodic jets of blue exhaust fumes and came to a coughing standstill outside Mains and Shearing's. It was a large and very noisy vehicle, but sufficiently powerful to pass more than half the private cars it encountered on the road. The rear of the lorry was covered by a large green canvas hood mounted on a wooden framework. There was no indication of its owners either on the hood or the front of the vehicle.

No sooner had the lorry quivered for the last time, than a crew of some half-dozen workmen leapt actively out of the back, bringing with them pickaxes, electric drills, shovels, iron stakes and other impedimenta of the road-breaker. They laughed, joked and shouted to one another in the true

116

tradition, and the few pedestrians in Lorrimer Street regarded them with a shrug and perhaps a muttered comment, 'Road up again!'

The foreman, who might have been recognised beneath his grimy make-up as Jed Ware, gave some rapid instructions. In next to no time, a space in front of Mains and Shearing's had been roped off, and the air was reverberating to the ear-splitting racket of pneumatic drills, punctuated from time to time with the clinking of pickaxes.

Strolling thoughtfully on his beat in the square, P.C. White naturally heard the racket and immediately made tracks in that direction. P.C. White liked to think that he was no ordinary policeman. Of course, he did not scorn an occasional motoring case; he had even been seen surreptitiously marking motor-tyres with chalk in order to check up on the time of parking. That, however, was merely a question of routine. Lorrimer Street was a very useful source of such cases, and P.C. White was never very far away when on duty. This, however, was very much by the way. Something had always told him that one day his Big Case would loom on the horizon, and he meant to be fully prepared.

Only the other day he had been reading an article in a periodical on the subject of famous hoaxes. One of these, apparently, was the uprooting of a section of the roadway in Piccadilly, which some bright young sparks had accomplished without any interference from the police. Constable White fumed inwardly when he read this. He bitterly resented such escapades at the expense of the Force. At the same time he made up his mind that he would never be taken in like that.

He came upon the scene almost at a run and demanded brusquely of the foreman, 'What the devil's going on here?'

Ware surveyed him quickly, then replied indifferently, 'We've had orders to take up the road.' He continued to give his orders and completely ignored the policeman.

By this time the lorry had been backed carefully, so that its rear number-plate was just level with the shop door of the jewellers.

'How long do you reckon it will take?' the constable was asking when a police sergeant came up.

'What's going on here, White?' he raged. 'The traffic's in a devil of a mess at the end of the street, and—'

'They're taking the road up, sir,' shouted the constable, above the din of drills and pickaxes.

'Damn it man, I can see that!'

The sergeant turned to Jed Ware. 'Why didn't we hear about this beforehand?'

'Don't ask me, I'm not the Corporation,' was the casual reply. A smaller lorry had now arrived and dumped a load of gravel further down the street, and men were shovelling it noisily. Incidentally, it had been unloaded in such a position that it was now impossible for traffic to proceed down the street.

'Look here, you can't do this!' shouted the bewildered sergeant. 'Why, the end shops are roped off!'

'Sorry, Sergeant,' coolly replied the foreman. 'You'll have to get on to the Corporation if you want to do anything about it.'

'And I certainly will!' fumed the sergeant, as a workman sent a shovelful of earth over his boots. He turned to the constable.

'White, get in touch with Inspector Hutchinson and report this. Then come back here. I'm going along to see Milford.'

Once more, he turned to Jed Ware. 'These men must not go on rooting up that pavement till I get back. You understand?'

'All right,' replied Jed Ware, indifferently.

The sergeant and constable went their respective ways. As soon as they were out of sight, the workmen relaxed visibly, though they still made some pretence of carrying on their jobs. The foreman went up to the lorry and was soon deep in conversation with the two men who sat in the driver's cabin.

Inside Mains and Shearing's, the electric lights glinted on the highly polished silver. They were on most of the day, for it was rather a gloomy interior, hemmed in by showcases which excluded a large proportion of the daylight. The shop had a low ceiling supported by pillars here and there, and at the far end of the counter were a couple of rather unusual alcoves in which visitors waited to interview the proprietor.

Whilst all the commotion was raging outside, Mr. Ronald Spears was quite oblivious to anything in the nature of a disturbance. Approaching fifty, and quite distinguished-looking, Mr. Spears had bought the business from Mains and Shearing some seven or eight years ago, and had paid quite a stiff price for it. But he would cautiously admit that he was beginning to see a return for his money.

At the moment he was blissfully engaged in trying to interest a lady customer in one of the latest watches, skilfully set in an expensive ring. The wife of one of the city's leading solicitors, she had caught something of her husband's distrust of mankind. She was dubious that such a tiny watch could keep correct time. But Mr. Spears was not discouraged. He was at some pains to detail the niceties of the movement.

'It really is a most attractive watch, madam,' he pleaded. 'I noticed Lady Friarholme wearing one at the Rotary Ball last week – they are particularly fashionable just now.' There was some sign of weakening his customer's sales resistance when the door opened swiftly. Mr. Spears looked up in some annoyance, then his expression changed.

Two masked figures stood in the doorway.

'If anybody moves, they won't live to tell the tale,' came the tense voice of Jimmy Mills. 'Get your hands up, everybody!'

The lady customer looked round, gave a loud shriek; her eyes seemed to bulge out of her head, and suddenly she sank heavily to the floor.

'It's all right; she's only fainted,' muttered Lucky Gibson, coming inside another couple of paces. Mills came up level with the counter.

'Where's the safe?' he snapped, pointing his revolver menacingly at Spears.

'I—I—assure you the most valuable stock is here,' stammered Spears, weakly.

'Keep back from that counter. If I catch you pressing any alarms, it'll be the last thing you'll ever press!'

Spears backed away nervously, still holding up his hands. This was an entirely new experience for him, and he had not the least idea how to cope with it. All sorts of wild schemes flashed through his brain ... should he take a chance and reach for that heavy silver cup? But the aperture of the barrel of Jimmy Mills' revolver loomed with ever-increasing menace.

'We're not interested in this junk,' snarled Mills. 'We want the Falkirk Diamond.'

There was dead silence for a moment. Then Spears spoke in a queer, choked voice.

'I assure you that—' The other cut him short.

'Get it!' ordered Mills furiously.

'All right,' agreed Spears, who had turned deathly white. He came round the counter. 'It's—it's in the safe downstairs,' he murmured. Mills nodded to Lucky Gibson to follow him. Their footsteps receded down the wooden stairs. His revolver still alert, Jimmy stood near the door, which was presently opened. Swan Williams thrust his head round the door.

'You'll have to get a move on. Jed's had the boys get back in the lorry.'

'What the hell's the game?' demanded Mills.

'Things are getting warm. The cops'll be back any time now – and Jed's pretty sure they smell a rat,' was Williams' warning.

'O.K.,' snapped Mills, moving the inert form of the woman with his foot, as footsteps sounded on the cellar stairs once more, and Lucky's head hastily reappeared.

'Got it?' demanded Mills.

'Yes,' replied Lucky, breathlessly.

'Right. Come on.' He paused to wedge a large showcase against the cellar door, which should effectively prevent Mr. Spears from making his escape, and they backed out of the shop with a final look round, then leapt quickly into the lorry which stood there with its engine spluttering.

'Keep low at the back!' advised Swan, speaking through a tiny partition. Jed Ware let in the clutch, and the lorry shot forward with a jerk, accelerating swiftly from the scene of the crime. None of its occupants saw a police-car approach from the square, discover that the street was impassable and back out again as quickly as possible.

Lucky Gibson removed his mask. There were beads of perspiration on his forehead, and Mills noticed that his hands were unsteady. He took a flask from his hip-pocket and handed it to Lucky, who drank deeply.

'I say – I want to get rid of this rock – I shan't get any rest till it's safe,' whispered Lucky hoarsely.

'All right,' growled Mills. 'Lina and Brightman will be waiting just outside Ashby. Step on it!' he called through the partition to Jed Ware, and the lorry swayed and skidded through the suburbs until the frame which carried the canvas creaked and groaned again.

They had travelled very nearly two miles before Jimmy Mills suddenly clutched Lucky as he gazed at the receding road.

'Cops!' he hissed, rattling the partition vigorously. 'They're after us!' Jed Ware nodded grimly and pressed his foot firmly on the accelerator. Now they came to a loop-road which took them along narrower streets. Lucky peered behind them ... the police-car was slowly gaining, despite the fact that the lorry must have been travelling at nearly sixty miles an hour, to the consternation of the other road-users. There were several sharp corners at which Jed had no alternative but to brake heavily, otherwise the lorry would have overturned.

At each of these the police car gained appreciably, until it was no more than fifty yards behind. Round the next corner a level-crossing became visible, and when they were some thirty yards away the gates began to close. A long goods train was puffing its laborious way towards the crossing – it was still a quarter of a mile away. Jed Ware gritted his teeth and stepped hard on the accelerator.

'You'll never do it! Stop!' screamed Swan Williams.

'Can't stop now,' replied Jed.

There was just about six feet of space between the gates as they came up to the crossing. They caught a glimpse of a very indignant signalman leaning out of his box at the side of the road and waving his arms wildly. Swan Williams flung his arms before his face. Jed Ware clung grimly to the wheel.

There was a bump which shook the vehicle, but Ware held it to its course and they clattered on. The men in the back could see that one of the gates had been hung off its hinges and was lying across the roadway. The police-car had managed to stop just in time.

Meanwhile the signalman, armed with a red flag, ran down the line to stop the goods train. By the time the road had been cleared of its obstruction and the police-car was able to proceed, the lorry was very nearly half-a-mile ahead. However, the police were not to be denied, and along level stretches their car came into sight once more.

'They're coming again,' growled Mills, rattling the celluloid partition. The lorry swayed perilously on the wrong side of the road as they took another corner, twice they missed oncoming cars by what seemed the merest fraction. Fortunately for them the country was fairly flat, and there were no hills of any size to slow down the lorry to any appreciable extent. It was beginning to grow dusk now, though it would not be lighting-up time for some twenty minutes.

The police-car drew nearer. It was not more than twenty yards away now. Jimmy Mills went right to the back of the lorry and closely scrutinised their pursuers.

'Why, there are only two of 'em,' he announced, with a short laugh. Which was quite true, for the police had not anticipated anything out of the ordinary. Jimmy Mills returned to his seat by the partition and shouted some instructions to Jed Ware, who nodded, and narrowed his eyes in intense concentration on the road ahead.

The lorry swung down the next side-turning and was soon bumping down a narrow lane, which it almost filled. They continued in this fashion for the better part of a mile. The police had switched on their headlights now, and the men in the lorry let down the canvas at the back. Mills suddenly shouted to Jed, who brought the lorry to a standstill. The police car pulled up some five yards away, and its occupants alighted.

As they came level with the back of the lorry the masked faces of Jimmy Mills and Lucky Gibson were thrust through the canvas.

'Were you wanting anything?' demanded Jimmy in the politest tones he could muster.

'Yes, you're coming along with us,' curtly replied one of the police, 'on a charge of—'

He broke off abruptly as he saw he was facing two revolvers.

'I don't think so, Constable,' replied Jimmy smoothly. 'If you're wise you'll put up your hands quickly – both of you – come on now!' he snapped, as he noticed one of them make an involuntary movement towards his belt.

Slowly the policemen raised their hands.

'All right, Jed,' shouted Jimmy, and Jed Ware slid swiftly past, flung open the bonnet of the car and wrenched vigorously at various wires.

'That'll take 'em a couple of hours to put right,' he announced grimly, at length. He made his way back to the driver's seat of the lorry, which presently rumbled on its way, leaving two very disgruntled policemen standing with their arms above their heads in the middle of a deserted country lane.

By carefully watching the signposts, they managed to find their way to Ashby, where Brightman's luxurious American saloon was waiting just outside the town. On the way they had dropped the workmen at the railway station, after Swan Williams had handed each of them a bundle of pound notes.

124

'What are you going to do with the lorry?' asked Brightman, when they had reassured him concerning the Falkirk Diamond.

'Leave it up this lane here,' decided Jed Ware.

'But the police are sure to find it.'

'Yes, and a fat lot of good it will do them!'

They all piled into the back of the saloon car, which headed swiftly for London.

'What about the diamond?' queried Lucky, anxiously.

'Keep it till we get to town,' advised Brightman, busy at the wheel.

'I'd sooner 'ave it out of me 'ands,' protested Lucky.

'All right, Lucky,' smiled Lina, speaking for the first time. 'I'll take care of it.' Brightman threw her a suspicious glance, but Lucky handed over the stone thankfully.

'Blimey! I'm glad to be shot of that!' he declared fervently.

Back in the shop Mr. Ronald Spears and the police sergeant were busily endeavouring to restore the lady customer, who had recovered from her swoon, only to lapse into a fit of hysterics when she recalled what had happened.

'It's no use, Sergeant. She can't tell you any more than I have,' Spears pointed out.

'I must have her statement,' insisted the sergeant. 'Now come along, madam …'

For a moment, the lady looked quite intelligent.

'They wore masks!' she said, softly, then once more relapsed into incoherence.

'Pull yourself together, madam, please,' urged the sergeant, turning his attention once more towards the jeweller.

'Who else was in the shop when it happened?'

'Only the three of us, sir. This lady, whom I was attending to at the time, and this gentleman.'

'Eh?' snapped the sergeant, sharply.

'This gentleman was sitting in the recess over there, waiting to see me on a small business matter.'

The sergeant turned to the man who had come forward as though reluctant to intrude.

'Then I take it that you saw everything, sir, the same as the others?'

'Everything.'

'H'm – could I have your name, please?'

'With pleasure,' said the customer. 'The name is Hargreaves – the Reverend Charles Hargreaves.'

CHAPTER XIV

At Bramley Lodge

Paul Temple always spent as much time as possible at Bramley Lodge, his house near Evesham, in the spring. Standing on a slope, this ancient Tudor mansion commanded a view of the Worcestershire orchard-country calculated to send any artistically minded spinster into ecstasies. In fact, you often saw them at blossom-time, seated at their easels, and busy with their water-colours.

After the attempt to kidnap Steve, Temple had insisted on bringing her to Bramley Lodge, where, he assured her, the country air would build up her health and the placid tempo of rural life would soon restore any nervous deficiencies. He added lightly that she might even feel impelled to start her book.

There followed five days of complete, peaceful serenity. Temple forbade her even to read the papers, declaring that sixteen-point headlines are calculated at times to produce a disturbing effect even on an ex-reporter.

But he read the papers himself. So he was not surprised to see Sir Graham Forbes' huge roadster sweep round the curve of the drive one fine May morning. Steve heard it too, and was waiting in the hall when the Chief Commissioner was shown in.

Sir Graham looked very haggard, which was not surprising, as he had been investigating in Nottingham for the better part of the night.

'I expect this business at Nottingham gave you a nasty jolt,' sympathised Temple.

'That's putting it mildly. Have you seen the papers?'

'Yes,' said Steve promptly, smiling sweetly in reply to her husband's frown. 'I can't quite see why the Front Page Men should trouble themselves over a small jeweller's in Nottingham.'

'This particular jeweller,' quietly interposed Forbes, 'had the Falkirk Diamond.'

'Phew!' whistled Temple, rising and walking over to the window, where he pensively regarded his beloved orchards for some moments.

'The Falkirk Diamond?' repeated Steve, somewhat puzzled.

'Yes,' said Forbes. 'So far, we've kept it out of the papers, but the story is bound to break sooner or later.' He drummed his fingers moodily on the arm of his chair.

'Did you come down from town?' asked Temple.

'No, I've been in Nottingham all night. I motored down there with Mac and Hunter.'

Temple nodded, and resumed his thoughtful contemplation of the scene outside.

'We're in a jam, Temple,' growled Sir Graham, 'and believe me it's a pretty bad one. Sir Stephen Frost came through on the phone first thing this morning. Apparently the P.M.'s in a devil of a rage. Something must be done about the Front Page Men, and done quickly.'

He thumped the table to emphasise his anxiety, then relapsed into gloomy silence.

'Have you made any further attempts to find that warehouse?' asked Temple.

'My dear fellow, the river police have been literally combing the Thames-side,' Sir Graham wearily informed him.

'No luck?'

Forbes shook his head.

'What about these men who committed the robbery at Nottingham?' asked Steve eagerly, her reporting instincts now fully aroused.

'The only information I seem to be able to extract is that they wore masks. We haven't got a decent description of any of them with the exception of one or two navvies, who were probably toughs just got up for that particular hold-up.'

Steve leaned forward and stirred the log-fire which was still lighted in the mornings. Her husband, who had been perched on the window-seat, came and settled himself in an armchair.

Forbes filled his pipe with nervous fingers and thoughtfully puffed smoke-rings in the direction of the fireplace.

'Temple, you remember that man, Andrew Brightman?' he began, reflectively.

'Perfectly,' said Temple.

'I'm just a shade doubtful about that gentleman. Never liked the looks of him from the start.'

'I could mention a few hundred people who are something of an eyesore to me,' grinned Temple, 'but that would hardly constitute evidence that they have any connection with the Front Page Men. Or even that they are criminals.'

Sir Graham nodded glumly.

'All the same,' he went on, 'you remember Brightman told us that, acting on instructions received from the Front

Page Men, he deposited a suitcase containing eight thousand pounds in the cloakroom of the Regal Palace Hotel.'

'Well?' queried Temple.

'He cashed a cheque for eight thousand all right, but he didn't deposit the suitcase in the cloakroom.'

Temple and Steve sat up and began to look interested.

'How do you know?' asked the former.

'Because,' said Forbes quietly, 'they won't let you deposit a suitcase in the cloak-room of the Regal Palace Hotel. They have a luggage depot in Villier Street.'

'Smart work,' commented Temple.

'Hunter happened to find that out,' conceded Sir Graham, a little reluctantly.

Steve was quite excited now. 'You think that this man Brightman might be the leader of the Front Page Men?' she demanded.

Forbes frowned. 'I wouldn't go so far as to say that, Mrs. Temple.'

'But there must be a leader,' argued Steve.

'Yes, there's a Front Page Man Number One all right,' agreed Sir Graham, 'but somehow I don't think it's Brightman.'

'No,' said Temple evenly, 'neither do I.' But he did not offer to give his reasons, and they sat in silence for some time, each debating the point in his mind.

'I can't help thinking that, whoever he is, Front Page Man Number One must be a sort of genius,' announced Sir Graham at length. 'Yes, a genius,' he repeated emphatically, 'with a strange, fantastic type of mind.'

'Why do you say that?' asked Steve.

'Well, take the name of the gang, or organisation ... it's also the title of a very successful thriller, written apparently by a woman called Andrea Fortune – who nobody knows anything at all about.'

'Perhaps she's Front Page Man Number One,' suggested Temple, diffidently.

'Yes, that's possible,' conceded Sir Graham, but he was prevented from enlarging upon the theory by the telephone's shrill ring. Temple answered it, and with barely a word handed over the receiver to his guest.

'That was Inspector Nelson,' Sir Graham told them, as he replaced the receiver. 'I don't think I told you he's been trailing Goldie.'

'You mean the piano-tuner?' asked Steve, her eyes lighting up. Forbes nodded.

'Well?' said Temple. 'Apparently, Mr. J. P. Goldie spent the afternoon in Nottingham on the day of the hold-up.'

'That's interesting,' smiled Temple. 'Were there any customers in the shop when the robbery occurred?'

'Yes, but they can't tell us a great deal, unfortunately,' said Sir Graham, with obvious regret.

'Goldie wasn't there by any chance?'

'No.'

'By the way,' put in Steve, 'have you had any news of Sir Norman Blakeley's child?'

Once again Sir Graham had to admit defeat. This seemed to irritate him so much that he suddenly announced that he must return to London at once. He refused the Temples' pressing invitation to lunch, declaring he had no time to lose. They saw him to his car. With one foot on the running-board, he hesitated.

'Temple, if you should happen to think of anything ...' he murmured tentatively. 'Or if by any chance you come across some clue ...'

'I'll do all I possibly can, Sir Graham,' Temple assured him. And the eight cylinders roared in unison as the huge car shot down the drive.

'He looks terribly worried, doesn't he?' commented Temple, as they stood on the steps and watched Sir Graham disappear.

'Yes,' agreed Steve, 'I wish he'd stayed to lunch. Carol says he misses half his meals when he's on a worrying case, and a man of his age can't be expected to ...'

'Steve darling,' her husband admonished her gently, 'for a moment I thought you were about to launch upon woman's favourite lecture of all time!' They both laughed, and went back to the hall.

'I wonder if they'll get away with the Falkirk Diamond,' Steve speculated.

'I don't know,' said Temple, lighting a cigarette, and flicking the match accurately into the heart of the fire.

'Anyhow, the Nottingham robbery seems to show they don't intend restricting their activities to abduction and murder.'

'There never was any restriction on their activities, Steve,' he replied. 'This is the biggest organisation of its kind that we have had in this country. And something tells me that we haven't heard the last of them by any means.'

'This Mr. Goldie,' Steve broke in. 'Do you think he is ...'

A quiet smile flickered around her husband's mobile mouth. 'I don't know quite what to make of Mr. Goldie,' he declared. 'In fact, up to date, he presents the most intriguing problem of the whole business.'

There was a sound of screeching brakes outside, a car door slammed abruptly, and Steve ran to the window.

'Why, it's Gerald!' she announced, greatly surprised, and went to open the door.

'Hallo, Gerald; do come in,' Temple heard her call out, as he rose to welcome their second visitor that morning.

Gerald Mitchell seemed very excited. He crushed the brim of his felt hat nervously in his hands as he came into the room, and occasionally his face twitched oddly, distorting his features in an unpleasant fashion. He seemed to be keyed up for some sort of ordeal.

'Paul, I'm frightfully sorry bursting in on you like this,' he apologised, 'but I simply had to see you.'

'Yes, yes, of course,' said Temple, soothingly.

'Do sit down, Gerald,' invited Steve.

Mitchell shifted nervously from one foot to the other.

'No, I'd rather stand, thanks, Steve.' He put his hat on a side table, then picked it up again, and began fingering it in a manner which irritated Temple.

'Have a drink, Gerald,' suggested Steve, but he shook his head. 'Then you must stay to lunch,' she decided. 'What you want is a good square meal.' She caught her husband's amused glance, and subsided.

'Paul, I'm worried, hellishly worried,' said Mitchell. 'I've just heard something, and—oh Lord—I don't know what to think.'

'What you need is a good stiff whisky,' began Temple, but Mitchell waved him aside.

'No, no, I'm all right,' he protested.

Temple and Steve regarded each other in some perplexity. Suddenly Mitchell took out his handkerchief and mopped his brow.

'I saw Reed yesterday afternoon,' he said. 'And he told me about what happened that night Steve disappeared.'

'You must have won your way to his rugged Scottish heart,' smiled Temple, disarmingly.

'He told me that Steve received a telephone message from Carol Forbes.'

'No,' interposed Steve. 'It turned out that the call wasn't from Carol.'

'But—but you thought it was Carol speaking on the phone, didn't you?'

Steve nodded. 'I was positive. I've known Carol quite a while now. I both like and respect her, and I'm sure she was telling the truth when she said that she didn't phone me.'

'But—the voice ...' broke in Mitchell, urgently.

'The voice was Carol's. I'm sure of it.'

'No, no, it wasn't! It wasn't!' cried Mitchell.

Temple took his arm. 'Gerald, what is it?' he demanded firmly.

'I'm sorry,' stammered Mitchell, 'but I'm so worried about Ann.'

'Ann?' repeated Steve, taken aback. 'What's Ann got to do with all this?'

'Oh, nothing!' hedged Mitchell, a note of alarm in his voice. 'Nothing—only—before we were married Ann was on the stage, you know ...'

'Well?'

'She did impersonations.' Mitchell seemed to get more and more distressed.

'I don't quite follow ...' Steve was beginning, when Mitchell shouted hysterically, 'Don't you see? She can copy almost anyone's voice perfectly – quite perfectly.'

CHAPTER XV

Mr. Tony Rivoli Visits Scotland Yard

Sir Graham Forbes sat at his desk listlessly stirring a cup of very black coffee. He had had comparatively little sleep during the past week, and there was a network of tiny wrinkles around his tired, grey eyes. For the first time in his life, the Chief Commissioner felt every one of his fifty-five years weighing upon him.

His nerves, too, were suffering, and when the door was suddenly opened he started perceptibly. Hunter was the visitor, his face betraying the fact that he brought news.

'Sir Graham, that youngster of Blakeley's …' he began, excitedly.

'Yes?' queried the Chief Commissioner, a little wearily.

'He's been returned!'

'Yes—yes, I know.'

Hunter was astounded.

'You know?'

'I had the information last night.'

'But—he was only brought back this morning.'

Sir Graham managed to raise a smile. Then his face became serious once more.

'Hunter, I want you and Mac to pick up a fellow called Lucky Gibson. You'll find his record in the files. I've a feeling he had something to do with the Nottingham affair.'

'Yes, sir,' assented Hunter, and at that moment the door opened, and Paul Temple was shown in.

'I've got some news for you, Sir Graham,' said Temple briskly, after they had interchanged greetings. 'Whether it's important or not, I don't know.'

'Yes, and I have some news for you too. Blakeley's boy has been returned.'

'Is he all right?' demanded Temple, obviously rather startled.

'Yes, he's all right, but somehow, he can't remember things.'

Temple looked up quickly.

'Amashyer?'

Forbes nodded. 'Looks like it. They must have given the poor kid a tidy dose of it.'

'How did you find him?'

'Oh, one of our men found him,' answered Forbes, with rather studied indifference, which did not deceive Temple. He seemed to be waiting for further information, so eventually Sir Graham continued, 'Temple, I'm going to take you into my confidence. Wrenson's working on this case.'

'Wrenson? I thought he retired about four years ago.'

'So he did. But this Front Page Men business intrigued him so much that he asked me to take him back. And, quite candidly, I was rather glad he offered. He was always inclined to be a bit theatrical, but, by Jove, he gets results!'

Temple nodded thoughtfully. He remembered Wrenson quite well.

'Do the others know about this – Reed and Hunter, and …'

'No,' said Sir Graham, 'I've kept it a pretty close secret. Wrenson always plays a lone hand better if he receives no official recognition. Seems to act as a sort of spur. Already he's begun to get results.'

'Very glad to hear it,' murmured Temple.

'Now let's hear your news,' went on Sir Graham, who seemed to have recovered some of his vitality by now.

Temple seated himself casually on the corner of the Chief Commissioner's desk. 'Shortly after you left Bramley Lodge yesterday, Mitchell arrived,' he told Sir Graham.

'Yes, I passed him just as he was turning into the drive. Nearly bumped my right wing. What did he want, tearing along in a hurry like that?'

'Apparently Reed had told him about someone imitating Carol's voice on the telephone.'

'Oh, and why should that worry him?'

'Because,' Temple explained, 'his wife is apparently a very good impersonator.'

'Ann Mitchell? H'm, that's interesting.' Sir Graham traced a series of lines on his blotting-pad with his paper-knife.

'Have you known her long?'

'Off and on for about two years – since Mitchell started publishing my stuff.'

'They were married when you first knew him?'

'Yes. Unlike most actresses, she never discusses her past successes.'

'What about her husband? Has he always been in the publishing business?'

'No. He used to be a reporter on the *Morning Express*.'

Forbes' eyebrows were raised a trifle as he asked, 'H'm, so he can write?'

'I wouldn't go so far as to say that. He was on the *Morning Express*.'

If Sir Graham saw anything funny in this remark, he chose to ignore the fact. 'I was just wondering,' he went on thoughtfully, 'whether Gerald Mitchell is really Andrea Fortune, author of *The Front Page Men*. After all, he published the book.'

The rather abrupt entry of Chief Inspector Reed prevented any further speculations, 'I'm sorry to be interrupting ye, Sir Graham, but Mr. Rivoli's called to see ye. He says it's verra important.'

'Rivoli?' repeated Forbes, impatiently. 'You mean ...'

'Tony Rivoli, who runs the Medusa Club in Piccadilly,' supplied Temple.

'Ay, that's right,' nodded Reed.

'You mean the fellow we were talking about that night we traced the telephone call to the Manhattan Club? All right, show him in, Mac.'

Reed turned briskly on his heel, and presently returned with the little Italian, who looked rather insignificant out of evening dress, though he affected a pair of immaculate spats which would have done credit to any City director.

'Good morning, Mr. Rivoli,' welcomed Sir Graham, rising to greet his visitor, and motioning Reed to remain.

Tony was by no means ill at ease in these surroundings; in fact, his manner retained all that charm so appreciated by his wealthy lady clients.

'I hope I do not intrude, Sir Graham?' he began, with a deprecating gesture.

'No, no, not at all,' Forbes assured him. 'May I introduce Mr. Temple?'

Tony shook hands with the novelist. 'Ah yes, Mr. Temple – I see your name on the posters. They say "Send for Paul Temple", no?'

Sir Graham coughed. He considered that particular episode better forgotten. Tony turned to him.

'Sir Graham, I think you know all there is to know about me. In the past I 'ave been a little foolish, perhaps – and maybe a little naughty.'

'Ay!' confirmed Reed with some emphasis.

Tony turned a bewitching smile on him.

'Ah – the Inspector – he remembers me, yes?'

'I do that!' declared Mac with a glint in his eye.

'But now,' smiled Tony, 'I 'ave a pretty swell business. The Medusa Club in Piccadilly; the High Spot at Waring; my restaurant in Bruton Street.'

'Mr. Rivoli, what is it you wanted to see me about?' demanded Forbes in a tone which implied that he supposed these aliens must be tolerated.

Quite undismayed, Tony nodded his head vigorously, and proceeded.

'Sir Graham, I am a little confused. On Tuesday I read in the paper about that business at Nottingham. Oh, ver' bad news. And every night since I lie in bed and think ... and I say to myself: "Tony, it is ver', ver' strange." Then last night I wake up and say: 'Tony, put two and two together – and go to Scotland Yard, and tell them ...'

'Yes—er—quite so,' rumbled Forbes, who was obviously at sea.

'Mr. Rivoli, I'm afraid you are just a little confusing,' explained Temple, diplomatically.

'Ay,' grunted Mac, who had understood less than anyone.

'Would you mind talking a little slower, Mr. Rivoli?' suggested Temple.

'O.K,' smiled Tony, obviously eager to oblige. 'Well, I lie in bed, and I think that the night before this robbery at Nottingham some men come to my club and take a private room for talk and dinner. Now this is ver' strange, because I remember that they come before – several times. And after one of them there is a big bank robbery at Margate ...'

The Chief Commissioner looked up curiously. 'So these men have patronised your club before?'

'Yes, yes, that is what I say. An' always after they meet there is something in the paper about the Front Page Men. One time it is the Margate bank, one time Sir Norman Blakeley's child is kidnapped, and last week it was ...'

'What are these men like?' snapped Forbes, now very intent upon his visitor's story.

Tony shrugged expressively. 'Oh, they are not what you would call 'andsome.'

'Yes,' growled Forbes impatiently, 'but what do they look like?'

'One is tall and—'ow you say?—plump?'

'Dark or fair?'

'Dark.'

'That,' ruminated Forbes, 'might be Brightman.'

'It might,' murmured Temple, 'be any of a million men in London.'

'He call 'imself Mr. Blake,' put in Tony, trying to be helpful.

'What are the others like?' asked Forbes.

'One is 'ver ugly. He 'as a scar across 'is face.'

'How many of these men are there?'

'Usually five. And of course the girl.'

Sir Graham leaned forward intently.

'Oh, there's a girl. What's she like?'

'Ver' nice indeed,' smiled Tony pleasantly. 'She 'as ver' beautiful legs.' He made an expressive gesture.

It was Temple who patiently pointed out to Tony that there were scores of young women with beautiful legs, and that the only way they could hope to recognise the young lady in question was by a description of her features.

'Ah yes, Mr. Temple,' laughed Tony, 'she is so pretty!'

Forbes gave it up as a bad job. He made a sign to Mac and addressed Tony once more. 'I want you to go downstairs with Chief Inspector Reed. He'll show you a lot of photographs, and if you see a picture of one of these people, tell the Inspector.'

'Oh yes, sir, I do that,' agreed Tony eagerly. 'An' – you will not close my beautiful club, no?' he pleaded.

'No, no, of course not,' said Forbes, gruffly.

Tony followed Reed, highly delighted.

'What do you make of that?' demanded Forbes, after the door had closed behind them.

'I have a feeling he was telling the truth,' said Temple, simply.

'Yes, but look here,' protested Forbes, 'the Front Page Men aren't going to use the Medusa Club as a meeting-place.'

'Why not?'

'But it's bang in the middle of Piccadilly.'

'Precisely,' smiled the novelist. 'And who would think of looking for the Front Page Men in the middle of Piccadilly? There is method in their madness, Sir Graham.'

Forbes paused to consider the proposition, and had to admit that there might be something in it.

'Well, supposing the Front Page Men do meet there ...' He stopped and shook his head. 'No, it's much too obvious, Temple.'

But the novelist did not appear to hear him.

'What's worrying you, Temple?'

Temple came to life and smiled. 'Nothing, Sir Graham – nothing at all. In fact, I was just thinking that a little night life might do me a world of good.'

He wished the Chief Commissioner a pleasant good morning, sauntered to the door, and let himself out, exchanging a brief quip with Sergeant Leopold.

CHAPTER XVI

Paul Temple Receives a Warning

After lunch that morning Temple reflectively stirred his coffee. 'What would you say if I suggested we went to a night club this evening?'

'Yes!' answered Steve promptly, and they both laughed.

'Now tell me the subtle motive underlying this invitation,' pouted Steve.

'And what if I refuse?'

'I shall come anyway. I've just bought a new gown from Molyneux, and it's got to be worn before the week's out. Where are we going, Paul – some low dive?'

Her husband pretended to be shocked.

'On the contrary,' he rebuked her, 'we are going to the highly respectable Medusa Club. At least, the proprietor assures me it's respectable, and I'm inclined to believe him.'

'The Medusa? Carol's often been there. She loves it.'

'Then I hope you won't be too bored.'

'I'm never bored when I'm with you,' she smiled. 'But why this sudden urge to visit the Medusa Club?'

'If you think there's going to be a lot of unlawful excitement, I'm afraid you'll be disappointed,' said Temple.

'All the same, I'd like to know ...'

He laughed. 'It's quite simple. We have reason to suspect that the Front Page Men have been making use of the Medusa Club as a meeting-place.'

'And so ...' prompted Steve.

'And so, my sweet, I'm going to take a quiet look round, and see if I recognise any familiar faces.'

For an air of discreet opulence, the Medusa Club's dining-room was probably unsurpassed in the West End. Its furnishing was the last word in lavishness, the lighting was softly effective, calculated to take at least ten years off any woman's age. Indeed, the Medusa Club was particularly popular with the fair sex, who, as Tony argued, invariably have the last word in choosing where an evening shall be frittered away.

In keeping with the lighting, the music was similarly restrained. Ray Carmino engaged the most expensive musicians in London for his ten-piece band. They were reputed to cost him over £400 a week. In fact, their efficiency seemed almost monotonous, if you did not happen to be a dance enthusiast.

Steve and Temple had a table about half-way down the room, on the edge of the dance-floor, which was now packed so tightly that they had given up the idea of dancing for the time being. Occasionally the swaying couples brushed a napkin off the Temples' table, or bumped gently into one of the chairs.

'No wonder Tony believes in going straight,' commented the novelist. 'He must be making a small fortune out of this place.'

'I rather like it for a change,' confessed Steve.

'All right in small doses,' was Temple's laconic opinion, as a particularly artificial blonde brushed his shoulder, and coyly smiled her apologies, when her partner wasn't looking. The band concluded a popular dance number, and amidst the applauding dancers Temple espied Tony Rivoli threading his way towards their table.

'Ah, Mr. Temple!' cried Tony extravagantly, when he was still some distance away. 'Welcome to the Medusa Club!' Several couples stared curiously. Rather embarrassed and somewhat annoyed at this unwelcome publicity, Temple rose to shake hands with Tony.

'Steve – this is Mr. Rivoli – my wife.'

'How do you do? This is most charming,' cried Tony. 'Please you come often to the Medusa Club, yes?'

'We hope so,' laughed Steve. 'I'm enjoying myself immensely. Do sit down for a moment.'

'We must 'ave some champagne to celebrate your visit,' went on Tony. 'Leon!' He snapped his fingers and whispered an order to a waiter, who presently returned with a bottle of champagne. 'My favourite brand,' confided Tony as he filled their glasses.

'Now, Mr. Temple, you tell me what you think of the Medusa. Everything is perfect—yes?'

'Absolutely,' smiled Temple, who saw no reason to mention the fact that the place's one drawback was its popularity. After they had drunk the health of the club, Temple leaned forward and asked quietly, 'Tony, did you recognise any of the pictures they showed you?'

'Ah yes, yes!' cried Tony, excitedly. 'I recognise one man, and I tell the Inspector. He said 'is name was …' Tony broke off abruptly, as the sound of loud voices penetrated across the room, almost drowning the band, which straggled into silence. A group of men were pushing their way across the floor.

'What is the matter? Who are these men?' shouted Tony, leaping to his feet.

'Paul, they're police,' whispered Steve, urgently.

A broad-shouldered, authoritative man stood in the middle of the floor. 'Kindly keep your seats, please,' he shouted. 'We won't detain you any longer than is necessary.'

'Mr. Temple, what is this? What is the reason for raiding my club?' cried Tony, wringing his hands, and looking the picture of abject misery.

Temple could only shake his head helplessly.

'Is your name Rivoli – Tony Rivoli?' asked the man in charge, coming up to them.

Tony nodded and began to protest in voluble Italian.

'I have a warrant for your arrest.'

'For my—arrest?' gabbled Tony incoherently.

'Look here, officer,' began Temple, but the newcomer interrupted him.

'Are you Mr. Temple?'

'Yes.'

'My name is Low, Inspector Low. Sir Graham Forbes asked me to deliver this note to you.'

'Thank you,' said Temple, rather nonplussed. He read the scrap of paper, and turned to his wife. 'We'd better go, Steve. Sir Graham is waiting for us at the flat.'

'At the flat?' echoed Steve, in some surprise.

'I'm sorry I can't give you a lift there, sir,' said Inspector Low respectfully, 'but we have orders to search this place from top to bottom.'

'No! No!' protested Rivoli, energetically, but he was rushed away while the Temples stood watching helplessly.

'Come along, Steve,' said Temple at last. 'Sir Graham will be waiting.'

'I'm afraid it hasn't been a very successful evening from a social point of view,' said Temple, as they sat in the taxi on their way home.

'One can't have everything,' murmured Steve.

'I'm sorry for Tony Rivoli – he was so gay – just like a child with a new toy. I'll never forget that look in his eyes when they dragged him away.'

'Poor devil! This business will break his heart. I can't think what made Forbes have the place raided. Something pretty drastic must have happened.'

Steve considered this for some moments.

'It isn't like Sir Graham to break his word,' she decided. 'Though this business has got him pretty well worked up lately.'

'Even so ...' began her husband, but just then the taxi slid to a standstill, and he broke off to delve in his pockets for some loose silver. 'Got your key, darling?' he asked, when the taxi had driven off and they stood in the entrance hall of the flats.

'Yes, of course. But if Sir Graham's up there, Pryce must have let him in.'

For some unaccountable reason, Steve shivered as they stood in the lift, and neither spoke until it stopped at their landing.

'Close the gate, Paul,' she said as she stepped out. 'You know how irritating it is to find somebody has left it open.'

'Funny, there isn't a light in the drawing-room,' mused Temple, peering through the glass panel of the outer door as he fitted the key.

Having heard them enter, Pryce came to inquire if he should prepare sandwiches and coffee.

'But where's Sir Graham?' demanded Temple, immediately.

'Sir Graham, sir?' repeated Pryce, in some confusion. 'He hasn't called, sir.'

'I see,' said Temple quietly. He crossed over to the telephone and rapidly dialled the Chief Commissioner's private number.

'Paul, you don't think it's a trick?' asked Steve.

But he did not reply.

'I hope nothing is the matter, sir,' said Pryce anxiously. 'I'm sure if Sir Graham had called ...'

'That's all right, Pryce,' nodded Temple. He returned to the telephone.

'Hallo, Sir Graham? This is Temple. Sir Graham, did you send any of your men to the Medusa Club?'

Steve noted with alarm Temple's change of expression.

'Well, look here,' went on Temple, 'meet me at the Medusa Club in twenty minutes ... better get Reed if possible. No, I can't explain now.'

He slammed down the receiver and turned to Steve.

'Paul, what is it?'

'I must go back to the Club right away,' he told her. 'That was a faked raid. I've got an awful feeling that something's happened ...'

'I'll come with you,' offered Steve.

He regarded her dubiously for a moment.

'I hardly like to take you in case ...'

'With half Scotland Yard there – and me an ex-reporter?' she laughed.

'All right, then come on, darling. Don't wait up, Pryce.'

'Very good, sir,' murmured Pryce, holding the outer door open for them.

They ran across the landing to the lift.

148

'It's at the bottom,' announced Steve. 'Somebody must have used it since we arrived.'

'Damn them!' growled Temple, vigorously pressing the button, with no result. 'They must have left the gate open. It won't work!'

'Oh lord!' groaned Steve. 'What a waste of time! Come on, we'll have to walk down …'

Temple suddenly clutched her arm. 'Listen!'

Up the lift-well came the echo of the sharp snap of closing gates.

'H'm, they've thought better of it,' commented Temple, pressing the button once more.

The lift came whining towards them.

'I wonder who closed that gate,' pondered Temple, as the top of the lift came into sight. Before it jerked to a stop, Steve screamed in sheer horror.

A squat form in evening dress lay huddled in the bottom of the lift.

'My God! It's Tony Rivoli!' cried Temple.

A slim-looking knife had been plunged into the little Italian's back, and a dark stain was already spreading slowly over his tail-coat.

Steve turned away as Temple opened the gates.

'There's something written on his shirt-front,' he said. Entering the lift, he bent over the inert form, and read the crudely scrawled message:

He interfered, Mr. Temple!
 The Front Page Men.

CHAPTER XVII

The First Circle

Inspector Hunter was beginning to wonder whether his knowledge of London's underworld was quite as comprehensive as he had imagined. He had boasted at one time that he could put his hand on any man whose record was held by the Yard within twenty-four hours. But Lucky Gibson had eluded him for over a week. Furthermore, none of Lucky's former associates could offer any clue to his whereabouts. Of course, some of them were lying, but there were others who would have been only too ready to betray Lucky if there happened to be a chance of a reward.

Hunter had frequented every disreputable haunt known to him, including several which had only opened during the past few weeks, and were likely to vanish in a like period. Their proprietors were ne'er-do-wells, whom Hunter had met before, usually when they were running some other establishment of a similar nature. They did not exactly welcome him with open arms, but they were quite pleasant to this ex-Oxford graduate, for they knew that he was not interested in any point concerning the licensing regulations. He was merely looking for somebody. Besides, some of them were Oxford men themselves!

It was hardly encouraging to have to return to the Yard every morning, encounter Sir Graham's keen look of inquiry, and report that there was nothing doing. It depressed Hunter more than a little. Moreover, he was suffering from splitting headaches, which left him in the throes of depression.

He could feel one of these headaches hovering over him one night after a particularly exhausting day in the less savoury purlieus of Limehouse. He had walked back, thinking the fresh air might drive away the headache, and on reaching his favourite coffee-stall on the Embankment, he decided that a cup of coffee might also help in this battle with migraine.

The proprietor, Bert Styler, was quite a friend of Hunter's, since the latter had been able to help him on a small problem concerning his pitch, and had been of some assistance in smoothing out the matter with the authorities. Bert was a typical chirpy Cockney, in the middle thirties. He usually looked on the bright side of life, and this trait was just as much a part of him as the wart on one side of his nose.

With sleeves rolled up, he was vigorously wiping cups and plates, to the accompaniment of unceasing clatter. Fortunately the crockery was extremely substantial and withstood Bert's rough handling. Hunter often wondered if those plates would break if they were dropped on the floor. Bert turned and grinned cheekily at the detective.

'Hallo, guv'nor! You look a bit down in the dumps. What's up now? Somebody pinched the 'Ouses of Parliament?'

Hunter leaned against the garishly lighted stall and felt rather better. He was the only customer. The steam from the coffee-urn strayed towards him. It smelt tempting. He leaned his elbows on the counter.

'I'm looking for a man named Lucky Gibson,' he announced rather wearily. 'I don't suppose you've seen him by any chance?'

'Never even 'eard of the cove,' replied Bert, anticipating Hunter's order, and pushing a cup of coffee towards him. 'I don't get many crooks 'ere, you know. 'Course they 'as to eat and drink just like you an' me, but they seems to 'ave the money to go to the posh places these days. Mind yer, I gets a card-sharper and a pickpocket or two now and then, when trade ain't bin too good wiv 'em. Then there's Steeple Bill – they tell me 'e does a bit o' cat-burglin' now and then.'

'Oh?' queried Hunter, with a little more interest. 'What's he doing now?'

'Six months,' answered Bert, evenly. 'They copped 'im last time 'e was out on the tiles. Mind you, 'e 'adn't actually broken in anywhere, but it looks a bit suspicious when they find you 'angin' on to somebody's spouting just after midnight. 'E told 'em that 'e was mendin' the roof, but 'e couldn't find nobody to back 'im up. Lost me a good customer for six months that did.'

Hunter stirred his coffee, reflectively.

'Supposing you wanted to get away from the police, Bert,' he murmured, 'where would you hide yourself?'

'South America,' replied Bert without a moment's hesitation. 'That's one thing about this job, guv'nor; it gives me time to read Edgar Wallace!'

Hunter laughed for the first time that day.

'But supposing it wasn't possible for you to go abroad, Bert – what then?'

'Then,' replied Bert, thoughtfully, polishing his copper urn, 'the game would be up. The blinkin' police are everywhere these days. There'll soon be more police than soldiers. What with these courtesy cops and—'

But Hunter interrupted him. He had enjoyed the doubtful pleasure of listening to Bert's harangues on the subject of courtesy cops on many other occasions.

'It's funny, Bert, but I feel hungry for the first time since breakfast.'

'I *thought* there was something the matter with yer,' said Bert with visible concern. 'You didn't ought to go missin' yer grub like that, guv'nor. Now if you could see the hinside of your stomach at this minute—'

'God forbid!' shuddered the detective.

''Ere, what about a nice sausage roll?' pursued Bert.

'I don't think they agree with me,' smiled Hunter.

'Then what about that night you ate fourteen of 'em right off the reel? Fourteen! Coo, I'll never forget that night. What with the crowd round the old stall – it might 'ave been a blinkin' circus. That was the best advert I ever 'ad. I suppose you ain't feelin' that way tonight?'

Hunter shook his head.

'I might manage one, or even two,' he replied. 'But fourteen … I wonder I'm alive to tell the tale.'

'There's nothin' in them rolls that would 'urt a new-born babe,' protested Bert, indignantly.

Hunter bit into his roll and shook his head reproachfully.

'This wasn't baked today, Bert – or even yesterday.'

'Maybe not, guv'nor,' Bert cheerfully agreed. 'But that's all the better for yer digestion.'

Hunter nodded thoughtfully and helped himself to mustard. 'You're very quiet here tonight,' he added.

'Yes,' said Bert, 'I don't mind admittin' I'm glad to see yer, guv'nor. It's a bit lonely 'ere at this time o' night, and what wiv these Front Page Men knockin' off everybody – by the way, guv'nor, what are you doin' about these 'ere Front Page Men?'

Hunter's face clouded again. 'If I even started to tell you, Bert,' he answered wearily, 'I'd be here till the tide turned. How's business with you these days? Is Mayfair still crazy about coffee-stalls – or have they tired of the novelty of eating with the down-and-outs?'

'Don't talk to me about business,' grumbled Bert, dumping a pile of saucers on a shelf, and quite pleased to change the conversation to a topic which gave him more scope for argument. 'The coffee-stall profession is simply going to the dogs.' He flung a handful of spoons into a drawer. 'It's these 'ere milk bars that's gone and done us in,' he announced fiercely. 'Sprung up like blinkin' mushrooms they 'ave, wiv all these blokes in the City backin' 'em. O' course they don't get what you might call the "class", but who does? If they comes 'ere, all they wants is a cup o' coffee. Strewth! You got to sell a lot o' cups o' coffee before you can save enough to retire on.'

'Oh, so you are thinking of retiring?' asked Hunter.

Bert placed his elbows on the counter and gazed dreamily across the river. 'As soon as I've made a few hundred quid,' he murmured, 'I'm givin' this old wagon of mine a real good-night kiss.'

'And then what?' Hunter teased him. 'I expect you'll blue it all on some second-rate nag in the two-twenty.'

Bert shook his head, firmly.

'Oh no, guv'nor. Not me. I'm off the 'orses good and proper. Me and the missus 'ave got our eye on a nice little pub out Rotherhithe way.'

'Rotherhithe!' repeated Hunter under his breath. Rotherhithe ... The Glass Bowl ... why hadn't he thought of it before? That was where Temple had met that poor devil Chubby Wilson, and Lucky Gibson too, for that matter. Hunter pulled his felt hat forward and signalled vigorously to a passing taxi. He was a hundred yards away before he remembered that he had not paid for his roll and coffee.

Bert wagged his head sorrowfully as he gazed at the disappearing vehicle. ''E'll be joinin' the courtesy cops next,' he cogitated gloomily.

Hunter dismissed the taxi nearly a quarter of a mile from his objective and threaded his way down the narrow streets leading to the river, which seemed particularly dismal and uninviting. Though he was wearing an old mackintosh, and a none-too-smart hat, he was well dressed compared with most of the men he encountered, and was eyed suspiciously on that account. The doleful creak of the signboard announced that he had reached the Glass Bowl. The electric lights shone yellowly through the dirty windows, and gusts of music came from the bar.

The florid Mrs. Taylor gave him a suspicious glare as he came in. She had never seen him before, and, in view of her past experiences, immediately concluded that he was connected with the police.

The detective sauntered over to the bar and ordered a small whisky and soda. Mrs. Taylor grimly poured out the minimum quantity of whisky, pushed it across to him, and did not offer to help him to soda.

'Is that clock right?' asked Hunter, at length.

'Ten minutes fast,' she replied, never taking her eyes off him.

'I wonder where he could have got to,' murmured Hunter, adopting the attitude of a man who is obviously irritated by the turn of events. This was too much for Mrs. Taylor's curiosity.

'Expecting somebody?' she asked, wiping the counter with a wet cloth, but eying him carefully as she did so.

'Yes. I arranged to meet a pal of mine here. Maybe he's looked in and didn't care to wait.'

'Would I know him?' demanded Mrs. Taylor cautiously. 'Is he one of our regular customers?'

'Yes, I believe so. A little fellow – name of Gibson – Lucky Gibson.'

Hunter thought he saw Mrs. Taylor's mouth tighten the merest fraction. But her voice was quite unperturbed.

'Never 'eard of the name,' she replied, casually. 'We got a feller who comes in 'ere named Bridson. But he ain't exactly lucky. Perhaps you'd better ask the Reverend over yonder, 'e might know the man,' she added. Without further ado, she beckoned to a man in clerical dress, who had just come in.

'Mr. 'Argreaves, there's a gent 'ere lookin' for somebody named Gibson,' she called out in a voice that could be heard all over the bar. Several men looked up suspiciously, and one or two slunk out at the first opportunity, when they thought their exit would go unnoticed. The Reverend Hargreaves came forward with some reluctance.

'Gibson, did you say, Mrs. Taylor?' He shook his head in deep deliberation.

'Yes, sir. I thought as 'ow 'e might be one of your flock, in a manner o' speaking.'

Again Hargreaves shook his head. 'No, I'm sorry, sir, I'm afraid I cannot help you. And if you will excuse me, Mrs. Taylor, I must run along now. My evening service starts in just five minutes. Good night, everyone.'

Hunter drank his whisky and ordered another.

Then he turned to question Mrs. Taylor again, but she was gone, and a very forbidding-looking barman stood behind the counter In vain, he tried to get into conversation with other habitues of the bar-room. He even strolled into the tap-room, to see if Mrs. Taylor was there, but the place was deserted. Eventually he had to give it up as a bad job, and soon after half past eight he left and caught a bus back to the West End. Once more he was feeling depressed. The whisky had not been of particularly good quality, and seemed likely to bring on his headache. Then there was the prospect of facing Sir Graham again in the morning. Mac would be inclined to look down his nose too.

He jumped off the bus in the Strand, and was making for his flat near the Adelphi when a small sports car suddenly drew in to the kerb beside him. He only had a back view of the driver until he came level with the car. Then he recognised her.

'Why, Sue! This is a surprise!' he cried in delighted tones.

The girl at the wheel looked up at him and grinned. A multicoloured silk scarf could not hide entirely her attractive chestnut curls.

Hunter's acquaintance with Sue Marlow dated back to his Varsity days, when he had often joined in the triumphant procession accorded the principals of the D'Oyly Carte Company back to their hotel after the show. Sue had been a small-part player in the company, and seeing her come out of the stage-door one night when the leads were borne off in triumph, Hunter felt sorry for her. As a matter of fact, Sue was feeling more than a little sorry for herself at that moment. So she did not require much persuading to accompany this personable young man to supper. After that, Hunter always looked forward to her visits, which usually numbered two or three a year, generally in musical comedies. Her parts grew less and less insignificant, and Hunter occasionally visited her in London, when she was appearing in the West End. Lately she had grown tired of musical comedy, and had been trying to make good in various spineless comedies on tour.

'I've been trying to get you on the phone all day long,' she told him. 'Are you busy or something?'

'Out on a job,' explained Hunter briefly, climbing into the tiny car, which rather cramped his longish legs.

'I even telephoned you at Scotland Yard. They put me on to three different offices,' smiled Sue, letting in the clutch. 'Everybody was terribly polite till I came to a Scotsman, he sounded just like somebody out of a play.'

'That would be Mac,' grinned Hunter. 'He's all right when you get to know him.'

'I don't think I particularly want to, thank you all the same. One Scotland Yard man is quite enough in my young life.'

'I thought you were on tour somewhere,' remarked Hunter, as the car was held up in a considerable traffic block.

'I'm always on tour somewhere just lately,' Sue sighed. 'And this one dried up beautifully. The leading man got temperamental, the backers went bust, and the play even bored the author. Have you ever been stranded at Hanley?'

'Never,' replied Hunter, firmly.

'I wouldn't advise it,' she murmured, taking a lipstick from her bag and proceeding to use it to the edification of the passengers of buses on either side.

'Isn't it in the Potteries somewhere?'

'I really couldn't tell you, darling. I only know the digs are dreadful and there's a sort of gloom hanging over everything. Still, perhaps that was just through being stranded,' she added, in generosity to Hanley.

'This car doesn't look as if you were particularly hard up,' said Hunter.

'Oh no. The Hanley business was over a month ago. Since then, I've broken into films up here. Had some pretty good jobs too. And, of course, this car was secondhand, through a friend of mine.'

This was Sue's strong point. She had a friend in practically every trade and profession, and never dreamed of paying cost price for anything of any value. Hunter often teased her about it, but she always paid him back in his own coin. 'You're jealous,' she would retort. 'Nobody loves a policeman.'

At last the traffic block moved on twenty yards, then came to another standstill.

'You look pretty stunning, I must say,' commented Hunter in admiration, as he noticed she wore an attractive evening dress under her light coat. 'Why all this gala atmosphere?'

'I got so depressed hanging around doing nothing. This is the first free day I've had since I started filming. I spent the morning going round the agents, and that's enough to depress anybody. Even a policeman. Or don't policemen get depressed?'

'This particular policeman has been very much down in the mouth right up to the moment he set eyes on you,' replied Hunter.

Ignoring this, she went on with her story. 'So I decided to get myself up fit to kill, and you are going to do the same. How long will it take you to slip into a dinner-jacket?'

'How do you know I've got one?'

'Don't you need one when you raid clubs?' she demanded, innocently. 'I suppose you live in the same poky little flat?' she continued, turning in the right direction, and at the same time, managing to extract a cigarette from the case he offered her.

'You don't seem to realise,' and Hunter frowned severely as he spoke, 'that I have just finished a very hard and thankless day's work.'

'Then you most certainly need a change.'

'You seem to overlook the fact that a policeman's salary hardly encourages him to entertain film stars.'

'Don't let that worry you,' she smiled, as the car drew up outside Hunter's flat. 'We'll go to a new roadhouse that's just been opened by a friend of mine. It'll cost practically nothing, and I'm lousy with money anyway.'

'That,' said Hunter, fumbling for his latchkey, 'rather alters the complexion of things.'

While he changed into evening dress, she perched on a chair near the open bedroom door and plied him with questions.

'What have you been doing all day?'

'I thought I told you. Looking for a man named Lucky Gibson. I suppose you didn't come across him in Hanley by any chance.'

Sue considered this. 'No, I don't think so,' she decided at last. 'Is he nice?'

'Dreadful piece of work.'

'Then why look for him?'

'He's wanted – by the police.'

'Then he can't be so very lucky after all,' declared Sue in the tone of one who has made a discovery.

'The luck's been with him today all right,' replied Hunter grimly.

'I once knew someone named Lucky Lorrimer,' said Sue rather irrelevantly. 'But that was a girl, and they called her Lucky because she was just the opposite.'

'You stage people do the quaintest things,' commented Hunter, with a touch of sarcasm that was lost on Sue.

'Yes,' she replied, complacently, 'don't we?'

Some sounds of struggle emerged from the bedroom as Hunter wrestled with his tie.

'Would you like me to do that for you?' asked Sue. 'I used to be frightfully good at that sort of thing.'

'Then I hope you haven't lost the knack,' growled Hunter, coming out of the bedroom. In less than two minutes, the tie was adjusted to the satisfaction of both of them. Sue stood back and surveyed him.

'You really do look rather sweet when you're dressed up,' she announced. 'Nobody would ever take you for a policeman.'

He bowed gravely. 'Much obliged, I'm sure.'

She picked up her bag. 'We'd better go if you are ready. It's quite a way out of town.' They clattered down the stairs.

'Where and what is this place?' asked Hunter, after they had settled themselves in the car.

'It's just off the Great West Road – a place called The First Circle.'

'Why?'

'How should I know?'

Hunter lit a cigarette. 'I just thought your friend might have explained,' he grinned.

'Now you come to mention it, I rather think he did. But I wasn't paying much attention at the time. It was something to do with the Pyramids from what I remember.'

'The Pyramids?'

'Yes. Aren't they covered with circles and squares and things?'

'I wouldn't be at all surprised.' The little car suddenly roared, cutting between a tramcar and an oncoming lorry.

'It is my painful duty to remind you that you are proceeding at forty-five miles per hour in a built-up area,' said Hunter solemnly.

'But you can't arrest me, darling. You aren't in uniform.'

'I can arrest anybody at any time, given sufficient reason,' he declared, firmly.

'Wouldn't it be fun, darling? To see you in court. I mean, swearing this, that and the other. Then giving your evidence … "on the tenth instant, your honour, I was proceeding in the direction of Hendon …" I wonder why policemen always "proceed". It fascinates me.'

'Not nearly so much as you would fascinate the policemen.'

She gravely wagged a finger at him. 'Don't overdo the compliments, Inspector.'

'You make it very hard for us poor policemen,' plaintively murmured Hunter. They looked at each other and laughed. Hunter was feeling better than he had done all day. The fresh night air had driven away his headache, and he was beginning to feel distinctly hungry.

'What have you been doing lately?' she asked. 'Anything exciting?'

'I'm always doing something exciting.'

'Didn't you go round the world or somewhere after leaving the Varsity?'

'It was the world,' said Hunter, giving an extremely bad imitation of Noel Coward.

They were on the Great West Road now, and the little car whizzed along at a speed that was quite amazing.

'I do wish you wouldn't go so fast,' he reproached her.

'It's perfectly safe.'

'Then you might consider my reputation. Suppose you were pinched while I was with you. What do you think the magistrate would say?'

'I haven't the faintest idea. But, ten to one, it would be very good publicity. Magistrates always say the quaintest things. We turn off somewhere here, and these arterial roads all look the same to me ... I think this is it ...'

Presently the red-and-blue neon and cleverly contrived floodlighting of The First Circle came into view. Sue steered the little car into the most advantageous position among some thirty others and the engine sighed to a standstill.

Collecting her things together, she paused. 'Darling, I knew there was something I'd been meaning to ask you for quite a while. It's often worried me, and I knew you'd be just the man to tell me all about it.'

'Well?' smiled Hunter.

'Darling – who are these Front Page Men?'

Hunter leaned back in his seat and roared with laughter until she thought he would never stop.

As might be expected from its name, the roadhouse was designed in the form of a circle, and the idea was also maintained in the interior planning. Most of the rooms were semicircular in shape and attractively decorated. All the furnishing and equipment was of the best, and the lighting was a joy to the eye of an artist. Hunter felt at peace with the world.

Sue introduced him to her friend the proprietor, whose name she had temporarily forgotten, though it didn't seem to matter particularly. The proprietor was a young American, very confident of himself, and proud of this, the first of a proposed chain of Circle roadhouses.

Over dinner, Hunter and Sue continued the flippant conversation which was proving such a pleasant relief to him after days of tight-lipped interchanges.

'Sue, after all these years I do believe I'm falling in love with you!'

'Don't be silly, darling!'

'Oh, I'm not being silly,' said Hunter. 'Oh dear, no! I know the symptoms all right.'

'You sound to me disgustingly experienced,' said Sue.

'I am experienced,' said Hunter, helping himself to another glass of wine. 'Didn't I ever tell you about the time I was in love with a schoolmistress?'

'Not a very good schoolmistress, of course?'

'Of course.'

'What happened?' asked Sue.

'It took me a long time to get over it. A very long time.'

'You did get over it?'

'Oh, rather! It was in Halifax.'

'I beg your pardon?'

'I said, I got over it in Halifax.'

'And do you think you'll get over your love for me, too?'

'I can hardly believe so at the moment,' said Hunter, 'but deep down inside of me something seems to tell me I shall.'

'That's a pretty useful "something" you've got deep down inside of you,' laughed Sue. 'But supposing I fell in love with someone else?'

'I should travel and try to forget.'

'Wouldn't it be cheaper to go straight to Halifax?'

Hunter laughed. 'I have only one retort to make to that remark, young lady: you are about to dance with a policeman!'

*

On their way to the dance-floor, they decided they might as well take a look at some of the other rooms. Hand in hand, they walked leisurely along heavily carpeted corridors, pushed open doors, looked round and walked out again. Until they came to a door which led into a tiny room shaped like the segment of a circle, and intended for a very modern equivalent of the old-fashioned snug. Four men sat there playing cards. Glasses of various shapes and sizes littered the small tables around them. Three of the men Hunter did not recognise. But there could be no mistake about the fourth, who sat facing him. Hunter gripped Sue's hand tightly.

'The luck has changed,' he breathed. For the fourth man who was busily dealing the cards was none other than Lucky Gibson.

CHAPTER XVIII

'Taxi, sir!'

Paul Temple was becoming more than a little familiar these days with the Chief Commissioner's office at Scotland Yard. He began to wonder whether the carpet was beginning to look shabby as a result of his pacing over it so often.

On the morning after the discovery of Rivoli's body, Paul Temple felt profoundly depressed. He had conceived quite a liking for the little Italian, with his flashing eyes and extravagant enthusiasm. Temple was inclined to speculate morosely on the possibility of ever bringing these alarming outrages to an end.

After considerable argument he had persuaded Steve to take breakfast in bed, as she had slept very little, and he himself had come on to the Yard in response to a telephone call from Sir Graham.

The Chief Commissioner had sat up with Temple, Reed and Hunter until the small hours, trying to reconstruct the murder of Tony Rivoli. Temple had given them a minute description of the man who called himself Inspector Low, but this had proved to be of little assistance so far, as there was no trace of this individual in the Yard's comprehensive files. Even now, Temple was sitting by Sir Graham's desk listlessly looking through a batch of photographs which Hunter had passed on to him as likely suspects.

'Come to think of it,' suggested Temple for Sir Graham's benefit, 'there was nothing to prevent the Front Page Men engaging a bunch of out-of-work actors to stage this raid – telling them it was just a lark – and then taking Rivoli off their hands when he was supposed to be under arrest.'

Sir Graham nodded gloomily. 'They never seem to be lacking in ideas,' he acknowledged.

'Maybe the note will tell us something,' said Temple hopefully. 'Glad I decided to keep it – I might easily have crumpled it up in the heat of the moment and left it there.'

'I've got Nelson working on it now.'

'I didn't know he was a handwriting expert.'

'Yes, that's his pet sideline. Pretty good at it, too. I've always given him the important stuff ever since the Holborn forgery case.'

There was a knock at the door, and Sergeant Leopold entered with Inspector Nelson's report, which he placed before Sir Graham.

Silence fell upon the room while Forbes frowned over the document, and Temple flicked aside another half-dozen pictures rather restlessly.

'Well?' he demanded, at length.

'I'm afraid this doesn't tell us a great deal,' Sir Graham informed him reluctantly. 'According to Nelson, the note was definitely written by a man, but apparently we haven't any record of the actual handwriting.'

Temple shrugged impatiently. 'What about fingerprints?'

'From what I gather, they're somewhat blurred. For once in a way, Nelson seems reluctant to commit himself.' He tossed the report over to Temple, who glanced at it casually.

'We seem to strike a dead end in every direction,' he declared irritably. 'What about Brightman; have you been in touch with him lately?'

'No,' answered Forbes. 'But I've got a very good man on his tail. I've some pretty strong suspicions about Brightman, and I'm just hanging on until something more definite comes along.'

'And then there's Wrenson – you told me the other day that he was working in his own mysterious way. Has he had any luck so far?' pursued Temple, determined to explore every avenue.

'Wrenson's always pretty vague when he's busy on a job,' said Sir Graham, 'but he did advise me to pick up Lucky Gibson and Jimmy Mills.'

Temple looked up inquiringly as the last name was mentioned.

'Our old friend Jimmy, eh? Does Wrenson suggest they are Front Page Men?'

'He seemed fairly sure of it.'

'Then you've had them brought in?'

Forbes shook his head.

'Not yet. There was a time when we could always lay our hands on Lucky Gibson, but just lately he seems to be giving a pretty good impersonation of the Invisible Man.'

The telephone, which had been constantly interrupting them throughout the morning, rang again.

This time it was Steve.

'Really, darling,' Temple protested, with a humorous grimace at Sir Graham, 'you ex-reporters have no respect for Scotland Yard conferences. And besides, I told you to stay in bed …'

'Paul, do be serious,' she interrupted. 'Mr. Goldie's here.'

Temple's expression changed at once.

'Where is he?'

'In the flat below.'

Temple thought for a moment.

'Get hold of the porter, Steve,' he instructed, 'and tell him to keep Goldie in the building – yes – anything that occurs to you ...'

He rang off and turned to Forbes. 'Sorry, I'll have to be off, Sir Graham. Mr. J. P. Goldie is in Eastwood Mansions. And I particularly want to see him.'

'Oh, why?' asked Forbes, obviously more than a little interested.

Temple picked up his hat and smiled.

'I had some thought of changing my piano,' he declared cryptically. He had almost reached the door when it was opened by Sergeant Leopold.

'Inspector Hunter is here, sir, with Gibson.'

'At last,' said Forbes. 'Better hang on, Temple, and see what he has to say.'

Temple hesitated. 'No,' he decided, 'I'll give you a ring later, Sir Graham.' He nodded briefly to Hunter, who stood in the doorway, and wished Sir Graham good morning.

Forbes beckoned to Hunter to enter.

'Bring in Gibson now,' he ordered. But Hunter closed the door after him.

'Sir Graham, I rather wanted to have a word with you first,' he began, seriously.

Forbes looked up interrogatively. 'Oh – anything wrong?'

Hunter seemed worried.

'I picked up Lucky Gibson last night at a roadhouse called The First Circle,' he reported. 'He seemed all right when I first spoke to him, but on the way here in the taxi he was, well, peculiar, to say the least.'

'What do you mean?'

'It's rather difficult to explain,' replied Hunter. 'When I first spoke to him, he answered my questions sensibly. Now he seems in a sort of daze – as if he can't remember things. Then without the slightest warning, he suddenly becomes hysterical.'

'H'm,' grunted Forbes, 'did you leave him on his own at all?'

'Why, no ... at least ...' Hunter hesitated. 'He did go into one of the other rooms at the station this morning,' he admitted. 'Said he'd left his raincoat there.'

'Did you go with him?'

'No. I knew he couldn't escape that way, because the sergeant told me there was only one door, and—'

'That isn't the point, Hunter. You should have stayed with him.'

'But really, sir, I don't quite see ...' Hunter had begun to protest when Sir Graham silenced him.

'While he was in there, if I'm not mistaken, he gave himself a pretty good injection of this Amashyer drug.'

'Then that accounts for what Mac said!' cried Hunter, suddenly enlightened. 'Eh?'

'When I brought Gibson in just now, Mac said he had the same look about the eyes as the Blakeley child when he was returned.'

He paused, considering this. 'The Blakeley child wasn't hysterical, was he, Sir Graham?'

'No. It probably affects people different ways. I expect Lucky Gibson was fairly shot to pieces to start with.'

'I daresay,' agreed Hunter. 'We've hounded him around pretty well these past few days.'

'Tell the Sergeant to bring him in,' Forbes ordered.

Hunter went to the door and gave the necessary instructions. There was a pause, then a gentle shuffling was heard outside. Lucky appeared in the doorway, blinking in the strong light from the window behind the Chief Commissioner's desk. Hunter took him by the arm and dismissed the sergeant.

'Sit down, Gibson,' said Hunter, leading him to a chair and pushing him gently into it.

Nobody spoke for a moment. Lucky Gibson was obviously quite bewildered and far from his normal self. His mouth hung loosely and his eyes were glazed.

'What have you brought me here for?' he mouthed, very slowly.

Forbes went across to him and spoke distinctly.

'Lucky, when you did the Nottingham job, who went with you?'

'Went with you where?' whispered Lucky hoarsely, looking round as if seeking a means of escape.

Patiently, Forbes repeated his question.

'Went with me?' intoned Lucky, mechanically. 'I—I—can't remember—can't remember …'

His distress was obviously not assumed. Suddenly two large tears rolled slowly down his cheeks, and he began to sob hysterically. Forbes waited a while, then took him by the shoulder and shook him sharply.

'Lucky! Pull yourself together. I want you to tell me about Brightman.'

The mention of this name seemed to strike a responsive chord, and Lucky's hysteria temporarily ceased.

'Brightman!' he ejaculated in a strangled voice. 'He's all right, Brightman is. Why, only the other day he said …'

Lucky broke off, and the queer, lifeless expression was again visible in his eyes. 'Somehow – there's a mist – it's blotting things out …' he gasped. 'If only I could see through the mist, I'd be all right. Just—just—can't remember …' His head sagged.

'Take him to the hospital, Hunter,' advised Sir Graham. 'We'll never get anything out of him while he's in this state.'

With a considerable effort Hunter pulled Gibson to his feet and managed to get him out of the room. In the corridor, Sergeant Leopold came to his assistance.

Sir Graham went back to his desk with a baffled expression on his face. He collected the pile of photographs left by Temple, and pushed them carelessly into a drawer.

There was a cautious knock at the door, and Chief Inspector Reed appeared.

'Did the wee laddie talk, sir?' he asked.

'No. Hunter's taking him to hospital. He seems in a bad way.'

Reed nodded understandingly.

'Well, I canna find Jimmy Mills,' he sighed. 'I've searched every dump in the town.'

'Have you looked in the milk-bars?' suggested Sir Graham, a rather grim smile lighting his saturnine features for a moment.

Mac's face was a study. 'In the milk-bars?' he echoed.

'Yes,' said the Chief Commissioner. 'Jimmy Mills happens to be a teetotaller.'

Reed seemed quite incredulous.

'Ay, he may have told ye that, Sir Graham, but I well remember arresting him two years ago while he was holding a glass of fine old Jamaica rum – the smell took my breath away.' He sighed reminiscently. 'I remember it so well, because I let the wee laddie finish his drink. After a', he'd paid for it, and it seemed such a pity to waste guid stuff like that!'

With the help of Sergeant Leopold, Hunter managed to get his charge downstairs.

'Where's Morris with the police-car?' he asked.

'Out on a job,' replied the sergeant enigmatically. 'I'd better get you a taxi.'

Suddenly a fairly ancient vehicle seemed to appear from nowhere, and the sergeant signalled to it vigorously.

'Queen's Hospital,' called out Hunter, when he had seen Gibson stowed safely inside.

Lucky relaxed limply into one corner of the cab, and Hunter eyed him curiously.

'That's all right, Lucky,' he murmured, encouragingly. 'Just sit back and take things easily.'

'I feel—so—weak ...' whispered Lucky in that queer, lifeless voice. 'If only this veil would lift – can't remember—seen him before ...'

'Seen who before?' asked Hunter, suddenly alert.

However, when it became obvious that Lucky was referring to the taxi-driver, Hunter paid no further attention.

'It's this drug,' muttered Lucky. 'Wish I hadn't taken it.'

'They'll soon fix you up at the hospital,' Hunter reassured him.

'Oh! Oh! The hospital!' moaned Lucky. 'My head's like—like—like ...'

He appeared to be in some danger of relapsing into hysterics again, and Hunter watched him anxiously, wishing their journey were over.

Then, to Hunter's surprise, the taxi-engine spluttered to a standstill. He pushed back the glass partition which communicated with the driver.

'What's the trouble?' he snapped.

'Sorry, guv'nor – it's them there plugs. There's a garage on the corner. I'll get a couple o' new 'uns in a jiffy,' said the driver, jumping out and slamming the door.

'If you're not back in five minutes,' said Hunter irritably, 'we shall get another taxi.'

'Leave it to me, sir,' the driver reassured him. He made off in the direction of the garage he had indicated.

'If only I could remember who he is,' rambled Lucky. 'It's like ... like a part of a dream before ... before ...'

'You're sure you know this man?' demanded Hunter, rather more interested now.

'Of course I know him, but somehow ...'

Hunter suddenly grabbed Lucky and flung open the taxi-door.

'Come on! We're getting out of this!'

All this rushing about had made Lucky Gibson more bewildered than ever, and he almost fell as he got out of the taxi. One or two pedestrians eyed the strange couple rather curiously.

'Hurry!' urged Hunter, leading his prisoner in the direction of the garage. They were still twenty yards away from their objective when there was a shattering explosion behind them.

Fragments of glass and metal showered around them. People were running towards the wreck of the taxi. One or two women were screaming. A figure lay very still in the gutter.

'Great Scot! A time-bomb in the taxi!' ejaculated Hunter. 'Phew! That was a near thing!'

In a grimy back alley, Jed Ware tossed his chauffeur's hat into a dustbin, substituted a large cap, felt the vibration of the explosion, and chuckled to himself.

CHAPTER XIX

Mr. Goldie's Mistake

Paul Temple stopped his taxi at three florists' on the way back to the flat before he was able to buy what he wanted. He came into the drawing-room carrying (rather self-consciously), a huge bunch of particularly fine lilies, the scent from which was already giving him a slight headache. His vision was somewhat obscured by the flowers he held before him, and for a moment he did not see Ann Mitchell sitting on a corner of the settee.

'Do take these flowers, darling,' he begged, handing them over to Steve.

'Good gracious, Paul, whatever made you buy lilies?'

'There's a sinister motive,' he laughed. 'Why, hallo, Ann! How are you?'

'I'm—I'm all right, thanks,' smiled Ann, nervously.

'She's worried, Paul,' Steve told him.

'Oh, what's the trouble?'

Ann hesitated. 'Everywhere I go,' she said at last, 'there's always someone following me. It's—awful.'

'Ann, you must be mistaken,' said Temple.

'No ... no, honestly I'm not. It's getting on my nerves.'

'But who can it be? Does the man do anything or say anything?'

'No ... he's just there ... always looking at me ...'

'But surely, Ann ...'

'I tell you it's getting on my nerves,' she blurted out, desperately.

'Have you told Gerald?'

'No. The poor darling has too many worries as it is. I was wondering if ...' She paused with a look of fear in her eyes.

'If what?' prompted Temple.

'It couldn't be—the police?'

There was silence for a moment.

Then Temple asked quietly, 'Why should the police follow you?'

'They might think that because Gerald published *The Front Page Men*, that I—I—wrote it.'

'Did you?' asked Temple, calmly.

'Why, of course not,' she replied, hastily.

'Then why worry?' he smiled. 'You're probably imagining things, Ann.' He was about to add further reassurances when Pryce announced, 'Mr. Mitchell has called, sir.'

Gerald followed him in almost immediately.

'Sorry to barge in, but I saw Ann's car outside,' he explained.

'I was just leaving,' Ann told him, and Steve thought she detected the merest trace of coldness in her voice.

'I wonder if you'd run me out to Croydon, dear,' he asked. 'One of my readers has just phoned to say he's spotted a real winner.'

'Then let's hope it turns out another *The Front Page Men*,' smiled the novelist.

'If it is, you can rest assured that I shan't publish it,' declared Mitchell, emphatically.

'Why ever not?' demanded Steve, in all innocence.

'My dear Steve, if you knew the sleep I've lost over that opus ...'

'But how perfectly ridiculous!' protested Steve. 'I don't believe for one moment that Andrea Fortune has anything to do with the real Front Page Men.'

'Off we go again!' laughed Temple.

'Yes, and talking of going ...' Mitchell drew on his gloves.

'I'm ready, dear,' said Ann.

'Don't worry, Ann,' Temple murmured to her, as Steve and Gerald went out ahead of them. Steve stood talking until they were in the lift, then returned to find her husband rather quizzically regarding the lilies he had bought.

'Paul, are the police really following Ann?' she asked, in a worried voice.

'Yes, I'm afraid so. I had to tell them about Gerald calling at Bramley Lodge with that story about Ann being a good impersonator.'

Steve nodded thoughtfully. 'Poor Ann, it seems a shame.'

'I do hope Mr. Goldie hasn't left the building,' Temple briskly interrupted her commiserations.

'I told the porter to detain him.'

'Good. Now get a vase for these flowers, darling.'

'What on earth possessed you to buy lilies?' she demanded, for the second time.

'You'll soon see,' he smiled, carefully arranging them in the large black vase she had given him. Having completed this to his satisfaction, he placed them on the piano.

'Not there, Paul,' cried Steve in dismay. 'They look ghastly, and besides, they might fall off if—'

The door opened silently, and Pryce informed them that Mr. Goldie was waiting.

'Show him in, Pryce,' said Temple at once.

He seemed very much the same Mr. Goldie, with the hesitant manner, and rather short-sighted trick of blinking behind his spectacles.

'You wanted to see me, Mr. Temple?' he murmured gently, as if reluctant to intrude. Temple went forward to meet him.

'Good afternoon,' said the little man, smiling pleasantly at Steve, who replied to his greeting.

'I heard you were in the building, Mr. Goldie, so I thought I would take this opportunity of consulting you,' began Temple.

'If I can be of any help at all, Mr. Temple, I shall be only too delighted.'

'Well—er—the fact of the matter is, I'm thinking of changing my piano.'

'Ah now,' protested Goldie, 'it's such a beautiful instrument – almost perfect, and there are very few like it in the country today.' As if to emphasise his dismay at the idea, he sat down and very quietly ran his fingers over the keys. Soon, he was apparently oblivious of his audience, and continued playing for some minutes.

'I—I—beg your pardon,' he apologised, coming out of his trance.

'Not at all, Mr. Goldie,' said Steve gently. 'You play very well.' He acknowledged her praise with a slight bow. Then, as if he could not resist the temptation, started to play again. This time it was the familiar *Liebestraum*. Temple leaned against the piano and gently lifted the lid.

'I'm sure it sounds better with the lid raised,' he began, when the vase of lilies fell to the floor with a crash.

'I told you those flowers would fall off, Paul,' cried Steve, irritated by the mishap.

'How very careless of me,' said Temple, lightly. 'And just look at the floor!' He went to retrieve the flowers, but she forestalled him.

'It's all right, Paul. I'll attend to it.'

Temple straightened himself and smiled whimsically at Mr. Goldie. 'I'm particularly fond of tiger lilies, aren't you, Mr. Goldie?'

The piano-tuner looked up quickly. 'Yes ... yes ... very much,' he replied politely. Goldie resumed his playing while Steve replaced the flowers in the vase, which fortunately was not broken.

'Well, what do you really think of the piano?' asked Temple, at length.

'I very much doubt if you would find a better instrument in this country, Mr. Temple.'

'Then that settles it. I did seriously think of buying one of those new Remsteins ...'

'No! No!' cried Mr. Goldie, almost in horror, 'This is far superior in every way.'

'Well, it's a comfort to know that,' said Temple, easily. 'I'm very glad you were able to call. Would you care for a drink or—'

'No, thank you, I really must be going I have an appointment in Chelsea.'

'By Timothy! You do get about!' smiled Temple.

'Oh, that's nothing,' said Mr. Goldie deprecatingly. 'I spent two days in Nottingham last week.'

'I shouldn't have thought it would have been worth your while to go that far.'

Mr. Goldie shook his head wisely. 'It really is surprising, Mr. Temple,' he murmured, and Temple imagined the grey eyes gleamed for a moment. Then Goldie bowed himself out in an old-world manner which greatly intrigued Steve.

'Well, what was behind that little scene?' she demanded, deliberately, when the door had closed.

'What little scene, my sweet gazelle?' riposted Temple lightly, placing an arm affectionately around her.

'Don't try to act the innocent,' she chided him. 'Why did you knock those lilies off the piano?'

'Just an accident, my pet.'

'An accident!' scoffed Steve, bursting into rather strained laughter. 'I'm particularly fond of tiger lilies. Aren't you, Mr. Goldie?' she mimicked him almost perfectly.

'Apparently he is,' said Temple coolly.

'What did you expect him to say?' challenged Steve.

'To be perfectly honest, I thought he would say: "Excuse me, Mr. Temple, but they are not tiger lilies."'

'Not tiger lilies,' said Steve with a puzzled look. 'Then what are they?'

'They're known as "Lily Regale", but apparently Mr. J. P. Goldie didn't realise it.'

'But ... but why should he?' asked Steve, in complete bewilderment.

Temple looked into her eyes.

'Steve, me old pal,' he murmured with mock seriousness, 'I think you're slipping, partner!'

CHAPTER XX

Concerning Lucky Gibson

Mr. Brightman was irritated. In the first place, he had, following the Medusa Club raid, been compelled to call a meeting of the Front Page Men at his flat in Hampstead, on the orders of Front Page Man Number One, and in spite of the fact that he had a shrewd suspicion that the flat was under police observation.

Secondly, the news he had received at this meeting was by no means reassuring. He had just had a report that Lucky Gibson was still alive.

'I can't understand it. What could have made them leave the taxi?' he queried impatiently for the second time.

'Lucky must have recognised Jed,' was Jimmy Mills' solution to the problem. But Ware stoutly denied this. 'He wasn't in a state to recognise anyone,' he asserted emphatically.

'Well, I'll tell you one thing,' said Mills, adding the merest suspicion of a splash to his whisky, 'we've got to get him. If we don't he'll talk.'

'Talk?' snapped Swan Williams. 'What the hell can he talk about, anyway? The police know all there is to know.'

'They've got a warrant out for Jimmy, and I've a hunch that I'll be the next,' said Brightman, moodily.

'They'll soon 'ave a warrant out for the lot of us, and then the only bloke who'll be sittin' pretty is the big noise 'imself,' concluded Mills rather bitterly. There was a short silence, during which everybody drank deeply and seemed none the better for it.

'I can't figure out how they managed to get back the Blakeley kid,' went on Brightman. 'It shows that somebody must know about the hide-out.'

'D'you think Ginger's talking?' queried Mills.

Brightman negatived the idea.

'I had a word with him yesterday. He's made more out of us in the past two months than he'd make out of that tin factory in two years. Ginger isn't likely to do any talking.'

'Well, we've got to find a new place to meet, and that's definite,' decided Mills.

Brightman was completely in agreement with this. In fact, he had been gazing uneasily out of the window and listening to every footstep ever since the meeting began.

'And for the lord's sake, let's keep away from Piccadilly,' implored Swan Williams.

'The Medusa was perfect,' retorted Brightman, somewhat offended, 'if Rivoli hadn't started putting two and two together.'

'Rivoli isn't the only man in the world capable of putting two and two together!'

There was a swift succession of knocks on the outside door, and Brightman started up at once and went to open it. They heard a woman's voice outside, and Lina came in, remote and self-possessed as ever, though she was slightly out of breath.

'You're late, Lina,' Brightman was protesting as they entered.

She nodded distantly, but offered no excuse.

'Did you see him?' eagerly demanded Brightman.

Lina slowly drew off her gloves.

'I spoke to him on the phone.'

'You mean Front Page Man Number One?' demanded Jimmy Mills.

'Yes,' said Lina. 'He was pleased about the Nottingham job.' She took a cigarette from her case and lit it.

'Gor blimey, so 'e ought to be!' cried Jimmy.

'But,' continued Lina, firmly, 'we've got to get Lucky before he talks.'

'That's impossible – he's under constant supervision at the hospital,' Brightman began to protest, but she quelled him with a look.

'It's got to be made possible. They're taking Lucky from the hospital this afternoon. He's due at Scotland Yard shortly before six. According to the present schedule, Hunter will be picking him up at about five-thirty.'

'Well, I'm not trying any fancy tricks this time,' flatly declared Jed Ware.

'There's no necessity for fancy tricks – but we've got to stop Lucky talking.'

'He's probably spilt the beans by now, anyway,' muttered Ware, dismally.

'No,' Lina contradicted, emphatically. 'Lucky hasn't talked – yet.'

They all looked at her inquiringly, and in answer to their unspoken question she murmured, 'The Chief told me.'

'The Chief!' echoed Swan. 'He certainly keeps himself up to date. I'll say that for him.'

'The Falkirk Diamond is in Amsterdam,' continued Lina, evenly. 'We shall get our share by the middle of next week.'

'That's what I call quick work!' approved Jimmy Mills, draining his glass and smacking his lips.

Lina ignored this interruption. 'The Chief told me to let you know that the hide-out on the river is quite safe. The police haven't spotted it.'

'Then 'ow the 'ell did the Blakeley kid do a bunk?' Mills questioned.

'I don't know,' answered Lina, quietly, 'and neither does the Chief.'

'Well, thank Gawd there's somethin' he don't know,' commented Mills expressively. 'Makes the bloke almost 'uman!'

'Did he say anything about the Jewellers' Ball?' asked Brightman, who was now rather more cheerful.

'Yes. He wants us to go ahead.'

'The Jewellers' Ball. What's that?' came Swan Williams' high-pitched falsetto.

'It's our next proposition,' Brightman informed them.

'If you ask me,' said Ware deliberately, 'it's about time we laid low for a while, especially if we've got to take care of Lucky.'

'No,' decided Brightman, 'we can't afford to miss a chance like this.'

'What's in it?' asked Jimmy Mills, pricking up his ears.

'A cool million,' stated Brightman deliberately, amidst startled exclamations from the others. Even Jed Ware seemed aroused from his lethargy. Brightman glanced questioningly at Lina, who signalled him to proceed.

'Every year the Birmingham Jewellers' Association holds a ball,' expounded Brightman. 'It is their custom to display valuable pieces of jewellery of all descriptions at this function. This year, they are bringing the Carter Collection over from Paris. It will be on exhibition in the main lounge of the hotel.'

'Yes,' chimed in Mills sceptically, 'with every flatfoot in the country practically sitting on top of it.'

'What exactly is the Carter Collection, and when does it arrive?' demanded Swan Williams, who had a technical interest in jewellery.

'It comprises an emerald necklace and two diamond-studded pendants. It's in London now, and a man called Paradise is taking the stuff up to Birmingham on Thursday.'

'That doesn't leave us much time if we're going to do anything about Lucky,' Swan pointed out.

Brightman nodded thoughtfully.

'Jimmy, you'd better look after Lucky,' he decided.

Jimmy looked dubious for a moment. 'What time does he leave hospital?' he asked.

'Five-thirty or thereabouts.'

'All right. I'll pick up some of the boys, and be back here by seven at the latest.'

'I should use the crowd we had at Nottingham,' advised Brightman.

Jimmy nodded and extracted an automatic pistol from his pocket.

'Leave it to me,' he said.

CHAPTER XXI

In Which Hunter Receives a Surprise

Entering the hall of the Queen's Hospital that afternoon, Hunter sniffed suspiciously at the antiseptic-laden air as he crossed the glassily polished floor. For some reason, he always felt rather uncomfortable in hospitals.

Intercepting a nurse who was hurrying past, Hunter asked for Doctor Henderson. At first she was inclined to be a little officious until he revealed his identity. Then she conducted him at once to a neat little office at the end of a long corridor.

Henderson came out of his office and smilingly shook hands with his visitor.

'Hello, Inspector. Sorry if I've kept you waiting.'

'That's all right,' murmured Hunter.

'I didn't ask you into the office because I expect you want to be getting along with the patient. He seems pretty fit, by the way – though he isn't exactly talkative.'

'He'll talk all right in time,' declared Hunter drily.

Doctor Henderson called a nurse and instructed her to fetch Lucky Gibson from Ward Nine. While they were waiting, he asked, 'How are you taking him back to the Yard? We've got an ambulance, if that's any use.'

'I've brought the police-car,' said Hunter. 'I'm taking no chances this time.'

'I don't blame you,' smiled the doctor, who knew all about the previous adventure.

It was a very different Lucky Gibson who emerged rather truculently from a distant door, in the company of the nurse. A few days of rational diet and correct treatment had completely restored his old *gamin* qualities.

'What the 'ell do you want?' he snapped at Hunter.

'H'm, a very charming greeting after all we've been through together,' grinned the Inspector, snapping a pair of handcuffs on Lucky's wrists before he could make any further protest.

'If you think you're going to get anything out of me, you're ruddy well mistaken!'

'Tut—tut—remember you're in respectable company,' Hunter reproved him. 'Come along now.'

He led his prisoner down the corridor and into the entrance hall. A muffled figure sitting on one of the chairs reserved for callers rose as they came through the door.

'Jimmy ...' gasped Gibson with fear in his voice. 'Jimmy, I didn't tell them—'

His words were cut short by two sharp revolver-cracks, and with a cry of anguish, Lucky Gibson crumpled slowly on to the polished floor.

'If anybody moves from here in the next five minutes they'll get the same,' threatened Mills, as he backed out of the door, leaving Hunter and Henderson gazing at each other in blank amazement.

'He's—he's killed him!' stammered the doctor at last. 'In this hospital … my God, it's not possible!'

'Anything's possible with the Front Page Men,' said Hunter, waking into activity. 'Where's your phone?'

'In the recess over yonder.'

Hunter rushed across, and was about to pick up the receiver when the bell began to ring.

'Yes?' he demanded, impatient at the thought of delay. 'Oh … yes, this is Hunter speaking … who are you?'

He inclined his head as if to make more certain of catching the name of his caller. But the name came over so plainly that even the doctor could hear it five yards away.

'This is the Reverend Charles Hargreaves …' said the voice.

CHAPTER XXII

Concerning Lina Fresnay and Herr von Zelton

Brightman watched Lina light her tenth cigarette and wondered if he would ever really get to know her. She had appeared among the Front Page Men quite suddenly, and did not seem to be known to any of the habitues of London's underworld. He suspected that she had hitherto operated mainly on the Continent in rather more delicate propositions than those undertaken by the Front Page Men.

All the same, she had been introduced by the Front Page Man himself; in fact, she was their main contact with him. Of course, she was his mistress, reflected Brightman rather enviously. Yet you never knew with Lina. She was almost as big a mystery as Front Page Man Number One.

And Brightman was beginning to mistrust all this mystery. After all, they were partners in the organisation; they must stand or fall together. What if the Chief proposed getting rid of them one at a time, just as he had instructed that Lucky Gibson should be taken care of? Then, having skimmed the cream of the spoils, he would be able to vanish discreetly with Lina – back to the Continent, no doubt.

Brightman told himself that it was hardly fair that he, a prominent City man, with a considerable reputation at stake, should be kept in the dark like this. After all, his brains had helped considerably in the various coups. In fact, several of them would never have gone through without him. Look how he had covered up the Blakeley Case, for instance.

It was all very well for the Chief to keep rushing them into new jobs, but every one was twice as dangerous as its predecessor, with the police getting confoundedly unpleasant. And there was that queer customer Paul Temple hovering about in the background. Brightman had felt all along that the attempted abduction of Temple's wife had been a mistake. It had gained them nothing, and only resulted in putting the novelist on his mettle. Everybody's hand was against them now. Just one more coup, and then ...

But Brightman betrayed none of these thoughts as he methodically attended to the wants of his guests. Plied the men with plenty of whisky – offered to mix Lina a cocktail of his own invention.

'I don't think we ought to have let him go alone,' Swan Williams was saying about half an hour after Jimmy Mills had departed.

'Jimmy'll be all right,' said Ware, confidently. 'He'll make a quick get-away. Always does. Look at the Nottingham job. As neat a bit of—'

'We are not interested in that any longer,' interposed Brightman. 'The next proposition is Birmingham.'

Lina nodded approvingly. 'The Chief is particularly anxious to bring this off,' she informed them. 'Afterwards, he proposes that we let up for a while and take a rest.'

'We'll get a rest all right – in clink if we don't watch our step,' muttered Williams.

'Has the Chief any ideas about how we're going to land this stuff?' asked Ware.

Lina shook her head. 'Not yet. He's waiting for more information.'

'One thing is quite certain,' said Brightman. 'We mustn't try anything at this end.'

'Why not?' asked Lina, with the merest lift of her narrow eyebrows.

'Because,' declared Brightman, impressively, 'there isn't a 'tec in Town who won't be watching the station on the day Paradise leaves for Birmingham.'

The other men nodded in agreement.

'All the same,' said Williams, 'I hope you're not working on any fancy ideas of raiding the hotel. I've hung around affairs like this before today, and believe me, we shouldn't even get a sight of the stuff.'

'I agree, the hotel is out!' said Brightman. 'The train is our opportunity.' He paused, then added thoughtfully, 'Swan, I think you'd better trail this fellow Paradise. You can start tomorrow.'

'That suits me,' agreed Williams.

'We must know in advance what train he intends to leave on. That's very important.'

'What's he like, and where do I find him?' asked Swan.

'He's a little man about forty. Rather grey about the temples, small moustache and a bit of a beard – French style, you know. He's staying at the Grand Palace Hotel in the Haymarket. You shouldn't have much difficulty in finding him there.'

Brightman turned to Lina.

'Who is going to handle this stuff if we get it?'

Her eyes narrowed as she replied. 'There's only one man who can handle it.'

'And that is?'

'Von Zelton.'

'But, he's a German,' put in Ware.

'What of it? Nobody in this country is big enough to handle a proposition like this.'

'Yes, but von Zelton,' protested Williams, 'I wouldn't trust him out of my sight. Why, what's to stop him—'

'The Chief will look after our interests,' retorted Lina.

'All the same, even if we get a straight deal, von Zelton will want at least twenty-five per cent,' Williams pointed out.

'That's pretty steep,' commented Brightman.

'It's got to be von Zelton,' Lina told them quietly, but firmly. 'That's the Chief's orders.'

The argument was still raging when there came four quick knocks on the door, and Jimmy Mills was admitted. Without a word, he went to the sideboard, poured himself a stiff drink and gulped it down.

'Did anybody see you come in?' asked Brightman, quickly.

Jimmy shook his head.

The others looked on in silence while he refilled his glass.

'What happened? Did Lucky—' began Brightman.

'He didn't talk!' snapped Jimmy, with a short, savage laugh.

'You got clear all right? Nobody recognised you?'

'Of course they recognised me. What's the odds? There's a warrant out for me, anyway,' snarled Jimmy. He drank again, and presently became calmer.

'Well, what about the Birmingham job?' he asked.

'We haven't decided everything yet,' said Brightman. 'Swan starts trailing Paradise tomorrow. We've got to find out what train he's taking on Thursday.'

'Supposing he goes up by road,' suggested Mills.

Brightman smiled for the first time.

'So much the better,' he chuckled.

CHAPTER XXIII

Andrea Fortune Writes a Letter

If the Front Page Men were worried over their plans to steal the Carter Collection, New Scotland Yard was even more harassed in their attempts to prevent the robbery. Sir Graham had already called two conferences on the subject, and as his mind was still far from easy, he telephoned Paul Temple and asked him to drop in for a chat.

Having begun to formulate some rather interesting theories on the identities of the Front Page Men, Temple hardly welcomed the invitation, for he was anxious to work independently of the police. However, a summons from Sir Graham could not be ignored, and Temple duly presented himself at the appointed time.

'What makes you feel so certain that the Front Page Men will be interested in the Carter Collection?' he asked curiously, after Sir Graham had outlined some of his ideas.

'Because it's the most valuable collection in the country,' growled the Chief Commissioner. 'And if anything happens to it, I shudder to think what the papers'll say.'

'What do you think the collection is worth, at a rough estimate?'

'Difficult to tell,' grunted Forbes. 'A million at least, I should say.'

Temple appeared suitably impressed.

'Is this man Paradise to be trusted?' he asked.

'Considering that watching over the Carter Collection is his full-time job, I should imagine so. We've checked up on him all right, don't worry. He's been known to the Jewellers' Association for years.'

'Who's watching him?'

'Both Hunter and Digby will be on the train.'

'Actually with Paradise?'

'Hunter will travel in his compartment. I've got Digby on his own, so that if he sees anything at all fishy he can follow it up.'

'Not a bad idea,' approved Temple. 'It all seems fairly fool-proof – unless, of course, Hunter should be outnumbered …'

'He has instructions to pull the communication-cord at the first sign of anything suspicious – and the guard of the train will also be warned.'

'You're sure they won't try anything at this end, or when the collection is at the hotel?'

'They'll be unlucky if they do,' said Sir Graham. 'No, the train is the vulnerable spot, and I'm pretty certain that's what they will concentrate on.'

'You seem to have covered all contingencies there. Afraid I can't suggest anything more,' smiled Temple.

Sir Graham was obviously gratified.

'It was a great pity they got Lucky Gibson,' went on Temple. 'I think we should have found him useful – in time.'

'Yes, I'm sure we should,' agreed Sir Graham, taking off the glasses he wore for reading, and pitching them among the papers on his desk. 'I must say Hunter was damn lucky a bullet didn't come his way. That lad always has had a charmed life.'

'Very lucky indeed,' murmured Temple thoughtfully. He waited a moment before asking, 'Any news of Mills or Brightman?'

'No. They must be lying very low. But we'll get 'em all right before long.'

'There's no warrant out for Brightman?'

'Not yet. I'm still waiting for something rather more definite. Expecting it any minute now.'

Temple smiled. 'Wrenson?'

Sir Graham nodded. He quickly initialled several forms, then turned to Temple again.

'Well, any more news?'

'Yes, Sir Graham. It's about Ann Mitchell. You've got a man trailing her, haven't you?'

'That's right. After that story you told me about her being an impersonator ...'

'Yes, of course, I expected as much. But I'm afraid your man is hardly up to scratch. She's spotted him.'

'Damn!' said Sir Graham, making a hasty note on his blotter.

'Has he found out anything?' asked Temple.

'Nothing of any great importance, at least ...' He delved amidst a pile of papers and extracted a fairly lengthy report.

'Temple, do you happen to know if the Mitchells get on well together?'

Temple considered this for a while.

'Why, yes,' he decided at last, 'as far as I know. Why do you ask?'

'Because Ann Mitchell appears to rent a flat in Bloomsbury, and spends quite a lot of her time there. There doesn't seem to be anything sinister about it, though it may be that—'

'Well?'

'There might be another man.'

'Yes,' conceded Temple, 'there might.'

Now he came to think of it, he remembered seeing Ann out with another man – once at the Chelsea Arts Ball, and once at a private party. She was the type that would prefer the company of men, and Gerald's time was occupied a good deal with business affairs. It was hardly surprising that a good-looking woman like Ann Mitchell refused to deprive herself of male companionship. All the same, dinners and dances were rather a different proposition from taking a flat in Bloomsbury.

His reflections were interrupted by the entrance of Reed, who brought in a letter marked 'Urgent' for Sir Graham. With a muttered apology, Sir Graham tore open the envelope, and Reed quietly left the room.

Concluding that the letter was some matter of routine, Temple took little notice, and resumed his speculations about Ann Mitchell. Even an exclamation from Sir Graham did not disturb him, and it was not until the Chief Commissioner passed over the letter, that he suddenly realised it might concern him.

'What do you think of that?' demanded Sir Graham, more than a little excited.

Temple picked up the letter and read:

My dear Sir Graham,

Just recently there seems to have been a great many rumours to the effect that the author of the novel The Front Page Men is personally responsible for the amazing number of crimes committed by a gang of ruthless criminals, who for some unknown reason wish to be known as The Front Page Men. As the author of the book in question, I need hardly say that the rumours are without the slightest foundation, and that I deplore most fervently the wicked and criminal activities of this gang. I have been intending to write to you about this matter for quite a while, but circumstances over which I have no control compel me to conceal my identity. I trust, however, that you will readily believe me when I say that I am most certainly not connected with the despicable organisation who, for reasons best known to them-selves, wish to be known as The Front Page Men.

Yours sincerely,

Andrea Fortune.

Temple slowly re-read the letter, then held it up to the light and examined it carefully. There was no address at the top of the paper, which was of excellent quality. The signature was typed.

'Looks as if she used a portable typewriter,' commented Sir Graham. 'I'll get Watts on this straight away.'

'What about the envelope – is there a postmark?' asked Temple.

Sir Graham rummaged in his wastepaper basket and brought the envelope to light. For some moments he scruti-nised it under a powerful magnifying glass.

'This is interesting,' he pronounced at length. 'Funny we should be talking about Ann Mitchell's flat.'

'Oh,' said Temple, failing to see the connection. 'Why do you say that?'

'Because this letter appears to have been posted in Bloomsbury,' answered Forbes.

Before they could discuss the matter any further, the telephone rang, and Forbes picked up the receiver.

'Yes? Hello, Digby ... yes ... on the six-ten from Paddington. Well, tell Hunter to stick to him like glue, and if you see anything suspicious, just pounce on it for all you're worth. All right ... goodbye, Digby.' He thoughtfully replaced the receiver.

'Now we're all set,' he announced. 'Mr. John Leonard Paradise leaves for Birmingham on the six-ten with Inspector Hunter – and a million pounds' worth of jewellery.'

'Not a bad train, the six-ten,' murmured Temple, casually lighting a cigarette. 'Takes just two hours. Plenty of things can happen in that time, all the same.'

'That,' declared Forbes rather uncertainly, 'is just what I am afraid of.'

CHAPTER XXIV

Murder on the Six-ten

With its chocolate-and-yellow carriages gleaming in the evening sunshine, the six-ten slid away from the smoke of Paddington. Clattering through a series of grimy suburbs, it picked up speed until it was swinging along at a steady fifty miles an hour past the new housing estates which sprawl their way into the countryside.

On opposite sides of a first-class compartment sat Inspector Hunter and Mr. John Leonard Paradise, a dapper little man, who held a small attache-case very carefully on his knees. When he spoke, he talked in prim, rather clipped tones. He was meticulously dressed in a blue serge lounge suit, of irreproachable Bond Street cut. His shoes were small, pointed and beautifully polished.

Mr. Paradise had agreed with Hunter that it would be better for both of them to remain in their compartment, rather than take the slightest risk by venturing to the dining-car. Mr. Paradise went over in his mind the dinner he had ordered by telephone, which would be waiting for him when they reached their destination. For Mr. John Leonard Paradise was something of a gourmet.

Hunter found his gaze returning time and again to the attache-case, until he almost imagined that he could see beyond that glossy brown cover to the sparkling diamonds that lay inside. Hunter's nerves were on edge, and Mr. Paradise was hardly a soothing influence. He fidgeted constantly, not from nervousness, for he was quite accustomed to carrying the Carter Collection around with him. In fact, he was inclined to be rather amused at all the precautions Scotland Yard were taking.

From time to time they carried on a desultory conversation, but both were inclined to be somewhat reticent.

'What time do you make it, Inspector?' asked Paradise, presently.

'It's about seven-forty. We should soon be getting into Leamington.'

'H'm, fairly good train this.'

'One of the fastest in the country,' replied Hunter indifferently. 'I suppose you have made all your arrangements in Birmingham?'

'Yes, I'm staying at the hotel where the ball is being held, so that simplifies matters.'

'Well, as soon as I've seen the collection safely locked away I'll shoot back to Town,' decided Hunter. 'One of our men will call round in the morning to see if everything's all right, and he'll come back with you on Saturday.'

'You people don't seem to leave much to chance,' commented Paradise, with a faint smile.

'We can't afford to – with a million at stake.'

The roar of the train changed its note as the brakes were gradually applied. 'This must be Leamington,' announced Hunter, as a few isolated villas came into view, to be followed by the rather disappointing railside suburbs of the royal spa.

'Not many people about on the platform,' commented Paradise, peering out of the window.

'No, it's rather late,' explained Hunter.

'What sort of a place is Leamington?'

'I've never actually stayed there for any length of time,' said Hunter. 'I've passed through occasionally by road. It's very like most of these spas – wide avenues, big shopping street, parks, gardens and so on.' Before he could add to this description, the form of a ticket-collector appeared in the doorway of the compartment.

Waiting for him to clip the pieces of pasteboard he had handed over, Hunter glanced casually out of the window and saw a man in policeman's uniform running along the platform.

'Hello, what's the matter with this fellow? He seems in a devil of a hurry,' remarked Hunter, as the man in uniform came up to their compartment.

'Why, it's Sergeant Lewis!' exclaimed the ticket-collector, in a surprised voice.

'Hello, White,' said the police sergeant.

'Anything the matter?' asked the ticket-collector.

'Yes, I'm looking for a man named Hunter – Inspector Hunter. He's supposed to be on this train.'

'What is it, Sergeant?' snapped Hunter.

'I beg your pardon, sir, but—'

'This is Inspector Hunter,' Mr. Paradise informed the sergeant.

'Oh, I'm sorry, sir. You're wanted on the telephone, urgent. I believe it's the Chief Commissioner. We have special orders to hold the train.'

'Oh,' said Hunter, rising. 'Where is the phone?'

'In the second of those huts, sir,' replied the sergeant, indicating some temporary buildings which had been erected during alterations to the station.

'I'll find it. You stay here, Sergeant.'

'That's all right, sir. The Chief Commissioner explained about Mr. Paradise.'

'Good!'

Hunter left the compartment and made his way along the platform. He had no difficulty in locating the hut indicated, but it was some seconds before he saw the telephone in a rather gloomy distant corner.

The receiver was dangling by its cord, and he snatched it up quickly.

For quite two minutes he failed to get any response. Then suddenly, to his surprise, he heard the train moving away.

'Hello!' called Hunter, desperately. In his excitement, he snatched at the cord which connected the instrument to a box on the wall. It came away in his hand.

Hearing a slight noise behind him, Hunter turned sharply. Three men stood there. Two wore rather dark and untidy mackintoshes, and he had never seen them before. By the crude light of the oil-lamp suspended from the ceiling, however, Hunter recognised in the third, the familiar features of Mr. Andrew Brightman.

Mr. Paradise sat blandly clutching his attache-case. The ticket-collector and the sergeant had retired to the corridor, as if they were reluctant to intrude upon his privacy.

If Mr. Paradise had listened carefully to their voices, he would have noticed that the sergeant's had undergone a complete change from the gruff tone adopted in keeping with his appearance. Swan Williams had now resumed his high-pitched falsetto in addressing his colleague.

'Are the boys ready?' the ticket-collector was asking.

'Yes, they're standing by at the end of this coach,' said Swan. 'What about Digby?'

'Don't worry. He's been taken care of.'

Feeling a slight vibration, Swan looked out. 'We're off!' He beckoned to the other to return to the compartment.

'My word, the Inspector will have to be quick,' said Paradise, as they opened the door.

'You'll be all right with me, sir,' Swan assured him, adopting his gruff voice once more.

Nevertheless, Paradise was obviously a trifle alarmed as the train cleared the platform and headed for the Warwickshire countryside.

'Get the blinds down,' suddenly hissed Swan Williams.

'O.K.' The ticket-collector snatched down a blind in each hand.

'What—what is—this?' stammered Paradise, now plainly scared.

'If you open that mouth of yours ...' threatened the falsetto voice.

Mr. Paradise fumbled in his coat-pocket and rather gingerly produced a revolver.

'If you don't stand back,' he declared with terrified determination, 'I warn you I shall shoot!'

His assailants backed a pace or two towards the corridor door. Then Mr. Paradise made the mistake of glancing desperately in the direction of the communication cord. The moment his eyes moved, Swan Williams suddenly thrust out a foot with amazing agility and kicked the revolver out of Paradise's hand.

There followed a terrific scuffle, and Paradise managed to let out a stifled scream a split second before Jed Ware – his ticket-collector's uniform all awry – placed a large hand over the little man's mouth.

'Open the door!' panted Jed, who had taken control of the situation. 'We'll have to get rid of him.'

'You're not going to throw him out?' shrieked Swan, hysterically.

'Get that door open!'

'But Jed, for God's sake—'

Suddenly the door swung open and a rush of air fluttered the blinds. Paradise still struggled desperately, clinging to Jed with terror in his eyes.

But the burly Ware freed himself, and with a tremendous heave flung the shrieking Paradise out on to the line.

Jed pulled the door to with a resounding bang, and he and Swan collapsed on the seats quite breathless for a few moments. Then, in about a couple of seconds, Swan deftly opened the attache-case, ascertained its contents, and closed it again nervously as a train rushed past with whistle screaming.

'My God ! Another train—and—he's on the line!' whispered Williams, in terror.

'Pull yourself together. He was done for, anyway,' roughly retorted Jed Ware. He was more interested in the contents of the attache-case.

CHAPTER XXV

Visitors at Eastwood Mansions

'Speak up, Digby, dammit, man, I can't hear a word!' barked Sir Graham Forbes in a voice which almost shattered the telephone. Apparently Digby obliged, and the Chief Commissioner was silent for a few minutes.

'H'm,' he grunted at last, in no better humour. 'That's a lot of good, I must say!' There was a sound of protest from the other end. 'All right, call me back,' snapped Forbes, planking down the receiver with a tremendous sigh.

He pushed the instrument away from him and relapsed into deep thought. When Reed came in, he hardly gave any sign of noticing him.

'I've seen Hunter,' announced Reed. 'He's recovered consciousness. My, but that's a lucky laddie. The doctor says that if that crack had been an inch to the left he wouldna be alive to tell us anything.'

'What did he say?' demanded Sir Graham, anxiously.

'They told him he was wanted on the telephone at Leamington, and he left the train. That's when they got him.'

'Does he remember what the men were like?'

'Ay.' Mac paused. 'He says he's pretty sure one of them was Andrew Brightman.'

'Ah!' exclaimed Sir Graham, slowly nodding. 'Anything else?'

'No, Sir Graham. I only had a wee talk with Hunter. He's still pretty groggy.'

'There'll be hell to pay over this,' suddenly burst forth Sir Graham.

'According to Digby, there was a parson laddie on the train who was acting rather suspiciously,' pursued Mac. 'He was in a compartment a wee bit further along, when—'

'I know, I know,' impatiently interrupted the Chief Commissioner. 'Digby's a damn' fool or he'd have guessed there was something afoot as soon as he saw Hunter leave the train. My last instructions to him were ...' Forbes shrugged his shoulders with a helpless gesture. 'What's the use?'

Mac pursed his lips and shook his head.

'I can't get that poor devil Paradise out of my head,' said Forbes.

'Ay, he might have stood a chance if it hadn't been for that other train.'

'A pretty poor chance, I'm afraid.' Forbes straightened himself abruptly. 'We've got to get the Front Page Men, Mac. No matter what happens, we've got to get 'em!'

'Ay,' said Chief Inspector Charles Cavendish MacKenzie Reed, but without much enthusiasm.

Steve crossed to a window and closed it, excluding the roar of traffic from below.

'Was he married, Paul?' she asked.

Temple looked up from some notes he was scribbling on a pad.

'Who? Oh, you mean Paradise. I really don't know, darling. But he didn't seem the marrying type.'

'I do hope he wasn't,' said Steve earnestly. 'It's all so dreadful.'

Temple nodded without speaking.

'You don't seem very upset about it, Paul.'

'I've come to expect anything from the Front Page Men. Besides, Sir Graham's doing enough worrying for six men, so I'm trying my utmost to keep a clear head.'

'But these Front Page Men can't go on forever, Paul,' Steve argued. 'Sooner or later they are bound to be caught.'

'So they are,' agreed Temple, quite cheerfully, 'sooner or later.'

'Didn't you say there was a warrant out for two of them?'

'There has been for some time. They seem particularly elusive.'

Steve considered the position. Then she stirred again.

'Paul, where does Mr. Goldie fit into all this? Does he fit in?'

'Certainly,' replied Temple imperturbably.

'Then do you think he is—'

'Andrea Fortune? No, darling, sorry to disappoint you.'

'No, no. What I was going to say was—'

But the entry of Pryce prevented her saying it. To the patent surprise of his master and mistress he announced that Mr. Mitchell had called. After they had exchanged inquiring looks, Temple ordered Pryce to show in the visitor.

'Hello Gerald,' smiled Steve, rising to meet him. 'Is Ann with you?'

'No,' answered Mitchell, with some hesitation. 'I'm—er —quite alone.'

'You look worried to death,' said Steve. 'Is there anything wrong?'

'Yes,' said Temple, 'out with it, Gerald. Maybe we can help.'

Mitchell bit his lip nervously, then blurted out, 'Paul—Ann has disappeared!'

'Disappeared?' echoed Temple.

There was a pause.

'What exactly do you mean?' asked Steve.

'I'm afraid I can't explain clearly – it's all so confusing,' Gerald told them, sinking on to a chair and looking moodily out of the window.

'Try to remember – as much as you can,' suggested Temple.

Mitchell swallowed hard and seemed almost in tears. Presently, however, he began. 'I was rather late getting in last night – I stayed at the office till about nine reading some proofs. When I got home I found a note from Ann. She said that a girl friend of hers named Sandra Storm, who lives at Brighton, had been taken seriously ill, and that she had promised to spend the night with her. This didn't really worry me, because I knew that they had always been great friends, and that Ann would rush down there like a shot the moment she heard of Sandra being ill. This morning, though—'

He paused, overcome with sudden emotion.

'This morning, a card arrived for Ann. It was from Sandra, and was posted in Cairo.'

'Cairo!'

'Yes, Sandra Storm and her husband are on a cruise. They get back on the sixteenth – according to the card.'

'Then – Ann couldn't have gone to Brighton,' exclaimed Steve in some alarm.

'No, she can't be in Brighton,' agreed Mitchell, who was becoming more and more distracted. 'But where is she? Where?' He sunk his head in his hands, and Temple waited a few moments for him to recover before asking, 'Do you know what time she left the house?'

'The maid said about seven.'

'When was the last time you saw her?'

'Yesterday morning. We did arrange to meet for lunch, but she rang through to the office and cancelled our appointment.'

'Did she say why?' asked Temple, looking rather interested.

'No – I don't quite remember. I think she said something about having a headache,' answered Mitchell, vaguely.

Temple and Steve exchanged a glance.

'My God—I do—hope she's all right!' cried Mitchell, somewhat incoherently. Temple went to the sideboard and poured out a stiff whisky and soda, which he brought over to his guest.

'Am I wrong, or have you been rather worried about Ann this past few weeks, Gerald?' asked Temple.

'Yes,' said Mitchell quietly. 'She's been acting rather strangely just lately. I don't quite know why, but she seems to have been rather, well, furtive and underhand about various things.'

'Did she say anything to you about her being—followed?'

Mitchell looked rather alarmed. 'Then she told you, too? She was under the impression that there was someone trailing her. I did my best to convince her that it was just her imagination, and yet—'

'Yes?'

'I couldn't help remembering that night when Steve heard Carol Forbes on the telephone,' continued Mitchell.

'You still think it might have been Ann?' demanded Steve, swiftly.

'Oh no! No!' cried Mitchell frantically. 'It couldn't have been Ann.' Then his voice quavered. 'And yet, I— I—suppose it could!' He finished off the rest of his whisky.

'Paul,' he whispered presently, 'you don't think Ann could be mixed up with— with the Front Page Men?'

'I really don't know, Gerald,' admitted Temple, quietly. 'Gerald, you're quite sure that Ann can still impersonate people's voices? I mean she may have lost the trick, having left the stage some years.'

'No, she can still do it, I know. She does it at parties – she's always been able to – ever since she was a girl.'

'Did she act under her own name?' asked Steve.

'No, she had a stage name, Lydia Royal.'

'Lydia Royal,' repeated Temple thoughtfully. 'Now where have I heard that before?'

But Carol Forbes burst in on them and interrupted his reflections.

'Why, Carol! This is a nice surprise,' cried Steve. 'I forget whether you've met Gerald Mitchell.'

'Oh yes. How do you do, Mr. Mitchell?'

They shook hands.

'I think my wife introduced us at Lady Ronson's,' hazarded Mitchell, and Carol nodded.

'You never told me you knew Ann Mitchell,' said Steve to Carol.

'Oh yes, we knew each other – we met several times at parties,' explained Carol. 'Strangely enough,' she added, 'that was why I came here – it's quite a coincidence.'

Steve looked puzzled.

'You came here because of my wife?' asked Mitchell.

'That's right,' said Carol brightly. 'I had a letter from her this morning, asking me to meet her at a flat in Bloomsbury … well, read it for yourself.'

She handed Mitchell an envelope, from which he extracted a small sheet of notepaper and read:

Flat K, Tavistock Court, Bloomsbury.
 Dear Carol, I should like to see you tomorrow at about seven-thirty. Please come to the above address. Don't fail me; the matter is urgent.

 Yours,
 Ann Mitchell.

Rather dazedly, he handed the letter to Temple. 'That's Ann's writing,' he told them.

'I was worried about it,' confessed Carol. 'I kept thinking of that night when Steve received the telephone message. So I thought I'd try to discover if the note is genuine, because I haven't the slightest idea what Ann can want to see me about.'

'It's genuine all right,' Mitchell repeated.

'You're positive about the handwriting?' insisted Temple. 'Absolutely.'

There was silence for a few moments, until Carol suddenly demanded, 'I say, is anything the matter?'

'Yes, Carol,' said Steve. 'Ann Mitchell disappeared last night.'

While Carol was recovering from her astonishment, Temple asked, 'Gerald, did you know anything about this flat in Bloomsbury?'

'Good lord, no!' cried Mitchell, in complete bewilderment. 'This is news to me. Whose flat is it, anyway?'

'Presumably, it's Ann's.'

'But—but that's ridiculous!'

'Well, we can soon find out,' said Temple smoothly.

'What are you going to do, Paul?' asked Steve.

'If Carol has no objection,' continued Temple, 'I think it would be a good idea if we all kept that appointment.'

CHAPTER XXVI

Concerning a Flat in Bloomsbury

Standing in a Bloomsbury backwater, Tavistock Court is a substantial red-brick building of architecture which is more or less commonplace in that quarter. Its windows are flush with the walls, and the only outer protuberance is an uninspiring porch supported by two very substantial pillars. It is the sort of building you might pass every day for a year without being aware of its existence.

On rather a dismal evening, Carol and Steve found the approach to Tavistock Court singularly depressing, and did not fail to comment upon the fact. Temple and Mitchell were silent, and the latter spoke for the first time when they stood outside the building.

'It looks more like offices than flats,' he declared. 'Are you sure we're at the right place?'

'Here's someone coming,' said Steve. 'Perhaps we'd better ask.'

A light-hearted young man in evening dress came out of the entrance, pulled his scarf round his throat, and was about to walk away when Temple accosted him.

219

'Excuse me, is this Tavistock Court?'

The newcomer nodded pleasantly. 'This is Tavistock Court – and you can have it!' he announced grandiloquently.

Carol and Steve could not repress a smile.

'We were looking for Flat K,' went on Temple.

'That might be anywhere – absolutely cock-eyed place, this,' the young man informed them.

'I'm sorry – I thought you might be a resident,' said Temple.

The man was quite shocked at the idea. 'Sooner die than live in a hovel like this,' he announced. 'You'll find a lift at the end of the passage, but I won't guarantee that it works!'

'Thanks,' smiled Temple. 'Do you mind telling me if they are all flats in this building?'

'I believe so. Used to be a club for spinsters at some time or other.' The idea seemed to tickle him. 'Can you imagine the riotous gaiety?' he demanded.

'I suppose this is the only Tavistock Court in Bloomsbury,' put in Carol, tentatively.

'Heaven forbid there should be another!' declared the young man, as he hailed a taxi and drove off.

'How nice to have a cheerful outlook like that on life,' laughed Steve, as they walked to the end of the passage in the direction of the lift. This proved to be a tiny affair, which could only accommodate three people at the most.

'I wonder what has happened to the liftman,' said Steve.

'It's automatic, darling,' answered her husband, indicating a row of buttons. 'And our gay young friend was obviously right about it being a club. Look, it says: Restaurant, Reading Room, Sewing Room – and so on.'

'Not particularly helpful to strangers,' commented Steve, 'but I suppose we may as well get in and see where it will take us.'

They found it a bit of a squeeze, and Temple, who was last in, instructed, 'You press the button, Gerald, after I've closed the gate.'

Presently they were being taken upwards with a considerable amount of creaking and grinding. Their faces appeared a trifle strained in the glimmer of light from a tiny bulb in the lift. When it came to a standstill, Temple pushed back the gate and stepped out.

'What floor is this?' asked Steve.

'The fourth, I think. Might as well start from here as from anywhere, I suppose. There doesn't seem to be anybody about to direct us.'

The others left the lift and began to wander along a corridor. Suddenly Carol called out, 'Here it is, Paul.'

'Yes, by Jove,' confirmed Mitchell, 'it's on the door – Flat K.'

'By Timothy, I believe you're right!'

Temple paused, then knocked. As there was no reply, he rapped again, the knocks echoing dismally along the deserted corridor.

'There's no one in,' decided Steve, at length, and they regarded each other in perplexity.

'Paul, I hope there's nothing the matter,' muttered Mitchell, in some alarm.

'I don't like it, Gerald,' admitted Temple, shaking his head.

'The flat is obviously empty,' pronounced Carol, a little impatiently.

'Well, we'll soon find out,' decided Temple, taking a bunch of skeleton keys from his pocket. He was usually prepared for emergencies. In less than five minutes the door clicked open.

Temple entered first, with Steve close behind him. They were in a fair-sized room, but it was difficult to distinguish anything beyond this fact, for the windows were concealed by heavy curtains.

Steve's foot touched something, and with a stifled scream, she half turned towards the door. 'Paul, there's someone on the floor!'

'Just a minute, I'll strike a match,' he told her.

While he was fumbling, Carol called, 'I've found the switch,' and the room was flooded with light. Almost simultaneously, a scream from Steve pierced the air.

'Paul – it's Ann!' she gasped. 'She's dead!'

They all ran towards the corner where Steve was standing, supporting herself against the wall.

At her feet lay the body of Ann Mitchell.

'She's been stabbed!' cried Carol. 'Look, there's the knife!'

'Don't touch it!' said Temple, quickly.

'Ann!' shouted Mitchell, hysterically, bending over her. 'Ann! By God, I'll make the swine pay for this!' He was almost demented with fury, when Temple gripped him by the arm.

'Listen!' he ordered, forcefully.

They stood in hushed silence.

Faintly from the flat above came the wistful refrain of *Liebestraum*. It was the melody that Paul Temple instinctively associated with Mr. J. P. Goldie.

CHAPTER XXVII

The Flat Above

'Wait here!' said Temple, making for the door.

'Paul, where are you going?' demanded Steve, in alarm.

'Upstairs!' replied Temple, briefly.

'Darling, please don't!'

'It's all right, Steve.'

'I'll come with you,' offered Gerald Mitchell.

'No. You stay here, Gerald. I shan't be long.'

Temple pulled the door to behind him, and after a little while they could hear him running along the corridor.

Mitchell dropped into a chair.

'I wonder what made Ann come here,' he brooded.

Steve looked at the body and shuddered; Carol was rather nervily lighting a cigarette.

'What's behind all this, Steve?' demanded Mitchell frantically. 'Do you think Ann was—oh, my God, I daren't even think of it!'

'You'll have to pull yourself together, Gerald,' urged Steve, quietly.

'I wouldn't care if only I could get things in their right perspective,' continued Mitchell, desperately. 'But somehow everything seems so terribly confused. What made Ann send for Miss Forbes? Whose flat is this? Why should Ann deceive me?'

'Gerald – you're only torturing yourself,' murmured Steve, gently.

Mitchell clasped and unclasped his hands, ran them through his hair, then paced up and down the room. He was having great difficulty in refraining from breaking down.

'I am sorry, Gerald,' sympathised Steve.

Steve, too, was worried, and breathed a sigh of relief when the door opened and Temple came in.

'Was it Mr—?' Steve was starting to ask, when he cut her short.

'There was no one!'

'But that's ridiculous!' exclaimed Mitchell.

'Why, we heard the piano! Someone must have been there,' protested Carol.

'I tell you the flat is deserted,' retorted Temple, rather irritably.

'Darling,' said Steve gently, 'it's no use denying that someone was there.'

'I wonder if he's climbed on to the roof,' speculated Mitchell, thoughtfully.

'Yes, that is possible,' Temple admitted. 'In that case, he's almost certain to have got away by now.'

He returned to their immediate situation.

'Gerald, I'm afraid we shall have to get in touch with the Yard straight away about Ann.'

Mitchell nodded silently.

'I'm terribly sorry, old man,' continued the novelist, placing a hand on Mitchell's shoulder.

'You know, it's so difficult to believe. I keep looking at Ann and thinking of the last time we were together – she was joking about Steve's novel and I know it seems strange, but it's almost as if we were—' Mitchell's voice broke.

'Come along, Gerald,' said Steve, leading him to the door.

Temple paused to take a last look at the body of Ann Mitchell. Curiously, he examined the long, narrow knife. It might have been a duplicate of the one which had accounted for Tony Rivoli.

CHAPTER XXVIII

Mr. Brightman is Worried

Every meeting of the Front Page Men was growing considerably less pleasant than its predecessor. With the police chase becoming more acute and every proposition doubly difficult, even the iron nerves of Brightman and his associates were beginning to show signs of fraying.

Whereas they had previously been content to wait weeks for their share of the spoils, they were suspicious nowadays if this was delayed for more than a week. And although he tried to keep them in order, Brightman was slowly becoming as restless as the others. Once again they had met in his flat, which he did not use much these days, preferring to stay at various small hotels all over London in case his movements were under observation.

With his back to the mantelpiece, Brightman scowled at Jimmy Mills, who was perched on the edge of the table protesting vigorously.

'It's all very well talking, Brightman,' snarled Jimmy, 'but it's about time we saw some results.'

'For heaven's sake, Jimmy, try to use your head!' snapped Brightman, becoming more and more angry. 'Can I help it if the stuff doesn't come through? You know I've always shared out—'

'Listen, Brightman,' put in Swan Williams, 'we had a tricky job on our hands with that Carter Collection, and it's about time we had our cut.'

'Which means now – not next Christmas!' supplied Jed Ware.

Brightman spoke quietly now, though he was inwardly furious. 'You know as well as I do that the Carter Collection has not been disposed of yet.'

'Then it's about time it was!' rasped Jimmy Mills.

'What the hell's the idea of keeping us hanging round like this?' growled Ware.

'Things are getting pretty hot, Brightman, and you know it,' said Jimmy. 'We want that dough – and the sooner we get it, the sooner we can disappear.'

'What do you expect me to do about it?' demanded Brightman, impatiently. 'You know very well that the Chief is handling the Carter Collection.'

'As far as we're concerned, Mr. Brightman,' said Jimmy slowly, 'you are the Number One Man of this outfit.'

'But I'm just as helpless as you are,' protested Brightman, indignantly.

'If the Chief has got the Carter Collection, how do we know he isn't going to double-cross us?' pursued Jed Ware.

'Has he double-crossed you before?' asked Brightman, without much enthusiasm.

Ware ignored the question.

'Brightman, who *is* the Front Page Man?' he demanded.

There was a slight pause. Brightman shook his head helplessly.

'I don't know,' he confessed. 'Nobody knows – except Lina.'

'Then she's got to tell us!' cried Jimmy.

Jed Ware nodded a vigorous approval.

'She's got to tell us, Brightman,' insisted Swan Williams.

They looked at him expectantly, and for a moment he seemed lost in thought. Then, 'I agree with you,' he said suddenly, and rather to their surprise. 'We've been working in the dark long enough.'

The tension relaxed a little as it dawned upon the others that Brightman was speaking the truth.

'I thought the Chief was getting in touch right away with this German fence, von Zelton?' grumbled Ware.

'Blimey, 'e's 'ad long enough to get in touch with Greta Garbo!' exclaimed Jimmy Mills.

'It's just occurred to me,' murmured Brightman, thoughtfully, 'that supposing the Chief has been in touch and the stuff has already gone, then we've no means of tracing anything.'

'My God, if he has double-crossed us …' snarled Jimmy desperately, but the string of threats he was about to embark upon were cut short by Lina's familiar knock on the door.

As she came in, she read at once the expressions of doubt and suspicion on every face.

'What's the matter?' she asked.

Brightman placed a chair for her, and she sat down rather wearily.

'Well, what's the trouble?' she continued.

'Oh—er—nothing—' answered Brightman, smoothly. 'We've just been having a little chat.'

'H'm. It doesn't seem to have left you in the best of spirits,' commented Lina, sceptically. 'I wouldn't call any of you a ray of sunshine.'

'Listen to me, Lina,' burst in Jimmy Mills. 'I'm tired of beating about the bush. We want to know—'

Brightman cut him short.

'Jimmy! I'll handle this.'

Jimmy relapsed sulkily into an armchair.

'Now, Lina,' went on Brightman evenly, 'we were merely wondering if there is any news about the Carter Collection.'

Brightman thought he noticed her expression change for a moment, as though she resented the inquiry. But her voice was as calm and unemotional as ever.

'Von Zelton is flying from Munich,' she announced. 'He's meeting the Chief tomorrow night.'

'Good!' approved Brightman.

'If von Zelton closes the deal,' said Lina, 'you should make the best part of twenty thousand each.'

'We earned it!' snorted Ware.

'And what,' demanded Jimmy Mills with a note of sarcasm in his voice, 'does Front Page Man Number One get out of it?'

There was a significant silence for a moment. Then Lina looked round and said, 'Something's in the wind. You may as well tell me now as later.'

Brightman fidgeted uneasily.

'Lina, the boys are getting anxious,' he told her. 'They think it's about time the Chief came out into the open.'

'And what do you think, Andrew?' she asked, in a steely tone.

'I agree with them,' said Brightman. 'It's no good beating about the bush any longer. We must know who the Chief really is.'

Four pairs of eyes were focused relentlessly upon the girl, whose features betrayed no consciousness of the crisis thrust upon her.

'Before I came here tonight,' she announced, 'the Front Page Man gave me a message. He is meeting von Zelton tomorrow night at nine – at the Glass Bowl.'

'That's all very well,' said Swan Williams impatiently, 'but how are we to know—' Something in her expression reduced him to silence.

'The Chief,' said Lina slowly, 'is anxious for you all to be there.'

In the flat immediately below, a middle-aged man took off the headphones he had been wearing and thoughtfully rubbed his ears.

CHAPTER XXIX

Wrenson's Report

'Mr. Temple, sir!' respectfully announced Sergeant Leopold, and Sir Graham Forbes rose from his desk to welcome the novelist.

'Hallo, Temple, I hope I haven't dragged you away from a pleasant dinner,' he began.

'No, not at all, Sir Graham. I was rather late getting your phone message,' answered Temple.

He placed his hat on one end of the Chief Commissioner's desk and threw his gloves down beside it.

Forbes opened a drawer and produced a postcard.

'I thought this might interest you.'

The Front Page Men are meeting at the Glass Bowl tonight at nine ... a Friend of Justice,

read Temple. He turned the card over. 'H'm – seems pretty crude, doesn't it?' he commented reflectively.

'Yes, that's what I thought,' agreed Forbes.

'Have you had it tested?'

'Yes. Apparently it was written by a woman.'

'That's fairly obvious, even to an amateur like myself. Haven't you any idea who wrote it?'

Forbes shook his head. 'It's nothing like the handwriting of the woman who sent the letter signed Andrea Fortune.'

'At the rate we're progressing,' murmured Temple, 'half the underworld of London will be involved in this case before we have finished.'

Sir Graham threw the card back into his drawer with an impatient gesture.

'By the way,' continued Temple, 'have you heard anything from Wrenson lately?'

'I had his report through this morning.'

'Ah, this sounds more like it,' approved Temple, who always admired Wrenson. 'What does he say?'

'He seems to have been fairly busy.'

'Really?'

'Yes, he advises me to pick up Jimmy Mills, Brightman, Jed Ware, Swan Williams, and a girl named Lina Fresnay.'

Temple, who had been nodding thoughtfully as each name was mentioned, looked up inquiringly at the last.

'Lina Fresnay? Is that her real name?'

'As far as we know. There's no trace of her in our records.'

'H'm. Well, Wrenson appears to have the gang very neatly tabulated. Not quite so slap-dash and dramatic as some people seemed to think.'

'Yes, Wrenson's done well up to a point.'

'You mean?'

'He's obviously quite mystified about the identity of Front Page Man Number One.'

'And I would be the last to blame him for that,' smiled Temple. 'By the way, I hope Carol is none the worse for our little adventure the other evening. The poor kid was pretty upset at the time, I could see.'

'Yes, it shook her up quite a lot. She's been very quiet just lately. I'm hoping it won't get her down.'

'It set Steve back pretty badly, too, just as I was hoping she'd recovered from that last affair,' said Temple.

'Yes, and talking of nerves, we had Mitchell in this morning. He seems to be on the verge of a breakdown.'

'That was to be expected. He's a very nervy type, of course. Very easily flustered. I hope you didn't ask him too many awkward questions.'

'No,' grunted Forbes, 'no more than usual. And he couldn't tell us anything of any importance.'

Chief Inspector Reed came in with a sheaf of reports.

'I didn't realise Mr. Temple was here, sir,' he apologised.

'That's all right, Mac. We were just discussing the Bloomsbury affair.' Mac laid the reports carefully before his superior and slowly shook his head.

'A nasty business that, Mr. Temple. Must have been quite a shock to ye.'

Temple nodded. 'Who's on the job – Hunter?'

'No,' replied Sir Graham, 'Hunter was still pretty groggy at that time. He's made a grand recovery, though, and insisted on getting back on the case.'

'Ay, Hunter's a plucky lad,' conceded Reed, rather surprisingly, in view of his earlier antagonism towards his colleague. 'I'm thinkin' Hodges is havin' a tough time on this Bloomsbury case,' he added.

'Yes,' nodded Sir Graham. 'It's a complete mystery. I can't think how a woman like Ann Mitchell should get mixed up in this business.' He paused before adding thoughtfully, 'unless, of course, she should happen to be Andrea Fortune.'

'In that case,' argued Temple, 'why should the gang wish to destroy its master-mind? And what's more—'

He paused as the door opened noisily and Hunter came in. Physically, he seemed none the worse for his recent beating-up, but at the moment he was over-excited, and a scar on the side of his forehead was dyed deep crimson.

'What's the matter, laddie?' Reed greeted him. 'Ye seem a wee bit—'

'I've picked up Jimmy Mills!' announced Hunter, breathlessly.

'Good man!' applauded the Chief Commissioner.

'Jimmy Mills?' echoed Reed, very much surprised. 'Where in the world did ye find him?'

'I've been trailing him since three o'clock this afternoon,' panted Hunter. 'He's in a devil of a state, and I reckon he'll talk if—'

'Let's have him in here,' suggested Forbes, at once.

Hunter opened the door, and they heard the voice of Jimmy Mills engaged in heated argument with Sergeant Leopold. At a nod from Hunter, Jimmy was thrust into the room, closely followed by the sergeant.

'What the 'ell is the idea of bringin' me 'ere?' yelled Jimmy in angry tones. 'You've got nothin' against me!'

'If you'll be quiet for a minute, Mills, I'm going to charge you with the murder of Lucky Gibson, and also being impli-cated with the death of Sergeant Donovan, Tony Rivoli and—'

'You leave me alone!' shouted Jimmy. 'Leave me alone, or by God I'll—'

'You'll tell us the truth,' said the Chief Commissioner with one of his penetrating looks, 'and you can start by telling us who is the Front Page Man.'

Jimmy Mills' demeanour suddenly underwent a complete change.

'I don't know,' he whispered, hoarsely.

'Well, whoever he is, he's certainly sitting pretty, isn't he, Jimmy?' put in Paul Temple.

Jimmy saw the novelist for the first time since he had entered the room. 'Oh, so you're here, Mr. Temple,' he sneered.

'Yes,' replied Temple imperturbably, 'I'm here, Jimmy.'

'Think you're pretty clever, I dare say,' scoffed Mills.

'Not at all, Jimmy,' replied the novelist. 'You're the clever one.'

'What d'yer mean ? I've got my rights, I 'ave. You can't get me in 'ere and do as you like without any evidence against me.'

'Don't worry, Jimmy,' Temple smiled sweetly, 'you'll get what's coming to you.'

Paul Temple's composure seemed to upset Mills' air of bravado.

'Get—what's coming to me?' he repeated, nervously licking his lips. 'You don't mean that they'll—'

'Remember Lucky Gibson,' Temple softly reminded him.

'No – they can't do that!'

'Of course they can't,' agreed Temple, 'if they're inside!'

'Jimmy, I should strongly advise you in your own interests to talk,' said Sir Graham.

'Ay, ye've got nothing to lose,' Reed pointed out.

Mills seemed to be torn by an inward struggle.

'All right,' he gasped after a while. 'I'll talk!' Then he seemed scared of his decision, but Hunter was on him in a flash.

'Who is Front Page Man Number One?' he questioned.

There was silence for a few seconds. Then, 'Nobody knows,' whispered Jimmy, 'except—the girl.'

'You mean Lina Fresnay?' asked Temple.

'That's right.'

'Doesn't Brightman know?'

Jimmy shook his head emphatically. Once more he licked his lips. 'The gang's meeting tonight at the Glass Bowl,' he informed them.

'Ah,' grunted Forbes, 'the Glass Bowl, eh? What's the idea of this meeting?'

'A man named von Zelton is coming over from Munich. He's a fence – come to get the Carter Collection.'

'And he's going to be at the Glass Bowl?' asked Forbes.

'Yes, that's where he's meeting the Chief,'

'You mean the Front Page Man?' demanded Hunter, incredulously.

'Let's get this straight,' interrupted Sir Graham. 'You mean the Front Page Man will be at the Glass Bowl tonight with von Zelton – and the Carter Collection?'

'Yes,' cried Jimmy hysterically. 'Yes! Yes!'

'Take him away, Sergeant,' ordered Forbes swiftly, and turned towards Reed.

'I shall want the Glass Bowl surrounded, Mac. Take as many men as you want.'

Reed nodded briskly.

'And tell Thompson to watch all the airports for von Zelton,' went on Forbes, turning to Hunter, who hurriedly left the room to obey this order.

Sir Graham snatched up the telephone. His face was set and grim.

'Harcourt? This is the Chief Commissioner. I want the Flying Squad!'

CHAPTER XXX

The Flying Squad

As the first police-car came into sight, the small group of loungers outside the Glass Bowl vanished swiftly into the heavy mist which was swirling in from the river, and by the time the last car had lurched to a standstill there was not a soul to be seen. The police spread themselves silently around the tavern, and Reed marshalled the men he had detailed to accompany him.

In less than two minutes, a sergeant reported to Reed that the house was completely surrounded. The Chief Inspector took a last look round and pushed open the front door.

In the passage a down-at-heel young man was playing an accordion and singing. At the sight of the policemen, his voice quavered and the instrument wheezed discordantly into silence. He shrank against the wall, and the police pushed past him.

When they came to the door of the bar-parlour, the noisy chatter faded until the only sounds were those of uneasy shuffling. One man who had not realised what was going on swung round abruptly to ascertain what had caused the silence. His arm caught a tray of glasses on the counter and they swept to the floor with a crash which seemed almost as loud as an exploding bomb.

''Ere, what the 'ell d'you think you're playin' at?' screeched Mrs. Taylor, who was the first to recover her voice. 'I'll 'ave you know this is a respectable 'ouse!'

Reed stepped into the room.

'Ye're a pleasant conversationalist, Mrs. Taylor,' he retorted dryly, 'but I'm in no mood for chatterin' with ye tonight.' He rapidly surveyed the faces of everybody present, decided they were not the men he sought, and turned to his colleagues.

'Hunter, Rogers, Thornton, Deal and Priestly – follow me. The rest stay here.'

As he turned to go, he warned the customers to remain in the bar.

Reed then went along the passage to the tap-room. The only customers, however, were a couple of Lascar sailors and three local hangers-on, whom he recognised by sight.

'Upstairs!' commanded Mac briefly, and his men filed as noiselessly as possible up the narrow wooden staircase. At the top, Reed motioned to them to remain silent while he went along to each of the four doors and listened for some minutes. Outside the farthest door he paused, and, hearing a certain amount of desultory conversation inside, beckoned cautiously to his companions. At a signal from the Chief Inspector, each produced a revolver. He waited for a moment, then seized the knob firmly and flung open the door.

Three figures seated by the fire swung round as one man.

'The police!' cried Swan Williams.

'If any of ye move, it'll be the last time ye'll ever—' snapped Reed, but the rest of his words were cut short by a shot. Slightly behind the others, Jed Ware had quickly produced a gun, aimed at the electric bulb, and reduced the room to darkness. The four men dropped to their knees, taking cover behind chairs and any other article of furniture that was handy. Standing in the narrow doorway, the police offered an easy target, and they had to back out into the corridor, dragging Thornton and Rogers, both of whom had been hit, out of the line of fire.

Reed scratched his head in some perplexity and sent for more men. He had reason to suspect that Brightman and one of the others were *hors de combat*, and decided to force the issue. Ordering his men to bring along an ancient horsehair sofa which stood on the landing, Reed had it pushed into the doorway, thus affording them some measure of protection.

Two revolvers still blazed, but the police now brought a small machine-gun into play, and it was not long before the Front Page Men were silent.

Reed went into the room as the smoke cleared away, and curiously surveyed the inert forms by the light of a torch.

There was no sign of Front Page Man Number One.

CHAPTER XXXI

News of Hargreaves, Gilbert Wrenson, and Mr. J. P. Goldie

'Well, I must say you seem to bear a charmed life, Hunter,' said Sir Graham Forbes rather grimly the next morning. 'How are the others?'

'Thornton's pretty bad, sir,' Hunter informed him.

'Tut! Tut! And Rogers?'

'Oh, it turned out that he wasn't badly hurt after all. The lucky devil had his cigarette-case in his breastpocket, and the bullet went off that and just grazed his shoulder.'

'Is Mac all right?' asked Temple, who was standing by the Commissioner's desk.

'Not a scratch!' grinned Hunter. 'Heaven only knows how they missed him!'

Sir Graham handed round his cigarettes and slowly lit one for himself.

'It's a great pity you didn't manage to get your hands on Lina Fresnay,' he murmured, regretfully. 'According to a report I have here, she was in the bar-parlour when you arrived.'

'I can't understand it!' said Hunter, wrinkling his forehead. 'Both Mac and I looked round carefully. Of course, it was thick with smoke – even so, she must have slipped through the cordon somehow.'

'Bad management somewhere,' growled Forbes. 'What about Brightman?'

'He's in a pretty bad way,' replied Hunter. 'They all are, except for Swan Williams.'

'Have you questioned him?'

'Yes, sir.'

'H'm. Won't talk, I suppose?'

'He'll talk all right, but he doesn't seem to know a great deal.'

'Just as I expected,' said Temple. 'They were working in the dark most of the time. Is Brightman likely to be well enough to say anything soon?'

'He was a little better this morning,' answered Hunter. 'As a matter of fact, Mac's with him at the moment.'

'We shouldn't have acted so hastily,' reflected Sir Graham. 'If we'd waited, we'd probably have got the Front Page Man. I shouldn't wonder if the sight of the police-cars scared him away.'

Temple puffed a neat smoke-ring into the air.

'The Front Page Man never had any intention of going near the Glass Bowl last night,' he announced, calmly.

'Why do you say that?' demanded Forbes sharply.

Temple leaned forward in his chair.

'Von Zelton arrives from Munich with the express purpose of buying the Carter Collection from the Front Page Men. But Front Page Man Number One has seen the red light. Things are getting a bit too hot. He therefore arranges for the gang to wait for him at the Glass Bowl, whilst he, personally, sees von Zelton elsewhere and clinches the deal. Of course, if it should happen that the Glass Bowl came to be raided that particular evening, well – that was a bit of bad luck for the gang.'

'You mean he double-crossed them!' said Hunter, excitedly.

Temple nodded.

'Then that explains the note I received – telling us about the meeting at the Glass Bowl,' deliberated Forbes.

'It does seem to fit in,' smiled Temple.

They heard a knock at the door, and Reed came in looking rather sorry for himself.

'Hallo, Mac. You don't seem very pleased to find yourself alive,' Forbes greeted him.

'I've just been having a friendly little chat with an oyster,' said Reed, glumly.

'Won't Brightman talk?' asked Hunter, with some interest.

'Talk! Ye have the devil's own job to mak' the blighter nod!' Reed ruffled his sandy hair in vexation.

'This affair is damned annoying!' muttered Forbes, with pronounced irritation.

'But Sir Graham,' Hunter put in, 'if the Front Page Man wasn't at the Glass Bowl ...'

'I'm not worried about that so much,' replied Sir Graham, briefly. 'I'm inclined to accept Temple's theory that he had no intention of turning up at the Glass Bowl. What I am worried about is the fact that the girl slipped through our fingers.'

'I'm afraid that was inevitable,' Reed explained. 'When they heard the shots, most of our men came upstairs.'

Sir Graham accepted this explanation rather gloomily.

'If it comes to that, who noticed the girl in the bar-parlour?' asked Reed. 'I'm sure I didn't.'

'Come to think of it, Mac, I did see a young woman – she was on the right-hand side. But it didn't occur to me that she would be Lina Fresnay.'

'Why not?' asked Temple, quickly.

'Well, she was rather muffled up, and not particularly well-dressed. I thought she might be one of the regular customers.'

'Ay, we expected to find her with the rest of the gang,' added Mac.

'She wasn't the only person missing from the bar-parlour, either,' continued Hunter.

Sir Graham raised his brows inquiringly.

'When we first entered, I noticed a parson sitting in one of the alcove affairs,' pursued Hunter. 'After the shooting, he seemed to have miraculously disappeared.'

'H'm, a parson,' repeated Forbes without much enthusiasm.

'Could it be our old friend the Reverend Charles Hargreaves?' queried Temple, pleasantly.

'Hargreaves!' cried Hunter. 'Why, that's the fellow who rang me up at the hospital to warn me that—'

The telephone rang. It was Sergeant Leopold, who told Sir Graham that there was a caller waiting to see him.

'Eh? I can't see anyone now,' barked Sir Graham. 'What's that? Who? Oh ... Hargreaves ... all right, send him in ...' He replaced the receiver.

'Why, this is the man I was talking about!' exclaimed Hunter, in complete amazement. Temple, too, was obviously interested.

'The Reverend Charles Hargreaves,' announced Sergeant Leopold, and all eyes were turned on the door.

With a slight smile curving his whimsical mouth, the Reverend Hargreaves shook hands with Sir Graham and then turned to Temple.

'I hoped we should meet again, Mr. Temple – and here we are,' smiled Hargreaves.

Hunter, however, was not to be denied.

'Sir Graham, this is the man who was at the Glass Bowl on the night of the raid – I'll swear to that!' he insisted.

The Chief Commissioner smiled rather grimly.

'That's all right, Hunter. He won't try to get away.' Sir Graham paused as if he were making a decision; then announced, 'Gentlemen, may I present an old colleague of mine – Gilbert Wrenson of the Intelligence Department?'

'How do you do?' Hunter managed to stutter at length.

'I'm very well, thank you, Inspector,' smiled Wrenson, pleasantly. 'Well, Temple, I hope we haven't been treading on each other's toes too often.'

'No,' laughed the novelist, 'but that get-up of yours had me completely baffled at first. I racked my brain for hours, trying to think where I'd seen you before.'

'Yes, it seems to have been fairly successful,' agreed Wrenson.

'No complaints from me,' murmured Sir Graham, 'you've certainly done as well as any of us.'

'What exactly happened upstairs at the Glass Bowl?' Wrenson was anxious to know.

'We picked up Brightman, Jed Ware and Swan Williams,' Sir Graham informed him.

'But we missed the chappie we're after, Mr. Wrenson – the Front Page Man.'

Wrenson seemed lost in thought.

'Gilbert,' said Forbes presently, 'who is this Front Page Man?'

Reed and Hunter eagerly scanned Wrenson's features, trying to anticipate his reply. Wrenson eased his clerical collar uncomfortably.

'I wish I knew,' he had to admit. 'Nobody knows except Lina Fresnay. Not even Brightman.'

With a muttered imprecation, Forbes leaned back wearily in his chair and closed his eyes.

'I think I've worked harder on this case, and taken more risks than ever in my life before, and yet, somehow, I haven't got the results I've aimed at,' admitted Wrenson. 'I fixed up a microphone in the Hampstead flat, and got Sir Graham to hold up the arrests of Mills and Brightman as long as possible, so that I could listen to their meetings. That was how I heard about the proposed attack on Lucky Gibson at the hospital. I got in touch with Hunter, but unfortunately was just too late. I also had a pretty good idea of how the gang worked the Nottingham affair; but at the time was unable to do anything about it – except be on the spot when it happened.'

'You've done remarkably well,' said Temple, with considerable respect in his voice.

'Up to a point, yes,' nodded Wrenson. 'I was damned lucky to get the Blakeley child back safe and sound. They'd taken him to a deserted tinworks on the river, owned by a rat-faced little devil named Ginger Ricketts. Your old pal Chubby Wilson was really responsible for my getting a clue in that business. I was in the Seamen's Hostel one night preparing for one of the weekly sing-songs, when a note came for Chubby. It said: "Be at Redhouse Wharf tonight at nine." I delivered the note, of course, then trailed Chubby for all I was worth!'

'And he led you to Ginger Ricketts' place?' asked Temple.

'Yes. I thought at first that I'd stumbled on their real hideout. But after finding the Blakeley kid, I realised that they'd more or less deserted the place, and were only using it on rare occasions.'

'What made you go to the Glass Bowl tonight?' demanded Forbes, curiously.

'I was there waiting for a gentleman I'd give ten years of my life to meet – Front Page Man Number One,' answered Wrenson, simply.

'But what made you think he'd be there?' Hunter was anxious to learn.

'If it comes to that,' answered Wrenson with a twinkle in his eye, 'what made *you* people think he'd be there?'

'Well, for one thing, I had this card,' said Forbes, handing it over. 'Also, we picked up Jimmy Mills earlier in the evening, and he decided to talk.'

'I see,' nodded Wrenson. 'Well, my information came straight from the horse's mouth. I listened in to a jolly little meeting they had the night before last. Lina Fresnay definitely promised Brightman and the gang that they would meet the Front Page Man last night at the Glass Bowl, together with another interesting gentleman named von Zelton.'

'Yes, Jimmy told us about him. I've had a warrant issued. Have you found out anything about von Zelton?'

'Not a great deal. He's the biggest fence in Europe, of course. And there's not the slightest doubt what he's over here for.'

'The Carter Collection!' said Reed.

'Exactly. I heard them talking about it in the flat.'

'Temple thinks, and I'm inclined to agree with him,' said Forbes, 'that the Chief intended to get the gang together at the Glass Bowl and then double-cross them.'

'That's what he intended all right, and he's got away with it. Our only chance now is if we can pick up von Zelton, and find out where he's arranged to meet the Front Page Man.'

'Maybe we'll get the girl yet,' hazarded Forbes.

'She was at the Glass Bowl last night, and in view of what's happened, that rather surprises me,' frowned Wrenson. 'I can't quite see why the Front Page Man should want to double-cross her. After all, she's the only person who knows his real identity.'

'Perhaps she was there for a purpose,' said Forbes.

'To see that all the gang turned up, for instance. You notice she didn't go upstairs to their meeting-place. She probably had an appointment with the Chief later on. Remember, she was his only contact with the gang, and he relied on her to keep him in touch.'

'Soon after the police arrived, she slipped out of one of the side entrances – that would be when the shooting started,' recalled Wrenson. 'I did my best to follow her, but it was very misty by the river. I made one interesting discovery, though.'

'Really?' said Temple curiously.

'She dropped her handbag, and there was this card inside.'

The card was just a plain piece of pasteboard, on which was scribbled, 'Mr. Wallace Sabina ... The Autumn Hotel.'

'Who on earth is Wallace Sabina?' asked Temple, leaning over Sir Graham's shoulder.

'If you look underneath, you'll see the letters "V.Z."' Wrenson pointed out.

'By Jove!' ejaculated Sir Graham.

'"V.Z." – that's von Zelton!' exclaimed Hunter.

'Great Scott! It's just occurred to me – Sabina must be the Front Page Man, and he's waiting for von Zelton at the Autumn Hotel,' said Wrenson, thumping the desk.

'Then von Zelton mustn't reach him, whatever happens,' decided the Chief Commissioner.

'Why not?' demanded Temple, to everybody's surprise.

'But surely, Temple, you see ...'

'I have always thought killing two birds with one stone rather a pleasant occupation,' said Temple, rather cryptically.

Any further argument was cut short by the telephone ringing. Reed, who was nearest, picked up the receiver.

'Chief Commissioner's Office … oh, hello, Thompson … *ye've what*? Good man! Stick to him like glue. Ay, bring him back here as soon as ye can!'

'Who was it?' asked Forbes.

'It's Thompson, speaking from Croydon,' replied Reed.

'What's happened?'

'They've got von Zelton. He's just arrived by special plane.'

'Thank God!' breathed Forbes.

'Well, whoever our friend Sabina is, it looks as if he's going to be very lonely, as far as von Zelton is concerned, at any rate,' smiled Wrenson.

Reed and Hunter made no attempt to conceal their delight. Paul Temple was the only member of the party who gave no sign that he welcomed the news.

A rather short, fairly well-built little man placed his elbows on the counter of the reception office in the dowdy lobby of the Autumn Hotel.

'Good morning, sir,' said the reception clerk.

'Good morning!' The little man spoke in a thick, guttural accent. 'I believe you have a gentleman staying here I wish to see.'

'What name, sir?'

'The gentleman's name is Mr. Wallace Sabina.'

'Oh yes, sir. Mr. Sabina is in Room Seventy-four. I believe he's expecting you.' He summoned a page.

'What name shall I say, sir?'

Mr. J. P. Goldie smiled benevolently at the waiting pageboy.

'My name,' he said softly, 'is Herr von Zelton.'

CHAPTER XXXII

The Autumn Hotel

If Mr. Wallace Sabina had met Mr. J. P. Goldie on any previous occasion, he showed no sign of recognition, though it must be admitted that Goldie's make-up would have defied many masters of the art. From every angle, his face had a genuine Teuton appearance, and his German inflection was in the true guttural tradition.

As the page opened the door, Mr. Wallace Sabina rose from a small writing-desk in the far corner of the room and came to welcome his guest.

'Mr. Sabina?' asked the little man.

'Herr von Zelton – I am delighted.'

'I am a little late, eh?' smiled von Zelton. 'I had to take a special plane and then this traffic – it was very difficult this morning.'

Sabina nodded understandingly. 'Did you have a good journey?' he asked politely, drawing up the one armchair for his guest.

'No journeys are good, my friend,' rasped von Zelton, 'some are bad, some not so bad. This was what you call—er—putrid.'

Sabina was amused by his visitor's quaint mannerism of speech.

'I'm sorry to have brought you all this way, von Zelton, but this matter is urgent, and I think well worth your journey.'

Herr von Zelton rubbed his hands.

'Let us forget about the journey. It is very nice to meet you after so much business we 'ave done together.'

'Business ... together?' repeated Sabina, rather puzzled.

Von Zelton nodded. 'I mean, indirectly.'

'Oh?'

'You see, my friend, whenever you do anything really big over here, it 'as what you call—er—favourable repercussions on my side.'

'I see,' smiled Sabina affably. 'Would you care for a drink, or—'

'No, no – thank you very much, but I am anxious to discuss at once this business you wish to see me about.'

'Ah, yes,' nodded Sabina, pouring himself a whisky. He slowly filled his glass with soda before asking in a more serious voice, 'Von Zelton, you've heard of the Carter Collection?'

Von Zelton was obviously impressed.

'But who has not, my friend?'

'Exactly,' nodded Sabina.

'It is, I am told, worth about two hundred thousand pounds in your money,' continued von Zelton.

'You seem to have been misinformed, my friend. It is worth ... a million!'

'A million!' von Zelton laughed sceptically. 'There is not so much money in the world!'

'All the same, I want two hundred thousand, and I want it tonight,' announced Sabina, with grim determination.

'It is a lot of money,' mused von Zelton.

'The Carter Collection is worth a million,' Sabina insisted earnestly. 'Why, even if the stones have to be cut, you'll make—'

'One moment! One moment, please,' gently interposed von Zelton. 'I am not in the habit of – as you English say – buying a pig in a bag. I shall want to see this collection.'

Sabina produced a key, went to the writing-desk, extracted a small case, and unlocked it. There, sparkling against their black velvet background, lay the Carter Collection.

'So, murmured von Zelton, very much impressed, 'this is the famous collection, wonderful, beautiful!'

'So you see,' pursued Sabina, 'you have only to get them out of the country.'

'That may not be so easy. The police are sure to be on their guard,' argued von Zelton, gently trickling the stones through his sensitive fingers. 'They are beauties, but it is a risk—'

The telephone shrilled, and with a muttered imprecation at the interruption, Sabina excused himself, and picked up the receiver.

'Hello – yes, this is Sabina.'

He recognised Lina's voice immediately. For once, she was excited, and no longer spoke in her unhurried, level tones.

'This is bad news,' she whispered, urgently.

'What do you mean? Where are you?'

'Not far from Scotland Yard. They've got von Zelton.'

'Don't be silly – he's here now!'

'I've just seen them take him into the Yard.'

'There must be some mistake.'

'You know I never make mistakes like that.'

'But I tell you, von Zelton is here!' Sabina was quite angry now. 'Lina, for God's sake, if this is a joke—'

'It's no joke for any of us,' came her steely voice. 'I can't stay any longer – there's a plain-clothes man just passed this box and—good-bye!'

Sabina slammed down the receiver, looking rather bewildered, then seemed as if he were about to pick it up again.

A strange voice suddenly interrupted him in his plans.

'Put that phone down, Mr. Sabina!'

The receiver clattered on to its rest once more.

'Then—then you're not von Zelton!' stammered Sabina, in alarm.

'No,' said the clear, firm voice, without a trace of accent.

'Then who the devil are you?'

'That is a long story, Sabina,' went on the other, 'and I am just a little weary. There is one more job for me, and then—'

'For God's sake put that gun down!' cried Sabina, desperately. 'If it's a question of money …'

'It is not a question of money,' coldly replied the other.

'Then what is it? What do you want?'

For a few seconds the men surveyed each other, as shrewdly as opponents in the boxing ring. Then the little man spoke again.

'I want revenge!' There was a soft, sinister inflection in his voice, which, however, grew louder until he was almost screaming. 'Revenge! Revenge!'

The revolver was thrust ominously forward.

'No! No!' cried Sabina. 'For God's sake—'

The little man recovered himself slightly. 'Do you remember Lester Granville, the actor?' he asked, in very deliberate tones. 'His child was kidnapped. His only daughter. He paid seven thousand pounds for her return.' He advanced a step, and once more his voice rose.

'But she was not returned! She was not returned!'

256

'Don't shoot!' begged Sabina, hysterically.

But Lester Granville shot four times with cold deliberation. Then he carefully replaced the diamonds in their box, which he thrust into his overcoat pocket, together with the revolver. With a final contemptuous glance at the body that had been Gerald Mitchell, he swiftly opened the door, and walked casually along the corridor.

CHAPTER XXXIII

A Surprise for Gilbert Wrenson

With determined expressions on their faces, four men got out of a police car and strode purposefully into the entrance hall of the Autumn Hotel. Their leader went up to the manager and introduced himself at once.

'I am Sir Graham Forbes, of New Scotland Yard.'

'You haven't lost much time,' commented the manager, admiringly. 'Why, it's only about five minutes since I telephoned.'

'Telephoned?'

'About the suicide.'

Sir Graham shot an inquiring glance at Reed, Hunter and Paul Temple. Then he turned to the manager again.

'I'm not concerned with your suicide at the moment. I'm making some inquiries about a Mr. Wallace Sabina.'

'But, it is Mr. Sabina!' cried the manager, excitedly.

'Show us his room,' ordered Sir Graham at once, and the manager led the way upstairs.

*

On the way, he explained that it was barely twenty minutes ago that a chambermaid had heard four distinct shots. She had been afraid to go and investigate, and some time elapsed before she had given the alarm and they had entered the room.

When he opened the door, and disclosed the body with its features grotesquely distorted, the three Scotland Yard men gasped.

Only Paul Temple betrayed not the slightest sign of surprise at the body of Gerald Mitchell.

Sir Graham began firing a string of questions at the manager, but the latter was not able to help him very much. He suggested that his reception clerk might know more about Wallace Sabina, and telephoned down for him.

'Well, if it's suicide, he made a pretty good job of it,' commented Mac, looking at the body.

'Suicide!' scoffed Forbes. 'How the devil could a man pump four bullets into himself like this?'

Paul Temple spoke for the first time since they had entered the room. 'Would you mind if I asked the reception clerk some questions, Sir Graham? I have rather an interesting theory about the murder, and if it all fits in—'

'All right, Temple, go ahead,' gruffly agreed Forbes, and just then the man arrived. 'This gentleman would like to ask you some questions,' Sir Graham told the reception clerk, and nodded to Temple to proceed.

'I am rather interested in the gentleman who visited Mr. Sabina,' began Temple, shrewdly surveying the receptionist.

'You mean Mr. von Zelton, sir?'

There was an exclamation from Hunter, but Temple ignored it.

'Exactly,' he continued evenly, 'I mean Mr. von Zelton. How old would you say he was?'

'Oh, it's difficult to say, sir. Perhaps about fifty-five.'

'When did he arrive?'

'About an hour ago, sir, as far as I can judge. He seemed a funny little man,' added the clerk, trying to be helpful.

'Then you've never seen him before?'

'No, sir,' was the very definite reply.

'How long had Mr. Sabina been staying here?'

'Well, he hasn't actually stayed, sir, in a manner of speaking. He only came in this morning about ten, and booked his room till Tuesday.'

'H'm. Has he had any other visitors during the day?'

'No, sir. But there were two telephone calls, sir. One came through while Mr. von Zelton was here.'

'Did you happen to overhear them?'

'Oh, no, sir!' the clerk replied, in an injured tone.

'Did Sabina say that he was expecting a Mr. von Zelton?'

'Yes, sir, he told me that as soon as he'd registered.'

'And this Mr. von Zelton – you're quite sure he was a foreigner?'

'I'd stake my life on it, sir,' replied the clerk, with considerable emphasis.

'I see,' murmured Temple reflectively. Then he dismissed the clerk, who went out with the manager.

'How the hell could it be von Zelton?' demanded Forbes, irritably, as Hunter closed the door.

'You don't think Thompson picked up the wrong laddie?' suggested Reed.

'Not a chance!' replied Hunter. 'The fellow we picked up at Croydon was von Zelton all right. I checked up on his pictures.'

'Yes, of course,' agreed Sir Graham impatiently. 'That was the real von Zelton.'

'Then who the devil was this fellow? He must have known a darn sight more than we do about the Front Page Men,' said Hunter.

'Ay, and he must have been a pretty good actor, too,' added Reed.

'By Timothy!' ejaculated Temple suddenly.

Forbes looked up suspiciously. 'Well, Temple, what is it?'

'Oh, nothing,' replied the novelist, looking rather embarrassed. The telephone started ringing, and saved him any further explanation.

Forbes answered it.

'This may be for Sabina,' he muttered. But it proved to be Wrenson, speaking from the Yard. The conversation did not convey much to the others, except the fact that Sir Graham was considerably startled by the message.

'Well, I'm damned!' he exclaimed, as he replaced the receiver. In response to the eager looks of inquiry from his subordinates, he announced, 'About five minutes ago a parcel was handed in at the Yard. It was addressed to the Reverend Charles Hargreaves.' He paused. 'It was the Carter Collection.'

His colleagues were duly impressed.

'It must have been taken from Mitchell by this— this fellow who impersonated von Zelton,' decided Hunter, wrinkling his brow. 'So, whoever he was, he couldn't have been a crook.'

Temple smiled quietly.

'Well, I'm off back to the Yard. Can't see much point in staying here. You fellows look after the doctor and the photographer when they get here,' ordered Sir Graham. 'Coming, Temple?'

Temple nodded. They walked downstairs, discussing the case, and while Sir Graham went to have a final word with the manager, Temple asked permission to use the telephone. He dialled the number of his flat, and soon heard Steve's voice.

'Hello, darling, I just rang up to warn you that I may be rather late tonight ... yes ... well, I couldn't say just how late ... oh, yes, darling, perfectly respectable ! As a matter of fact, I'm going to see an old friend of ours, yes, a Mr. Goldie.'

CHAPTER XXXIV

In Which Paul Temple Eats Far Too Many Muffins

It was tea-time the following day before Steve could get her husband to herself. All day long he had been at Scotland Yard, giving them the benefit of the information he had gathered, and comparing notes on the various aspects of the Front Page Men's activities.

Steve had only the sketchiest idea of what had happened, and her reportorial instincts were well and truly aroused. At the moment, however, her husband seemed to have but one purpose in life – reducing the pile of muffins arrayed temptingly before him.

'If Sherlock Holmes had married, his wife would have had my deepest sympathy,' sighed Steve, with the merest twinkle in her eye.

'I'm sure she would have been a terrible trial to him,' gravely replied Temple, reaching for another muffin.

'All the same, darling, I do think you're marvellous!' smiled Steve.

'So do I, by Timothy!' placidly declared her husband.

'I really don't know how you do it!'

'It's a gift,' solemnly announced Temple, with his mouth full. 'You simply buy a good old magnifying-glass, find a couple of clues, put two and two together, and then write a book about it. Tell Pryce to order some more muffins, darling. We'll have them for tea tomorrow and the day after and—'

'Paul—' began Steve, seriously.

'Yes, my pet?' He placed a hand cautiously on his diaphragm. 'I do hope these muffins aren't going to play me false.'

'Paul, do be serious. I want to hear all about the case.'

'Oh, you mean that little matter of the Front Page Men. Well, I suppose there should be no secrets between husband and wife.'

'Tell me, Paul, when did you first suspect Gerald?' Steve demanded, eagerly.

'The day he came to Bramley Lodge and told us about Ann being good at impersonating people. I couldn't quite see the point in that ... after all, if one is reasonably fond of one's wife, and discovers she has criminal instincts, one doesn't rush to the nearest police-station. Gerald knew I was almost bound to go to Sir Graham with such valuable information.'

'But what was his point?' persisted Steve.

'I haven't quite figured that out,' replied Temple, thoughtfully. 'He must have persuaded Ann to impersonate Carol over the telephone without her realising the significance of it. He probably bluffed her that it was just a practical joke.'

'Yes, but later she must have realised that—'

'Later, Ann realised many things, Steve, but I've a feeling he had some devilish hold over her in some way. That's why she tried to get away, and took that flat in Bloomsbury.'

'Gerald, of course, tried to throw suspicion on Ann.'

266

'Yes. Because he wasn't at all sure just how much Ann knew about him, and how much she had told the police. He was devilishly frightened. After all, except for this other woman, Lina, no one connected Gerald with the Front Page Men.'

'Then you think he killed Ann – suspecting that she was going to tell Carol Forbes all she knew?'

Temple nodded. 'Yes, he must have brought that off very cleverly. But it was at Tavistock Court that he first really gave the show away.'

Temple selected another muffin, and took a large bite.

'If you remember, Gerald tried to play the complete innocent about Tavistock Court. Yet he knew which button to press in the lift to take us to the right floor. How could he have known that without visiting the place beforehand? That's why I asked him to press the button.'

'Darling, you deserve another muffin for that,' smiled Steve.

'Thanks. And there was another point which rather interested me,' continued Temple. 'After we had heard Goldie in the flat above—'

'Then it was Goldie?'

'Of course. We had quite a little chat together.'

'But, you said the flat was deserted,' Steve reminded him.

Temple smiled. 'Yes, that little brainwave occurred to me on the way down. And Gerald said, "I wonder if he's climbed on to the roof!"'

'Would it have been possible for Mr. Goldie to have climbed on to the roof?'

'That's just the point. The flat was being thoroughly overhauled, and there was an opening above one of the windows, covered by a tarpaulin. Obviously, Gerald knew all about that.'

Steve poured her husband a second cup of tea before demanding rather casually, 'Who is Mr. Goldie?'

'Ah,' murmured Temple, with a slightly humorous twitch of his mobile mouth. 'Mr. J. P. Goldie – well, I believe he's rather a meek little man with a passion for horticulture. Of course, I've never actually met him.'

'Never met him!' repeated Steve in a startled voice.

Temple shook his head, and stared thoughtfully into his teacup.

'But, Paul—' Steve began to protest.

'Oh, yes, darling, I know what you're thinking. But our Mr. Goldie isn't *the* Mr. Goldie. In fact, he isn't a Mr. Goldie at all.'

'Then who is he?'

'His name's Granville – Lester Granville,' explained Temple quietly. 'Does that convey anything to you?'

'You mean the actor?'

'I do. And a pretty successful character-actor too, for many years. He had one child, a little girl. About two years ago she was kidnapped, and her father was instructed to pay seven thousand pounds for her return. He paid up all right. But, because he considered it was his duty, he also got in touch with Scotland Yard. Because of this, the child was murdered.'

Steve shuddered. She remembered working on the case with half a dozen fellow reporters in her newspaper days. It had been one of the most unpleasant cases she had covered.

'The effect on Granville was almost unbelievable,' continued Temple. 'He went nearly demented with fury, left the stage at once, and has since devoted all his time to tracking down the criminals responsible for his daughter's death. And Granville was no fool, Steve! He knew what he was doing all right. He realised from the start that it was quite hopeless for him to make a thorough investigation, unless he could first of all manage to conceal his real identity. And so—'

'He became Mr. J. P. Goldie,' prompted Steve.

Temple nodded and helped himself to more sugar. 'It was a clever move. Actually, Granville had known the real Mr. Goldie for quite a little while. He was, in fact, by way of being a friend of his. Fortunately, Granville was a pretty good musician, and had often discussed the technical problems of piano-tuning with Goldie. So he soon settled down to the work.'

'Yes, but darling, how did you discover he wasn't the real Mr. Goldie?' asked Steve.

'Well, I had my suspicions from the first. I knew he was either connected with the gang or making some sort of private investigation. Then one day I decided to visit Clapshaw and Thompson's in Regent Street. Goldie used to work there, remember. The fellow in charge described him absolutely to a T. It really did look as if my suspicions were unfounded. Then suddenly, just as I was leaving, the salesman said, "I expect the old boy is still crazy over lilies." That remark rather fascinated me, and I soon discovered my first clue. The real Mr. Goldie was considered an expert on certain flowers, and particularly lilies.'

Steve's face lit up. 'So that was why you brought those lilies home that day Mr. Goldie was here.'

'Exactly. I literally scoured London for the finest lilies in the country. But Goldie was quite unimpressed by them. He didn't even make a single comment. Then, as a final test, I deliberately called them tiger lilies. Now, no expert would stand for that! They were quite obviously nothing of the kind. But Goldie never contradicted me. In fact, to put it bluntly, as far as he was concerned, they might just as well have been the bluebells of Scotland!'

'Darling, your ingenuity leaves me breathless,' laughed Steve.

'Thank you, my pet,' murmured Temple affably. 'I also have the finest figure in the business – in spite of muffins.'

'But, Paul, how did you discover he was Lester Granville?' asked Steve, becoming serious again.

Temple shrugged his shoulders. 'Oh—er—deduction, just deduction, my dear,' he informed her with a deprecating air.

'Yes, but I don't see how you could arrive at that.'

'If you'll swear not to breathe a word, I'll tell you,' he whispered, looking into her eyes. 'Granville told me himself.'

For a moment Steve was taken aback. 'When did he tell you?'

'That night in Bloomsbury.'

'What was he doing at Tavistock Court?'

'Just keeping his eye on Gerald Mitchell. You see Goldie, or rather Granville, had already discovered that Gerald was Front Page Man Number One.'

'How strange for a little man like that to succeed where all Scotland Yard failed,' said Steve.

'Yes, it's rather a curious story,' continued Temple, thoughtfully. 'At the time when Granville's child disappeared, he was playing in a show called *Mist Over the Moon*. Lydia Royal, alias Ann Mitchell, also had a small part in the cast, and she became quite friendly with Granville's little girl. It was through her, in fact, that Gerald organised the kidnapping. Though Ann, of course, was quite ignorant of that.'

'What made Goldie first suspicious of Gerald?'

'Well, when the Front Page Men came into existence, Goldie suddenly realised that the novel, from which the gang apparently took its title, was published by none other than Lydia Royal's husband, Gerald Mitchell. This made him think. And suddenly he realised how very friendly Ann had been towards his little girl.'

'So he suspected Ann,' put in Steve, quickly.

'Yes, I'm afraid he did. Nevertheless, this helped to put him on the right track where Gerald was concerned. Oddly enough, however, his investigations led him to believe that Brightman was the leader of the gang, and it wasn't until the last week or so that he realised that Gerald himself was Front Page Man Number One.'

Steve frowned thoughtfully. 'I can't quite see why Gerald called his organisation The Front Page Men. It seems that by doing so he automatically drew attention to himself.'

'Exactly!' Temple thumped the small table until the teacups rattled. 'Don't you see that was really a brilliant psychological move? The police knew he was the publisher of the novel *The Front Page Men*. They knew he was telling the truth about the novel being submitted out of the blue by the mysterious Andrea Fortune. This put him in a really excellent position. In the eyes of the law, he was merely the bright, but somewhat bewildered, young book publisher. Certainly, it automatically connected him with the case, but it enabled the police to dismiss him as being an insignificant factor. The same move was made by Andrew Brightman, who deliberately brought himself to the notice of the police by saying that his daughter had been kidnapped. This, again, was a very carefully planned move on Brightman's part, for it also enabled him to throw suspicion on Mr. Goldie.'

'It was particularly clever of Gerald to contrive to be on both sides of the fence at the same time – why, he even went with you on that river trip,' recalled Steve.

'Yes,' agreed her husband, 'and he acted pretty scared, too. In fact, I think Gerald was a much better actor than Ann.'

'But this doesn't solve the mystery of Andrea Fortune,' went on Steve. 'Do you think she wrote that letter Sir Graham received?'

'I know she did,' replied Temple quietly.

Neither spoke for a few moments. Then Steve asked, 'What are you thinking of?'

Temple placed a hand lightly on her shoulder. 'Of a certain newspaper reporter I used to know. A girl by the name of Steve Trent ...'

'Was she – nice?' asked Steve, taking his hand.

'She was quite tall, and dark and very attractive in rather a special sort of way.' He paused, then added, 'and, of course, she was very, very clever.'

'Why do you say that?'

'Because she married a popular novelist,' resumed Temple, 'who was labouring under the impression that nobody in his family could possibly write anything except himself. And just to prove him wrong, what do you think she did?'

'Three guesses?'

He nodded.

'She wrote a book?'

'That's exactly what she did. And she sent it to a small literary agency, with strict instructions that all royalties be made payable to the London and General Hospital in Gerard Street. And the name of the book, my sweet, was *The Front Page Men*. And the name of the author was Andrea Fortune.'

'Paul, you know that—'

'I know that *you* are Andrea Fortune,' said Paul Temple, quietly.

'Darling, I'm so glad you know,' confessed Steve, impulsively. 'I've been dreadfully worried about the whole business. Of course, I knew that the book had nothing to do with the real Front Page Men, but I somehow couldn't bring myself to admit—' She broke off quickly. 'You're not annoyed, darling?'

'Of course not,' he told her gently. 'But, by Timothy, I hope you're not writing a sequel!'

Steve laughed. 'No, darling, I'm not. I think Andrea Fortune had better retire as gracefully as possible.'

'Yes, it might be an idea,' approved Temple, swallowing the last piece of muffin.

Steve poked the fire, then turned on him again.

'Paul, did you see Goldie – or rather, Granville – after you telephoned yesterday?'

'Yes,' replied Temple softly.

'Why ! If you knew all there was to know—'

'I realised that Lester Granville was the only man who could have impersonated von Zelton,' said Temple slowly.

'Then Granville murdered Gerald Mitchell?'

'He did.'

'Does Sir Graham know?' demanded Steve.

Temple shook his head. 'I haven't told him – yet.'

'Paul, what's going to happen? What are you going to do?'

Temple did not answer at once. 'Last night,' he said quietly, 'Granville told me the whole story. I don't think anyone will ever realise what the child meant to him, Steve. He was determined to get Mitchell – no matter what might happen to himself.'

'Paul, what are you going to do?' repeated Steve, anxiously.

'He talked about leaving for South America,' her husband informed her.

'But – aren't you going to stop him?' cried Steve, in alarm.

'Last night, I begged him to stay and confess. I told him, quite honestly, that after the terrible happenings of the past three months it was almost impossible to say what might be the result.'

'And if he doesn't stay?'

'If he doesn't stay,' repeated the novelist thoughtfully, '*Bon voyage*, Mr. Goldie!' And Paul Temple shrugged his shoulders expressively.

'I hope for his own peace of mind—' began Steve, then stopped, as the faint strains of the piano filtered in from the next room.

Someone with a gentle, almost wistful touch was playing the familiar *Liebestraum*.

Temple clasped Steve's hand, and they listened until the last melancholy note had faded into soft echoes. Then Temple looked up to see Pryce standing beside him.

'What is it, Pryce?'

'It's the piano-tuner, sir,' he said. 'A Mr. Goldie. Mr. J. P. Goldie.'